Shadows of
Bourbon Street

Books by Deanna Chase

The Jade Calhoun Novels
Haunted on Bourbon Street
Witches of Bourbon Street
Demons of Bourbon Street
Angels of Bourbon Street
Shadows of Bourbon Street
Incubus of Bourbon Street (Winter 2014)

The Coven Pointe Novels
Marked by Temptation (a novella)

The Crescent City Fae Novels
Influential Magic
Irresistible Magic
Intoxicating Magic (June 2014)

The Destiny Novels
Defining Destiny
Book Two in the Destiny Series (Fall 2014)

Shadows of Bourbon Street

A Jade Calhoun Novel

Deanna Chase

Bayou Moon Publishing

Acknowledgments

A big thank you to all my readers. Your enthusiasm for the Jade Calhoun Series is more than I ever dreamed possible. It's because of you that we're on book five. A special thanks to my editor Rhonda and the rest of my crew: Lisa, Susan, Angie, and Chauntelle.

Chapter 1

Foreboding wasn't the emotion a girl wanted to experience minutes before she was supposed to walk down the aisle. Yet that exact emotion was streaming off Lailah, my soul guardian. I tucked the skirt of my silver wedding dress up and walked to her side with all the nonchalance I could muster. "What's wrong?" I whispered.

"Huh?" She glanced up from her smart phone, startled.

Mom eyed us from across the bedroom. We were upstairs in the master suite, finishing the final touches before my wedding started at Summer House, the southern Louisiana home Kane had given me as a wedding present. Located in the small town of Cypress Settlement, it had been in his family for years and was where his grandparents had been married. Pasting a smile on, I waved at her, pretending nothing was wrong. The expression on her face softened and she went back to putting the final touches on her makeup.

"You're giving off a vibe that would make dogs whine," I said.

Lailah tucked a lock of honey-blond hair behind her ear, exasperation now clinging to her as she forced a smile. "I'm just doing my job. Nothing to worry about."

I could feel her trying to summon joy and excitement to mask whatever was causing her such turmoil. But she couldn't hide her emotions from me, an empath. "Don't try that with me," I scolded gently. "Something's going on. Is it Kane? He's here, right?" I'd been perfectly fine five minutes ago, ready to commit myself to the man who'd been by my side through all the crazy that had happened in the last year. Now nausea rolled through my stomach. What if he'd decided I was too much trouble? That life would be better spent with a normal woman? Not a witch-slash-empath with angel blood.

"Of course he is," she said, her eyes wide with surprise. "Why wouldn't he be?"

I took a deep breath and clutched my hand to my chest. "Sorry. Just a momentary bride freak-out."

She laughed, and more of the turmoil slipped from her. "I think we can let you slide this time. Don't worry. Everything is fine. Promise."

"Famous last words."

The door crashed open with a bang, rattling the small cluster of framed photographs hanging on the wall. "Jade," Kane's mother gushed as she fingered the half dozen strands of Mardi Gras beads hung around her neck. That wouldn't have bothered me if one of them hadn't sported flashing penises. On any other day I would have laughed, but on my wedding day I didn't appreciate it, and I had to bite back a scowl. "You look amazing, darling."

She wore a bright red, low-cut, form-fitting silk dress that was several inches too short for a woman in her sixties. Her lipstick, the shade a perfect match, was smeared slightly on one side as if she'd been making out with someone moments before. What was this? A frat party?

"Thank you, Shelia." I took another step toward Lailah, hoping I could avoid another of the inevitable bone-crushing hugs she'd bestowed on me five times already today. No such luck. She barreled into me, the strong scent of rum wafting from her.

Lailah gave me a sympathetic smile. "I'll go check and see how close we are to starting."

I glared at her over Shelia's shoulder and mouthed, *Traitor.*

"Shelia!" Pyper said as she strolled past Lailah into the bedroom, wearing a sleek woman's-fit tux. "Kane was just looking for you. It's time to seat the mothers." She paused and eyed my future mother-in-law. "Have you been outside flashing for beads again?"

Shelia grinned and touched one of the plastic penises. "It's Mardi Gras. What else was I supposed to do while I waited for this shindig to start?"

Pyper laughed, but when she saw my face, she covered with a cough. "Maybe it's better to wait until after the ceremony to partake in the parades."

"I'm here now, aren't I?" Shelia pulled off a strand of white beads with three miniature beer bottles attached. In the process, her dress slipped open, and Pyper and I were treated to a peek at her braless chest. I closed my eyes momentarily and prayed for patience. Kane had told me his mother was a little...*interesting.* "I didn't miss anything," Shelia continued. "Anyway, I was out there to get beads for Jade. She can't have her wedding Mardi Gras weekend and not wear beads." She moved forward with the beads outstretched as if she were going to settle the strand over my head.

"Whoa." I held my hands up. "I've already got beads on." I touched the intricate glass-bead flower necklace I'd made specifically for the wedding. All of my bridesmaids had something similar. I'd given Pyper a strand of roundels that matched the cuff links I'd made for Kane.

"And it's beautiful," Shelia said. "But those have nothing to do with Mardi Gras." She laughed. "Come on, Jade. Loosen up a little."

I stood frozen as she forced the tacky beads over my head.

"Perfect! Now we're ready to start." She flashed a sauced grin and sashayed out of the room, her hips swaying hard enough I was surprised she didn't throw her back out.

"Holy shit," Pyper said, smoothing back her jet-black hair. "She's worse than Kane said she was."

"Jade!" my mother called as she hurried over. "What are you wearing?"

"A gift from Hurricane Shelia." I started to sink down onto an ottoman, but Mom wrapped her hands around my arms to stop me.

"Oh, no. You're going to wrinkle your dress." Mom marched me over to the door. "Wait here. Your father will be up in a minute to get you."

"Okay." At this point, all I cared about was seeing Kane.

Mom eyed me one more time, sneered at the beads and then ripped them off me, nearly poking one of my eyes out with a mini beer bottle.

"Ouch!" I cried.

"Sorry, sweetie, but think of the pictures." She took off down the hall, her heels clattering against the old wooden floors.

Pyper put a hand on my arm. Her silent mirth rushed into me, and my mood brightened instantly. She shook her head. "Family. They're both crazy."

I laughed as her humor washed away all the apprehension that had built up over the last few minutes. "I'm pretty sure Shelia gets the crown."

"True." Pyper picked up the beads Mom had thrown on the ground and pulled them over her head.

I gave her a horrified look. "Pictures. Remember?"

"Oh, Jade," she mimicked in Shelia's voice. "Loosen up. It's a party."

"Hey!" Kat said as she strode into the room. "Where are my beads?"

"No one said anything about Mardi Gras beads," Lailah said as she followed her in.

"There are no beads. No one but Shelia is wearing beads." I turned to Pyper. "Take those tacky things off right this moment before I spell you into submission."

"Geesh," she said and did as I asked. "No need to be a bridezilla." Winking, she dropped them on the dresser. "Maybe if you wear them during the reception, that will appease Shelia."

"After the ceremony is done and the pictures are taken, anyone can wear them, but don't look at me. I'm not wearing that strand. I'm more of a wine girl. Unless we're talking about Guinness." I made a face. "I don't do Bud."

"Snob." Pyper stuck her tongue out, and we all giggled.

"True," I said. "Admission is the first step to recovery."

"I hate to break up the girl fest, Jade, but it's time." Lailah held her hands out. "Form a circle and we can start the spell."

Everyone sobered and we did as we were told.

"Nothing is going to interfere with this wedding," Lailah continued. "Not if I have anything to say about it."

The spell was my wedding present from my guardian angel. Since I seemed to have a penchant for attracting trouble, my one wish was that Kane and I would have a peaceful ceremony and reception. And with my history, we weren't taking any chances.

The four of us stood in a circle, our hands clasped, as Lailah chanted, "Four to one and one to four, combine our strengths forevermore."

A tingle sparked from her fingers to mine, ran through me, and transferred to Kat's fingers in my other hand. She let out a small gasp and tightened her grip.

"From north to south and east to west, we bind our hearts over this house. Over our friends. Over this day. No one uninvited shall trespass over this land. Let the day be full of love, laughter, and joy. From one to four and four to one, let our will be done."

We all parroted the last line, "Let our will be done."

The spark zapped our fingers one more time. Then a complete peacefulness settled over my nerves, and my heart filled with all the love radiating from my friends.

"It's perfect," I said to Lailah.

She shrugged, pretending nonchalance, but even if I couldn't feel the happiness and slight pride clinging just below her surface, I wouldn't have believed she didn't care. I knew her better than that. Lailah held her emotions close to the vest, and the only reason I could sense them was because we used to have a psychic connection. That was gone now, but her emotions still came through loud and clear.

I wrapped my arms around her and gave her a tight hug. "Thank you."

When we pulled apart, she grinned. "You're very welcome. Now let's get you married."

A knock followed by Lucien's voice filtered through the door. "Jade? It's time."

"That's my cue." Pyper gave me a kiss on the cheek. "See ya in a few minutes."

Lucien, the second in command of the New Orleans coven, dressed in a black suit and silver tie, was waiting to escort Pyper to Kane's side.

"You ready, gorgeous?" he asked her, but before she could answer, his gaze shifted to take in Kat. His expression turned to one of longing and quickly morphed into guilt. I wanted to say something, anything, to ease his suffering, but what could I say? *Sorry you're in love with my best friend and if you use any magic around her it could kill her?* No. He certainly didn't need a reminder. Not after she'd almost died last month. He was torn up enough.

"You look very handsome," Kat said and ran her hand over one of his lapels.

His smile turned tortured. Kat knew he had feelings for her. The feeling was mutual, and she was none too pleased that he was keeping his distance.

"Save me a dance," she continued in a voice so seductive it made me blush.

I made a face at Pyper.

Her eyes widened, and she gave me a short nod indicating she was on it. "Okay then. Lucien, let's get going before Kane sends someone else up to find me." Slipping her arm through his, Pyper dragged Lucien down the hall, not giving him a chance to answer.

Kat sighed. "One day he'll get over his fears."

"Kat, honey," I said. "He's only trying to protect you. And honestly, I'm glad. After what happened—"

She held up her hand. "That's enough. We've already been through this. He's not performing magic right now, and as long as he isn't, there's no danger to me."

"He's a witch. Sometimes magic occurs without us even trying."

"Jade's right," Lailah agreed. "Witches are unpredictable under the best circumstances—"

"All right!" Kat cried and held both hands up in surrender. "I hear you. Now let's drop this. We have a wedding to get on with." She smiled at me, a true and genuine gesture that warred with the sadness radiating from her heart.

"Oh, Kat," I said and wrapped an arm around her. "It will all work out. You'll see." I said the words but had no idea how we'd get rid of Lucien's curse. My mentor Bea, Lailah, and I had been trying to find anything that would reverse it for weeks. No such luck.

"Stop." She pulled away from me and gave me her don't-mess-with-me look. "Wedding." She cocked her ear. "Hear that?"

The first notes of the wedding music floated up the grand staircase.

She grinned, tears swimming in her hazel eyes as I leaned in for a hug. "Love you," she said.

"Love you, too. Now stop blubbering before you make me lose it."

She sniffed and then took off to meet one of the groomsmen at the top of the stairs. Lailah squeezed my hand and followed her.

I took one last minute to check my hair and makeup before grabbing my simple white rose bouquet and walking out into the hall.

"Hi, baby," my father said. Well, my stepfather, Marc. He was the man who'd raised me until my mother had forced him to go away. My biological father Drake was here somewhere, but we didn't have a relationship outside of my involvement in the angel world—more specifically, my job as a shadow walker that I was supposed to start as soon as Kane and I got back from our honeymoon.

We weren't close. We didn't even like each other much. Still, I was glad Drake had decided to come. He was my father, after all.

"What's wrong?" Marc asked.

"Huh?" I slipped my arm through his. "Nothing."

"That's not true. I can feel the apprehension strumming through you."

"You can?" I turned to him, unfocusing so I could see his aura. "You're not an intuitive. Your aura is blue. No outline of purple anywhere."

He chuckled. "I don't need to be an empath to know what's going on with you, Jade. I helped raise you, remember? I can tell your moods just by looking at your face most times."

I took in a sharp breath. "I look unsettled?"

"No. Not really. You look gorgeous, but there's this tiny wrinkle right here." He ran his index finger lightly over my forehead. "It only shows up when something's troubling you. And right now there's a faint worry line."

I rubbed my forehead, trying to smooth the skin.

"Gonna tell me what it is?" he asked.

I leaned into him slightly, liking that I finally had a father figure to rely on. He was tall and lean with a little gray in his blond hair. "I don't know, really. Lailah was worried about something, and I can't shake the feeling that something isn't quite right and it's going to ruin my day."

He ran a light hand down my bare arm. "With all the crazy crap you both have been through the last year, it's natural to be apprehensive on the big day. But try not to worry. Everything's fine. And you have that spell the four of you just wielded. I bet this is all nerves."

"I sure hope so."

"It is," he said. "Trust me."

Marc guided me down the hall and stopped a few feet before we came into view at the top of the grand staircase. "This is it. Ready?"

My heart seemed ready to explode. Our day was finally here despite the ghosts, the demon attacks, and the fact I'd almost died when my soul had been split. Kane had stayed by my side the entire time, and I couldn't wait to spend the rest of my life with him.

The music changed to the traditional wedding march, and tears sprang to my eyes as we appeared at the top of the stairs. A low murmur ran through the crowd below, but the only things I saw were Kane's love-filled eyes gazing up at me.

I floated down those stairs, all the foreboding forgotten. The love of the room pressed in on me and filled my heart to almost bursting.

When the minister asked "Who gives this bride?" both Mom and Marc answered. I hadn't been expecting that. In rehearsal we'd practiced Marc saying it, but I appreciated Mom speaking up as well. It finally felt as if I had a real family. Dysfunctional, yes, but one that cared about one another unconditionally. That was fine with me.

Kane, his expression full of admiration, held his hand out to me. Marc completed the transfer by placing my hand in Kane's. His fingers immediately tightened over mine and my knees went weak with the sheer emotion radiating from him. It was the most perfect moment of my life.

The minister said a prayer, followed by an earth blessing. Kane grinned at me and ever so slightly jabbed his head in his mother's direction. I almost laughed, knowing she was probably losing her mind over the earth blessing. She'd already told me no less than five times how out of place it was in the ceremony. But I was a witch. And there couldn't be a wedding without an earth blessing.

After clearing his throat, the minister continued with our Christian Pagan wedding. "If anyone here knows any reason why these two should not be joined in holy matrimony, speak now or forever hold your peace."

Silence.

"Excellent—"

A loud boom rippled through the ballroom, followed by a brilliant flash of white light. A collective gasp rose from our friends, and Kane instantly stepped in front of me, shielding me from whatever was to come.

I knew it was instinct, so instead of getting irritated, I just stepped out from behind him to find my real father and his consort Chessandra, the high angel, standing center stage between us and our guests. Anger coiled up from the depths of my soul. What the hell were they doing, and why were they dressed in their gold-embroidered council robes?

Before I could say anything, the high angel waved a hand, casting the entire room in a blue light, and said, "Jade Calhoun and Kane Rouquette, you are hereby summoned to the shadow world immediately."

"What? Now?" I cried. "We're getting married."

Chessandra leveled an unfeeling stare at us. "Change of plans."

Chapter 2

The room faded to black, and when my eyes adjusted, we were no longer at Summer House—at least, not the one filled with our wedding guests. No, this one was in disrepair with vines growing up the cracked walls and plaster falling from the ceiling. A sad emptiness clung to the air as thick as a hot, humid day.

"What the hell is going on?" Kane demanded in a tight and dangerous voice.

Chessandra bristled. "Watch your tone, dreamwalker."

My father took a step forward, holding a hand out in a "stop" motion. He was perfectly groomed, but his face was haggard as if he hadn't slept in days. "Hold on now. Let's all calm down."

"Calm down? Are you out of your mind?" I cried as Kane tightened his hand over mine. "Look at us. You ruined our wedding. And what about our guests? Aren't they going to be freaking out since Kane and I just disappeared?"

"Lailah and Beatrice can cast an illusion spell. They'll think it never started. You can work out the details later." Chessandra strode across the room, kicking up dust as she went. She stopped at a broken window and peered out.

"This shouldn't have happened," I said to Kane. "We cast a protection spell. No one should have been able to penetrate it."

Dad cleared his throat. "I was invited, remember? Chessa was my date."

"Figures," I mumbled and then glared at my father. "This is insane. I can't believe you went along with this."

He opened his mouth to speak, but Chessandra cut him off. "A witch's life is on the line. And unfortunately you're the only one who can help her. So forgive me if I ruined your special day." Her tone was clipped and sarcastic. She didn't give one flying monkey about our wedding.

I rarely experienced true hatred. Not within myself anyway, but I was dangerously close to the edge just then. How dare she?

Kane and I shared a glance. Every witch I knew was already at my wedding. "Who is it?" I asked, unable to tamp down my curiosity.

Drake, my dad, sent Chessandra a concerned look. "She works for the angel council and is stuck in the shadow world."

"So send someone else," Kane said and wrapped an arm around me. "We don't work for the council yet. I demand you transport us back to the wedding. Or else we'll take this up with the witches' council appointed to oversee shadow walkers."

"Weren't you paying attention?" Chessandra whirled and faced us. "There isn't anyone else. You two are the only chance to rescue her before she's stuck forever. You're not going back. Not until you find out what happened to her."

Tears glistened in Chessandra's eyes as she ran a shaky hand over her frazzled chestnut hair. She was moments from unraveling. Nothing about her resembled the sleek angel we'd met a few weeks ago when we'd negotiated the terms of our new positions.

"What do you mean, we're the only two who can help her?" Kane asked. "Where are all the other shadow walkers?"

The color drained from Chessandra's face, and a ball of panic started to filter through me. The outrage that had been consuming my mind started to dissipate. Something had gone terribly wrong, something that even the high angel couldn't fix, and we were being pulled right into the middle of it.

Drake put a hand on Chessandra's shoulder and faced us. "Others have tried. They have not been successful."

"Tried? What happened?" I was a powerful witch, I didn't deny that, but it wasn't as if I was expertly skilled. I'd only been an active witch for less than a year. My knowledge in all things magic was sadly lacking. If others couldn't save this missing person, I had no idea how I could.

"Maybe we should sit down?" Drake glanced around and gestured to a beat-up living room set. The tattered settee and both wing-backed chairs were covered in dust.

I glanced down at my dress and wanted to cry. "You can't be serious."

"Just say what you have to say." Something close to rage streamed from Kane. He was seconds from kicking some serious angel ass.

Chessandra turned slowly, her eyes wide and glowing red.

"Oh, crap," I muttered and pressed into Kane. Red eyes? Creepy. It was a sign she wasn't far from losing control.

"Matisse—Mati—was working on a spell to block the veil between Hell and the shadow world. It worked, but something went terribly wrong and now she's trapped…somewhere. Angels and shadow walkers alike have both come up empty."

I gasped. If they couldn't find her in the shadow world, then… "Could she be trapped in Hell?" Please, no. Not Hell. The last time we'd been there we'd barely made it back, and even then only because we'd had the help of two angels.

Drake quickly shook his head. "No. We don't think so." He shot Chessandra a glance. "She still feels a vague connection to her. If Mati were in Hell, Chessa would know. The soul-crushing oppression of Hell would be affecting them both."

That was something at least.

"Why us?" Kane asked. "If no one else can find her, what makes you think we can?"

"Because of this." Chessandra reached into her pocket and held her fisted hand out to me. "She gave this to me before we started working on the spell just in case anything went wrong."

She dropped a gleaming silver dragonfly into my hand. "It's important to her. When we set the finding spell, it always goes to the same place."

As we waited for her to finish the explanation, my impatience grew to obnoxious levels. "Dragging out the details for effect is not the way to get on my good side," I warned.

Kane hid a smile, and Drake let out a sigh.

The high angel narrowed those blood-tinged eyes at me. "It always ends up at your lover's club."

Startled, I jerked my head in Kane's direction. His eyebrows were raised. He was clearly just as surprised as I was. Why would she go to the club? Unless...

Recognition dawned in Kane's expression and we both said, "The portal."

"What portal?" Drake asked.

"Bea opened one to Hell at the club in order to banish an evil spirit," I said quietly. "But if the veil to Hell has been closed, I don't know that we'll be able to open it again."

"If it's truly a portal, and not a gate to Hell, it shouldn't be a problem. Open it, and you'll find our witch," Chessandra said with finality as if the conversation was over.

I glanced at Kane. His expression mirrored exactly how I felt: completely confused and extremely dubious. "So you don't really know if I can. You're just hoping that's the case, right? What if I do find her but then can't get back myself?"

"You'll find a way," Chessandra said. "Your power...it's unparalleled."

"Jade," Drake said. "Please. We need you to try."

We. The desperation filling the room pressed in, threatening to suffocate me. This seemed personal for both of them. I would help if I could. I'd never leave someone trapped in another dimension if there was something I could do about it, especially not with my history. My mother had been trapped in Purgatory for over fifteen years, and no one had tried to help her, not even the angels. I narrowed my eyes.

"Hey. Why are you suddenly worried about this witch? When Mom was taken to Purgatory after trying to help an angel, the council didn't step in then."

Chessandra hung her head.

Drake went to her side and bent to whisper in her ear. She nodded, and when she looked up, pink-tinged tears ran down her cheeks. Whoa, pink?

Drake noticed my alarm and said, "It's the blood of her ancestors."

Chessandra wiped the moisture from one eye and held her fingers up, staring at them. In a wispy, ethereal voice, she said, "We weep the blood of our own when they are at death's door."

Kane stiffened beside me. "Are you saying this witch belongs to you?"

"Not belong, Mr. Rouquette." Chessandra focused on him as her unearthly expression vanished. Those red-tinged eyes dilated and a fire lit in them. "Mati is my sister."

"Okay," I said quietly.

"Jade—" Kane started.

I held up a hand and turned to him. "I can't leave her there. You know I can't. You can't either. I know you."

He dropped his gaze and gestured to the gorgeous silver dress. "But what about the wedding?"

"I know." I grimaced. "But what else are we going to do? Say no?" I pulled away and shook my head. "I can't do that. Can you?"

He closed his eyes and sighed. "No."

I threw my arms around him, hugging him tight, overwhelmed at his huge heart and unwavering support. "I love you."

"I know, pretty witch."

I turned to the angels. "Fine. We'll help, but I have to get home to change."

"Bring her back," Chessandra said and waved an arm. The darkness faded as the world blurred around us. I groped for Kane's hand, coming up empty. When the world righted itself, my head was spinning, but Kane was standing next to me, holding me up. And right in front of us was his shotgun double in the French Quarter.

Kane put his hand on the small of my back and led me into the house. Once inside, he pulled me into his arms. "You okay?"

I swallowed. "Yeah."

Tenderness filled his deep-chocolate eyes. "You're amazing, you know that?"

I let out a choked laugh. "More like a walking nightmare. No one else has angels breaking up their wedding." I placed a hand over his heart, my own breaking from the rush of emotion I felt seeing him in his tux. "You're the amazing one for sticking with me through the crazy."

He covered my hand and then brought it to his lips. "I'm part of the crazy, too, love. The evil started at my club, remember?"

Tears filled my eyes. "I know." Sniffling, I met his penetrating gaze. "But you have to admit if it wasn't for me, you likely wouldn't be in this mess."

He brushed a lock of hair off my forehead. "Babe, without you, my life would be empty and incredibly dull. We'll do what we have to and then this wedding will go on. Now let's get you out of that dress and go kick some ass."

The way he said *get you out of that dress* made me go a little weak in the knees. Then I instantly felt horrible for my reaction. A woman's life was on the line.

I nodded and headed for the bedroom. A sense of loss filled me as I slipped out of my wedding finery. Why couldn't I have one normal day? Sighing, I hung my dress up and pulled on jeans and a T-shirt. There were about two hundred bobby pins and a gallon of hair spray keeping my hair in the fancy updo. It looked fairly ridiculous with my casual attire, but unless I spent the next half hour unpinning and then washing the product out, I was just going to have to live with it.

Kane changed into a similar uniform: blue jeans and a black T-shirt.

Clutching the dragonfly, I followed him into the kitchen. Hope and happiness streamed off Mati's talisman. She'd had positive energy before she'd been trapped. That was a good sign. "Ready?"

"Unless you think we should call in reinforcements."

I thought about that for a moment. Getting the coven members to downtown during Mardi Gras would take hours. And if we did open a portal, once we slipped into another dimension, their power wouldn't be useful anyway. Not unless they came with us. It was very tempting, though. Having others as backup was definitely preferable. But I shook my head. "I think we can at least check things out. See if we can find any clues first. I just hate the idea of leaving anyone trapped any longer than necessary if we can do something about it."

"Okay, but I'm not letting you go anywhere by yourself."

He wasn't kidding, either. He'd followed me into Hell once. "Got it." I held the dragonfly out. "I'm going to use this to create a connection to her. I want to see for myself where it goes." I pulled some herbs out of my rack and went to work with the pestle and mortar. Once the ingredients were ground together, I placed the dragonfly in Kane's hand.

He stood still, eyes locked on me. It was intense and oddly moving. This was the first time Kane and I were going to officially work together as shadow walkers. I smiled at him. Taking a pinch of the poppy seed and white willow mixture, I sprinkled the herbs over the dragonfly and said, "Goddess of the earth, we humbly offer the herbs of discovery." The dragonfly immediately started to glow. "May your sight see through the veils of the universe and lead us to our quest." Magic tingled from the center of my chest, and when I touched the dragonfly, it lit with sparkling white light.

For a moment, we stared at the pin. Then just as I was ready to give up, it fluttered to life.

"Wow. Impressive, Jade," Kane said, his eyes wide.

I grinned. It wasn't exactly a complicated spell, but the fact that it worked without having to call on the coven's collective magic pleased me. "Now we're ready to roll."

Kane held up a hand. "Wait. Better leave a note for everyone. They're bound to come looking for us sooner or later."

"Good idea." Our phones were still at Summer House.

Kane scribbled a note and left it on the counter. Pyper had a key. She'd find it.

"Go forth, dragonfly," I said. "Take us to Mati."

Kane and I followed the dragonfly out of the house, down his street, and then turned left into the crowds of Bourbon Street. The collective excitement of the crowd clung to me, both giving me a boost and draining me at the same time. No matter what I did, I couldn't block out the emotions of hundreds of people all at once. The crowd was the exact opposite of an emotional vampire, like a drug rush or something. But it also left me raw and unable to control any of it.

"Oh, damn." I waved a hand upward, forcing the dragonfly above the crowd. The last thing we needed was for it to get lost in the crowd, even though it seemed fairly obvious it was headed for the club.

Kane pressed against me, his hands on my hips as we fought our way through the hordes of people and the rogue strands of beads being thrown everywhere. Instant relief. His steady energy flowed into me, fortifying my own. I clung to him like a lifeline. It was slow going, but we'd gotten quite a few blocks before we were finally assaulted with a mass of flying beads. I ducked.

"Son of a bitch!" Kane cried and let go of me. The crowds instantly filled in the space between us and panic filled me, along with the crowd's collective energy. My body hummed with it, making me want to crawl right out of my own skin. The violation of hundreds of strangers' energy was something I wouldn't wish on anyone.

"Kane!" I cried, pushing against a large intoxicated man begging a woman to flash her tits for him. "Move."

When the man didn't budge, magic burst from my fingertips.

"What the fuck?" he sneered, rubbing his arm. "What the hell, bitch? You got a stun gun or something?"

I craned my neck and ducked around him.

"Jade." Kane grabbed my arm and staunched the invasion of energy once more. The panic fled until I realized we'd lost the dragonfly.

"Oh, man. Do you see it?" I called over the music blaring from the clubs.

Kane nodded and pointed ahead of us.

And sure enough, it was hovering right over the door of Wicked.

Chapter 3

"Let's go." Kane took the lead this time as I held on to him, and considering he was over six feet tall, he was able to cut a better path.

When we got to the front of his club, the dragonfly dropped and fluttered inside. I waved at Jim, the bouncer, and ignored his questioning glance. The two strippers who were trying to entice the crowds weren't nearly as tactful.

"Kane," a short blonde wearing two tiny strips of leather gushed. "What the heck are you doing here? You can't seriously be bringing Jade to the club for your honeymoon."

"Slight change of plans," he said and brushed past them.

"Don't let go of me," I said to Kane when we got inside. The club's energy was stale and held an echo of past patrons. I could block it out on normal days, but not after the onslaught of the crowds outside.

"I've got you."

We stood at the back of the club, watching the dragonfly. It hesitated and then took off fluttering in a circle high above the stage and the patrons. It moved slowly at first, then sped up, flying faster and faster until it was making a circle right over the spot where we'd opened the portal.

Kane's hand tightened around mine.

"She used it," I said, certain that was the case.

He nodded. "If what the angels said is true, then yes, I agree."

"But if the other shadow walkers followed it here, why didn't they see traces of it?"

"Maybe they weren't looking for it."

"Maybe." Snapping my fingers, I whispered, "Return." The dragonfly zoomed back to us and landed lightly in my palm. "Thank you." I tucked it into my pocket. "Are you ready?" I asked Kane.

"As ready as I'm gonna be."

I took a deep breath. "Okay, let's see what we've got."

It had been a few weeks since Kane and I had peeked into the shadow world. The ability had been an unexpected gift—or curse, depending on how you looked at it. At first, every time we'd touched I'd been plunged into darkness. But we'd finally found some sort of balance. It still happened, but we'd been working so hard to stay in this world it was weird to invite the shadows back in.

We clasped hands, and with a deep breath, I let my guards down. Lust and despair, combined with excitement from the club patrons, rushed into me at the same time the world faded to black and then resettled in shades of gray. The club patrons were still visible but muted now and seemingly wholly unaware of us.

Nothing about the club seemed out of the ordinary. There weren't any lost souls or even a trace of the portal. "That was unexpected," I said. "Remnants of the portal should be here."

"Now what?"

I inched forward, pulling Kane with me. People from our world unconsciously moved aside, parting for us in some mystical way. When we got to the edge of where I knew the portal had been, I crouched and placed a hand on the ground. A tiny spark sizzled at my fingertips. "It's still active. I think I need to call it."

Kane tugged on my hand, pulling me up. "Are you sure you want to do that?"

I worried my lower lip and shook my head. "No. I don't. But Chessandra said Mati was on the verge of death. What if we wait too long? What if she dies wherever she is because I'm too scared to go after her?"

Kane's reluctance was fierce as it slammed into me. "I won't risk you. Not now. Not ever."

My heart did a little flip in my chest. I reached up and placed my palm on his cheek. "I know. I feel the same. But can we just walk away from this? Can we live with ourselves if we do? Wherever she is, she's there because of the portal we opened."

"Fuck." He ran his other hand over the back of his neck. "All right. Call the portal, but at the first hint of trouble, we're backing away. Got it?"

I stifled a laugh. We were way past the first sign of trouble. "Let's just take it one step at a time." I crouched once more and placed my palm flat on the ground. Bolts of energy sparked over my hand. Focusing, I pushed my magic to my fingertips. The ground started to glow beneath my hand, and as I forced more and more magic out, the pool of light grew in a pale circle. When I was confident the light wouldn't fade, I stood and raised my arms skyward. "Portal of mine, do my will. Open for me. Let me see." It was a lame incantation, but it was the best I could do on the fly.

There was a low rumble that rolled across the club as the wind picked up. It was doing exactly what I'd asked. Then the world tilted, or at least mine did, because I was knocked off my feet and nearly flew headfirst into the fully formed portal, but Kane grabbed me and crushed me to his chest. He scrambled back and held tight, his heart racing frantically against my own.

"Holy shit," I said. "What happened?"

"The portal almost swallowed you."

I lifted my head and realized the wind was gone. All that was left was the glow of light three feet in front of us. "It's a lot calmer than when we opened it before."

Nodding, he glanced at it. "It feels different than last time, too."

He was right. The portal to Hell had been an inferno and completely terrifying. The energy of lost, angry souls had come through loud and clear, even to those not gifted with an empath ability. This one was...empty. Like a pit of nothingness but light.

Cautiously, we moved forward, trying to get a read on the portal and where it went. All there was to see was light. I glanced at Kane. "What do you think?"

He shrugged. "It doesn't exactly feel ominous. You getting anything we should be concerned about?"

"No." Not sure what else to do, I fished the dragonfly out of my pocket and held my palm out. "Find Mati."

The silver bug fluttered its wings and took off, right into the ball of light.

I turned to Kane. "I think we should follow it."

He hesitated then nodded his agreement. At the edge, I stopped and glanced up at Kane. "At least we're jumping together this time."

"If you jump, I jump, right?"

I snorted out a laugh. "Right, Jack."

He smiled down at me and brushed a thumb over my cheekbone. "Don't let go."

A strange mix of joy and disappointment clutched at my heart and made tears spring to my eyes. I blinked them back. "I can't believe we're joking about this right now."

"Better than hitting something."

"True. Ready?" I tightened my hand on his.

"On three." He counted, and a few seconds later we plunged into the light, our hands firmly clasped.

The world rose up and slammed into me, and Kane's hand ripped from mine as I crashed to the cold, hard ground. "Ouch. Damn, that hurt," I said, glancing around. I seemed to be sitting on a brick pathway with mist closing in all around me. "Kane?"

Eerie silence met my cry.

"Kane?" I called again, louder, a bit frantic. Had he hit his head? Landed somewhere else? Where the hell was he?

"Dammit! Answer me." I scrambled to my feet, twisting and turning, seeing nothing but mist. "Shit!"

Crouching, I frantically swiped my hands over the ground, searching. He had to be here. We'd come together.

"Kane!" I tried again when all I felt was brick. Standing, I moved cautiously, both anxious to search and also terrified I would put more distance between us. Instead, I sent out my emotional energy. If he was here, I'd get a read on him. Fear, mixed with intense curiosity and hope, brushed against my psyche. But it wasn't Kane. Every emotional signature was unique, like a voice, and I'd know Kane's anywhere. Whoever I was feeling definitely wasn't him. He was either knocked out or not close enough for me to reach him.

"Banish the mist," a feminine voice called from behind me.

I spun. A solid wall of gray met me. "What? Who are you?"

"Who are you?" she demanded, the irritation in her tone mirroring the irritation filling her.

"Mati?" I asked.

More silence.

"Matisse? If that's you, your sister sent me. Chessandra." I stood in the mist, becoming more terrified by the second that Kane appeared to be missing. And whoever this was wasn't helping matters. "Come on. I'm here to help," I said angrily. "It's my freakin' wedding day of all days. Now I'm stuck here, my fiancé appears to be missing, and if you're not Mati, then I'm seriously in the wrong place."

"It's your wedding day?" the woman asked, her voice high pitched with disbelief.

"Well, not anymore." I crossed my arms over my chest and clutched both arms out of pure frustration.

"Damn. That sucks. Chessa's such a bitch."

"Yes, it does. And yes, she is."

"Are you a witch? Or just a shadow walker?"

"Both." I took a step toward her voice. "Now what did you mean when you said to banish the mist?"

"You need to cast a banishing spell." Confusion rippled from her to me. "You said you're a witch, right?"

I huffed in frustration. "Yes. But I don't normally banish things unless we're talking about evil spirits." Now her energy turned to amusement. Seriously? "Look. If you want my help, you might want to start cooperating. Otherwise, I'm out of here." That was a lie. I wouldn't leave until I was sure Kane wasn't here, but dammit, this chick was pissing me off.

"You're the white witch, aren't you?"

I paused. She knew who I was? "Yes," I answered cautiously.

"Figures." She let out a long sigh. "This is the spell. *By my mind, by my heart, by the power of my will, may the mists part.*"

"Okay…but why don't you do it?"

"I can't." Her words were clipped, full of anger. "My magic has…well, it's not working."

"Oh." My heart broke for this girl. Ever since I'd come to accept my magic, it had become so thoroughly a part of me, I couldn't imagine it not working. Couldn't imagine how awful and helpless it would be to be without it. Anxious to find Kane and to see something other than mist, I touched the magic deep inside and repeated her words.

The mist retreated, leaving us standing on what appeared to be the waterfront of the Mississippi River. The dark-haired girl sat on the rocks, staring out at the normally brownish water. In this dimension it appeared to be black. She was rail thin but otherwise appeared unharmed.

I searched frantically for Kane but didn't see him anywhere. "No! Dammit, this is not supposed to happen."

The girl—no, woman—turned and regarded me with defeated eyes. The dragonfly pin was resting in her hand, no longer animated. "What wasn't supposed to happen?"

"Kane is supposed to be here. He jumped through with me. Where is he?"

Shaking her head, she closed her eyes. "Unless this Kane is a powerful witch, he likely can't come here."

"What? Where are we?"

She shrugged. "Damned if I know. But it doesn't mist in the shadow world, and this place is void of other souls."

Shock rippled through me. She was right. There wasn't anyone else here. Just us two. "We're not in Purgatory, are we?" I'd seen it before. Kane and Lailah had been stuck in a rundown shack. I hadn't seen anyone else then, either.

She shook her head. "No. This…feels different."

Of course she was right. Kane and I had already picked up on that. There weren't any lingering emotions. Most places had an echo of those who'd come before. This one didn't. My heart started to thump hard against my ribs. "Holy shit."

"What?"

"I think we're in a place where time stands still. It feels just like that room."

"What is today?"

"February twenty-first."

She shook her head again. "Not unless years have gone by since I went missing. As far as I can tell, I've been here about a week."

Relief flooded through me. "Yeah, that sounds right. Thank God for that."

She grunted. "Yeah, you hang here for a week by yourself with no one to talk to and no food or water. See how you like it."

That horror filled me again. How was she surviving? "No food or water?"

She shrugged. "Besides being really weak, the lack of sustenance doesn't appear to be a factor. But still, I'm about to go crazy with boredom. It's like I'm in limbo, waiting all the time for nothing. Because nothing comes."

"I did," I said. "And I'm going to get you out of here."

She raised her eyebrows. "How?"

"However I leave, you're coming with me." I glanced around again. No Kane. Where was he? Still back in the shadow world? Jesus, I hoped so. Otherwise I'd never find him. "How did you end up here? That portal I used was originally a gate to Hell."

Mati sat back down and buried her head in her hands. Then she jerked her head up. "I was working on closing the veil from the shadow world to Hell. Chessandra's orders." Self-righteous anger engulfed her and for a second I thought her eyes turned red. Whoa. Just like Chessandra's. "The spell seemed to work, too, but then it backfired and rushed through me." She shuddered, and a look of terror claimed her face. "I was on fire. It literally felt like I was burning alive." Her voice was low, shaking as she forced the words out. "I thought I was going to die."

The absolute horror of what she'd gone through rushed from her and slammed into me. Even the pain she'd felt hit me hard, making my knees almost buckle. I took deep, cleansing breaths, forcing the energy out of my system, praying I wasn't pushing it back on her. "What happened then?"

Tears streamed from her big whiskey-colored eyes, the red completely gone now. "I don't know. The rest of my magic sort of exploded, and when it was gone, I was left with nothing. Not even a spark."

She'd saved herself with her magic. "You must be a really strong witch."

"Not anymore."

"Bea can help," I said with confidence. No matter how much I learned, there was always something that I couldn't speak to. But Bea could. Or she'd help find an answer.

"Bea?"

"Beatrice Kelton. The New Orleans coven leader." I smiled. "She's back in charge until after the wedding...whenever that's going to be," I added, no longer irritated, just resigned.

She stiffened. "I don't think that's going to work."

"Sure it will. We just need to get you out of here." I was getting super anxious now. I prayed to the Goddess that Kane was waiting for me in the shadow world. Because I was not going to lose him today of all days. That was a hell. Fucking. No.

"I belong to the witches of Coven Pointe."

"So?" Most witches belonged to a coven. The collective power could accomplish what most witches couldn't by themselves.

She twisted her fingers together nervously. "You don't know, do you?"

Oh, crap on toast. Know what? I sighed and shook my head. "Obviously not. Why don't you fill me in on whatever it is?"

Maybe it was my eye roll that made her laugh. Or the fact that I seemed so clueless. But whatever it was, she seemed amused now. "You're the white witch who took over for Beatrice and you have no idea. This is just…" She shook her head. "She sure has her secrets. The witches of Coven Pointe live across the river."

"You mean Algiers Point?" It was the second-oldest neighborhood in New Orleans. They had a coven? I thought I knew all the witches in New Orleans.

She raised a sardonic eyebrow and nodded. "We call it Coven Pointe. Have you ever been there?"

"No."

"There's a reason for that. Before Algiers Point was founded, it was claimed by my ancestors and was called Coven Pointe. Over time, they were driven out. But fifty years ago, my grandmother and her siblings reclaimed what is ours. We've been at war—if you will—with the New Orleans coven ever since."

"What?" It was as if she were talking a different language. I'd never known Bea to not welcome a witch into the fold… unless… "Do your people dabble in black magic?"

"No," she said, clearly offended.

"Thank the Goddess for that."

"But we do experiment more than the NOLA coven."

"How?"

She gave a noncommittal shrug. "We just embrace more unorthodox methods."

I didn't have any idea what that meant. I didn't really want to know, either. The angel of the high council had sent me to get her sister. Whatever magic they used, it couldn't be that bad. I mean, her sister was a freaking angel, for God's sake. The high angel at that.

"But that's not why there's a war," Mati added.

I raised both eyebrows. "Are you going to fill me in? Because I have to say, this vagueness seems to be a family trait I'm not particularly fond of."

That actually got a smile out of her. Her entire face lit up, and just like that she morphed into a carefree, vibrant young woman. "Ha. Yeah, Chessa and I do that sometimes. Sorry. All I know is my auntie Dayla and Beatrice had a falling out over some man, and from that point forward, we never talked of or spoke to anyone in the coven on the east bank again. The details are vague, but for as long as I can remember, we've been kept isolated from the rest of the witches of New Orleans."

"That seems…crazy. No offense."

She shrugged. "Maybe. But Auntie Dayla is our coven leader and she's fair. I assume she has good reasons."

"Bea is fair, too." But doubt nagged at my mind. I trusted Bea, but I didn't know much about her past. "Never mind. That's their issue, not mine. Whatever war they have going on, it doesn't have anything to do with me. Let's just get out of here and we'll figure it out later."

She held her hand out to me. "Whatever you say, witch-girl. I'm more than ready to leave this hole."

Now what? Without knowing where to go, I opened up my senses one more time, pushing past all boundaries. Kane most definitely wasn't there. Nobody was. Only Matisse. But there was a tiny tickle of nondescript energy. I latched on to it, forcing the stream of consciousness to merge with my magic. A tug started in my belly and the world turned to mist.

Clutching Matisse's hand, I let my magic go. Everything faded and once again, I landed on my butt. Hard. Would I ever learn to get my feet under me?

"Jade?" Kane's voice penetrated my thoughts.

I jumped up and ran to his side.

He caught me in his arms, relief cascading from him in thick waves. "Where were you?"

"I…" I glanced around and realized we were back in the club but still in the shadow world. Souls milled around us, watching with dispassionate interest. They were ghosts who hadn't been called to either a higher or a lower plane. They just existed between worlds. It was sad, but I was grateful they hadn't ended up in Hell. "Where is she?"

"Who?" He glanced around and then back at me. "Mati? Did you find her?"

"Yes. Oh, son of a bitch."

"Jade?" When I didn't say anything, he took my hand and a moment later we were back in our world in the club. The music and the club's energy reverberated through me, making my stomach turn. "Let's go," Kane said. Tugging me after him, he took off toward the back door.

We climbed the three flights of stairs to my old apartment, the one still furnished with items he'd given me from his storage room. He'd told me he didn't want to rent it out so he could use it on the nights he worked late and didn't make it home. But that never happened. He always came home to me. I was pretty sure he kept it because my ghost dog lived there.

As soon as we opened the door, Duke, the golden retriever, bounded toward me, tongue lolling out the side of his mouth.

"Hey boy," I said and flopped on the bed, my hand covering my forehead.

He jumped up, landing on my stomach. I let out a surprised oomph. It wasn't like he weighed much…he was a ghost, after all. But he did dispel some energy. He must have missed me.

"You okay?" Kane asked.

"Yeah. Ghost dog jumped on me."

He chuckled and sat beside me. "What happened?"

I went through everything I'd learned and ended with how I'd lost her, just as I'd lost him. "It appears I'm the only one who can cross. Why?"

"Powerful white witch, love. What else could it be?"

I sighed. "Not powerful enough. She's still there."

"But she's not hurt, right?"

"No. She's awfully thin, though. She needs food. If she doesn't collapse from weakness first, she's likely to go crazy.

There's nothing there. No one. She just sits on the rocks in the mist without any power to even banish it. It must be awful."

"We'll find a way." He leaned down and kissed me. His lips were soft and tender, sweet, as if he was savoring me. Then his mouth turned heated, possessive, and his hands slid up my sides. He lifted me until I was sitting up. I opened my eyes and stared into the deep pools of his molten chocolate ones. "I'm never going to get used to that."

I smile against his lips. "You mean kissing me silly?"

His grip tightened. "That I can get used to, pretty witch. No, I mean thinking I might have lost you. When we were separated and I couldn't find you…well, dammit. I had no idea if you were coming back and there wasn't a damn thing I could do about it."

I pressed two fingers to his lips. "I know. I felt the same way when I realized you weren't with me. Every instinct told me to rush back, but I couldn't just leave. I didn't even know where I was. But yes, I do know. And I'm not a fan. We're supposed to shadow walk together. Right?"

"Of course. But you weren't shadow walking, were you? You were jumping dimensions again."

"Damn angels." I swung my legs over the side of the bed and stood.

"Where are you going?"

I stood frozen, wondering that myself. Where did we start? "We need to find Chessandra."

Chapter 4

Getting through town during Mardi Gras was worse than Hell. And I would know because I'd been there. Twice. It took us two hours just to get out of the French Quarter and over the Crescent City Connection Bridge. In order to get in touch with Chessandra, we needed Lailah, and she was still at Summer House in Cyprus Settlement. Along with everyone else we knew.

I spent the entire time wringing my hands, horrified that Mati was stuck in a world between. I was somewhat confident she was safe for now, but what a horrible existence. I wouldn't be comfortable until we got her out.

"Jade?" Kane asked.

"Hmm?"

"Will you marry me?"

His flippant tone startled me right out of my stupor and I actually laughed. "Sure. When?"

"As soon as I get the minister's ass back to Summer House."

I patted him on the knee. "Good luck. I'm pretty sure he had another wedding tonight." There wasn't one flippin' pig's ass of a chance that the minister was going to find a way back to Cypress Settlement. In this traffic? Yeah, no. But if Kane wanted to try, I could spare five minutes to say I do. Even if my gorgeous dress was back in town. I suppressed a sigh and stared out the window.

Kane did what he could, but our minister didn't even seem to remember us at all. Clearly someone had hit him a little too hard with a memory spell. As it was, we probably were going to need to find a new one altogether. When Kane ended the call, he shook his head. "Looks like today really isn't the day."

I ran a hand through his gorgeous dark hair and whispered, "I already belong to you."

His slow smile sent tingles to all the right places. We flirted and teased each other for the rest of the trip, and when we finally pulled into the long driveway of the house, I was almost relaxed. But then I saw remnants of the wedding, and pressure filled my chest, making it hard to breathe. All the planning. All the angst to get it done before Kane's parents left town, and now this. Goddess, my life was a clusterfuck sometimes. At least Kane was in it with me this time.

"Kane! There you are." His mother stumbled off the porch. The massive amount of beads wrapped around her neck actually made her look as if she might topple over at any minute. Or maybe that was due to the hurricanes. No doubt the half-full glass in her hand wasn't the first. "You missed Mardi Gras! The parades have already gone by. Where have you been?"

He gave her an indulgent smile. "We had some business to take care of. Looks like you had a great time, though."

She laughed and leaned in, placing her hand on his chest. "I'm so glad I wore an easy-access bodice, if you know what I mean."

Kane's jaw tightened, and I was torn between laughing and vomiting. Judging by her massive haul, she must've flashed her ass off, so to speak. "Mother," Kane said and sighed. "That's way too much information."

She giggled. "Oh, Kane. I'm not dead yet."

"Shelia!" his dad called from the porch. "Put that drink down and get your ass in here."

I raised surprised eyebrows at Kane. Did he always talk to her like that? I'd drink a lot, too.

"And make sure you keep your damn shirt on. The neighbors are complaining."

Apparently Mardi Gras in Cypress Settlement wasn't nearly the freak show it was in the French Quarter. There had probably been tons of kids. Ugh. We were going to be the talk of the town.

Kane shook his head and tugged me past both of his parents, disgust rippling off him. "Ignore them."

"Where are you going?" his dad called after us.

Kane quickened his pace, humiliation and pure frustration slipping from his hand to mine.

"Don't let them get to you," I said. "They'll be gone soon, back to wherever they go." His parents had spent the majority of his life traveling abroad, only sweeping into town when it was convenient for them. He'd been raised mostly by his mamaw. I wished with all my heart I could've met her. She sounded like an amazingly strong woman. Unfortunately, he'd lost her a few years back.

"That day can't come soon enough," he said.

I glanced at him, surprised by his clipped tone. Up until now he'd been mostly tolerant of their self-centered behavior. "Are you all right?"

He closed his eyes for a moment as if trying to get a hold of himself. "Yeah. They just annoy the shit out of me sometimes."

I squeezed his fingers, letting him know I understood. My family had issues of its own. We passed through the ballroom, and after one glance at all the lights and fresh flowers, I averted my gaze and stared at the floor. The house was still weddingized. Being slapped in the face with it was too much.

Relief consumed me as we slipped into the kitchen, until the trays of food assaulted my senses. Crab cakes, stuffed mushrooms, herb-and-cheese–filled turnovers. Lailah, Pyper, Kat, and Aunt Gwen stared at us from the table, their plates half empty. I waved and grabbed a plate. Once it was overflowing,

I sat between Lailah and Kat. Kane followed my lead, filling his plate, but stood leaning against a counter.

"Jade?" Aunt Gwen asked.

I glanced at her and tears threatened to spring forth. Her curly gray hair had been slightly straightened into a sophisticated wave, and she was dressed in a chic pantsuit. I'd never really seen her in anything other than blue jeans or coveralls. "Gwen, you look so lovely," I said unable to hold back the tears.

"Ahh, sweet girl, don't cry." She got up and pulled me into a hug. "It will be okay. The suit isn't going anywhere. You'll see me dressed up for the next round."

I blubbered out a laugh. "That's one good thing that came out of this, I guess."

She wiped my tears away and gave me a kiss on my cheek. "It'll be all right. I promise."

I eyed her, wondering as I always did if she'd had a vision. But I didn't ask. She wouldn't tell me anyway.

Kat got up and poured a couple glasses of iced tea. When she returned, she set one in front of me. "We've been worried," she said quietly.

"Yeah, I was ready to kick some serious angel ass for what they did today of all days," Pyper added. "It's a damn good thing they live in another realm or your mom might have beat me to it."

"Really?" I glanced around. "Where is she?"

"Upstairs." Gwen squeezed my hand. "She's working out her frustration by mixing some potions."

Alarm raced through me. "That doesn't sound like a good plan."

"Better that than formally summoning Chessandra and your dad," Gwen said.

"Can she do that?" I glanced around at everyone. My gaze landed on Lailah.

She shrugged. "If she gets the help of another angel. Meri would do it probably."

Meri was one of my mom's best friends and the one I'd shared my soul with at one point. It could be argued I'd saved her from demonism. It was likely Meri would help Mom do just about anything she asked. "Then I guess it's better she's playing mad scientist instead."

Mom was an earth witch and could make some interesting potions. Most were harmless, but not all. Especially the ones she made when she was pissed. Still, it was better than pissing off the high angel.

"All right. Enough chitchat," Pyper said, always the blunt one of the group. "We're dying here. Tell us what the hell happened."

I met Kane's eyes and noticed the easing of the tension in his face. It was doing him good to be around our friends. Waving him over, I nodded to an empty chair beside Pyper, his best friend. He needed this just as much as I did.

Once he was settled, I proceeded to explain everything that had happened since we'd been so rudely whisked away.

"The veil to Hell has been closed?" Lailah asked with wide eyes.

I nodded. "It appears so."

She stood and started pacing, her long honey-blond hair flowing behind her. "But how? I've never even heard of anyone coming close before. It's…well, impossible. I mean, the idea that angels can't fall anymore. I can't even… I just… Whoa."

Pyper and Gwen both chimed in with questions asking if demons could still cross, if witches could be taken. Was there still a need for soul guardians? Was black magic still accessible? Lailah didn't have the answers but was on her feet, ready to search for them, when Kat held her hand up.

"Hold on." Kat stood, demanding their attention. "I get that the closing of the veil is a big deal, but Jade said a young woman is trapped in some odd dimension. Isn't that more important right now?"

I sent my friend a grateful smile. Leave it to Kat to steer the conversation back to what was most important. Lailah's reaction was expected, but we had to focus on Mati now. "Can you call Chessandra?" I asked Lailah.

"Huh?" Her head jerked up, her expression still filled with wonder. "Oh, sure. But I can't believe she didn't give you a way to get to her directly."

I held my hands up. "She was more than a little distracted."

"I guess so." Lailah stood and moved to the middle of the kitchen. She raised her hands and without a word, a beam of pure white light filled our kitchen. The light twisted in on itself and then morphed into a translucent form of the high angel.

"Did you find her?" Chessa demanded.

"Yes."

A whoosh of breath rushed from Chessandra, and if she'd been in solid form, she might have lost her footing. "Thank the Goddess." She glanced around and her relieved expression vanished just as quickly. "Where is she?"

"In another dimension. I couldn't get her out. But I think she's relatively safe...for now."

Chessandra's eyes turned crimson once more. Then she pierced Lailah with her terrifying gaze. "Do what you have to in order to get her home safe."

Lailah stood tall and nodded, accepting her orders with grace. "Yes, your highness."

The high angel turned back to me and Kane. "Keep me updated." The light vanished, taking her with it.

"That was creepy," Pyper said.

We all turned and stared at her.

"What? It totally was. I mean, she had devil eyes. Right?"

Kane chuckled and covered her small hand with his. "Definitely."

I glanced at Lailah. Our eyes met and there was worry in her blue gaze. "Any ideas on where to start?" I asked.

She bent her head and pressed a hand to her forehead, thinking. "We need to know who her soul guardian is. He or she will have the closest connection to her soul. The guardian might be able to help her cross back over."

I frowned. "Then why didn't Chessandra start there?"

Lailah shook her head. "No idea. But didn't she say angels are shut out? Maybe that's why. I still want to find him or her. At the very least we might gain some knowledge about what Mati was up to and maybe find a way to reverse the spell if we have to in order to bring her home."

"That sounds like a solid plan. Still, we should start working on a spell to see if we can pull her out together." With the coven's combined energy, we might be able to make it happen. I glanced around the kitchen and frowned. "Where's Bea?"

"She left a while ago." Kat pushed a mushroom around on her plate. "I'm pretty sure she was planning to set some protection spells for you two."

"Really?"

"I think she's feeling somewhat helpless," Lailah added. "She can't help you when you slip into the shadows. She's your mentor. It's hard to let go."

My heart swelled with the knowledge Bea was still doing what she could. "But that was before we realized Matisse isn't in the shadows. It looks like we need to get on the road to the Garden District," I said to Kane.

"You're kidding, right?" Pyper scoffed.

"No. Why?"

"Hello." She waved a hand in front of my face. "Mardi Gras. The parades are headed down the Avenue. You'll never get through."

"She's right, love," Kane said as he got up and moved to stand behind me. The solid weight of his hands rested on my shoulders.

"Ugh." How could I forget? "Now what?"

Lailah held a finger up and pulled out her phone. "I can't imagine she went home anyway. I'll find out where she is." She got up and slipped into the other room.

"There you are," my mom said as she strode into the kitchen. She stopped and placed her balled hands on her hips. "What happened?"

"Drake," I said by way of answer.

She scowled. "That son of a bitch." Then she eyed me and her stance relaxed. "I'm so sorry, Jade. What a crappy thing to have happen today." Her high heels clattered on the tile as she strode over to me and squeezed my fingers. "Don't worry about a thing, shortcake. I'll take care of rescheduling this shindig."

Mom and I had our share of issues, but we were working on them. The fact that she was more concerned about my wedding being interrupted than the actual cause made me chuckle. Nothing was going to get in the way of her seeing her little girl walk down the aisle. "I love you, Mom."

"I love you, too, baby. Now tell me what that prick did this time." The fierceness in her voice, combined with the determination sparking from her, had me wondering if she was going to hunt him down and kick his ass. She probably would if she could get to him. I made a mental note to warn Meri in case Mom called in that favor.

I filled her in on the details, leaving nothing out. Curiously, she chose the tidbit about Coven Pointe to focus on. "Bea is at war with another coven? That seems...unlikely."

"I don't know, Mom. No one ever mentioned them. I thought I knew all the witches in town."

"Some wounds run deep." Gwen sipped her coffee. "If the feud has been going on that long, it could involve anything."

"Very true." Mom grabbed a diet soda from the fridge and headed toward the door. "I'm going to work on taking down the decorations so you don't have to stare at everything for now. Let me know when you need me for anything."

The door swung closed behind her, then slammed open again as Shelia stormed into the kitchen. "What's going on in here? I thought this was a party? Kane, get the crawfish boil going. Damn, I'm going to starve." She bypassed the multiple trays and chafing dishes and yanked the refrigerator door open. An instant later she had the fixings for another hurricane all spread out on the counter.

I slumped in my chair. I had to get out of there. She was too much.

Kane strode over to her and pulled the rum from her hands. "Maybe you should pace yourself, Mother."

She froze and stared at him dumbfounded for a moment. Then she yanked the alcohol back in defiance. "How dare you embarrass me in front of your friends?" Her tone was a loud whisper we all could hear.

"I think you're doing just fine on your own. In any case, if you want to keep drinking, be my guest. Drink yourself into a stupor if you want to. I don't give a shit. Just don't vomit on our furniture."

My mouth fell open in shock. I knew their relationship was strained, but I hadn't known about the hostility. Kane never talked about it. I could see why. I'd spent a significant amount of my life without my mother around, but it hadn't been her choice. Kane's mom had not only abandoned him but clearly had addiction issues. My heart swelled with admiration for the man he'd become despite his parents.

"Kane?" I said.

He tore his angry gaze from his drunk of a mother and looked at me. "Let's go. We have work to do."

Chapter 5

Filled with gratitude for all they were doing for us, we said a quick goodbye to our friends. On our way out, I gestured to Lailah to follow us outside. She was still talking with Bea and had been frantically taking notes on a napkin.

At the car, she handed me her phone. "Bea wants to talk to you."

Hope pushed away some of my turmoil. My mentor never let me down. "Bea, thank the Goddess."

"Jade, dear, I'm so sorry about the wedding."

A stab of irritation pierced me in the gut. I appreciated the sentiment, I really did. But it was dammed hard not to wallow in pity when everyone wanted to mention it. "We'll reschedule," I said evenly. "Right now, Mati is more important. Please tell me you have something for me."

"Not a lot, I'm afraid. Lailah said she already advised you to find her soul guardian. I don't know if that will help, but you can try." She sighed into the phone. "The Coven Pointe witches use a different form of magic than we do. Their spells come from a different source, so figuring out what *we* can do to help Mati is going to prove difficult, if not downright impossible."

"What do you mean, different?"

She hesitated.

"Bea? Is all of this really about some dude?"

"What?" There was genuine shock in her voice. "How did you get that idea?"

"Mati said that's why the two covens don't mix. That this all started over some man."

She laughed, a high-pitched tinkling sound. "Now, that's funny. If Dayla is spouting that story, then she's truly deluded."

Dayla. Mati's aunt and her coven leader. I was extremely curious about what had really gone down. But now wasn't the time. "Do you have any information that might help? Or a place to start?"

She hesitated. Then she took a deep breath. "I think you should go to Dayla in Coven Pointe. The best course of action is to restore Mati's powers. But you can only get that from one of her ancestors. Or more likely a few of them. They should have some sort of spell for that. You'll need to get them to trust you with their magic, though. And that will be the tough part. They aren't going to like giving you any of their power."

I could see why. If someone I didn't know asked me to give up some of my power, I'd be downright hostile about it. Who knew what they'd do with it? But I had to agree. If Mati could use her own power to cross back over, that would be best. "Am I going to be welcome there?" If our covens were in some crazy war—one no one even understood—what was I going to be walking into?

"Probably not. Tell them Chessandra sent you."

It sounded pretty simple. Just go get her power, restore her magic, and have her blast herself out. Right. Nothing was that easy. Not ever. And likely whatever spell they gave me would have consequences. They always did. "All right. But if one of them turns me into an ashtray, I expect you to come for me."

"Ashtray?"

"Yeah. An ashtray. Like those horrible metal ones kids make in school."

"Uh…all right, dear." I could tell by her resistant tone she thought I'd lost my mind.

I laughed, realizing she was probably right. "They are the ugliest things ever. I'm just saying I don't want to live life as a tin box smelling like tar and ash. That's all."

"I think you're safe," she said, chuckling. "But I promise I'll save you from eternal ash. Call me after you speak to her. Lailah has the address and a few notes."

"Thanks." After ending the call, I handed Lailah her phone and took the directions from her. "Kane and I are off to deal with the other witches. Why did no one tell me about them?"

She shrugged. "They keep to themselves and so do we. It can sometimes be hard to coexist with another coven. Mostly it's best to just ignore each other if each one doesn't want to make waves."

I stared at her dubiously. "Seriously?"

"Yes. I never mentioned them because I honestly don't think about them much. Bea is one of my assignments, as are you. I'm worried about what you two are up to. Not the coven across the river. As long as they aren't corrupting souls, I really don't care what they do."

Well, as long as they weren't corrupting souls. Alrighty then.

Kane placed a hand on the small of my back and led me to the passenger side of his Lexus. "It doesn't sound like I'm going to like this."

I turned into him, his fresh rain scent so familiar and comforting. "Do you ever?"

Brushing his lips over my temple, he murmured, "I like you."

That made me smile. "Good thing, Mr. Rouquette."

He tilted his head and leaned in, catching my lower lip between his. My fingers curled in his shirt as I pulled him closer and kissed him. It was a bittersweet moment, the two of us standing in front of Summer House, in the place we should have been leaving to go on our honeymoon. We broke apart, staring at each other for a moment. Then Kane said, "Italy will still be there."

I chuckled humorlessly. "It's lasted this long."

"There you go." He brushed back a lock of hair that had fallen from my fancy updo. "Ready?"

I shook my head no but walked to the car anyway. He followed and opened the door for me. I waved at Lailah, who had retreated to the front porch to give us privacy. "I'll call you as soon as we know anything."

She nodded and disappeared back into the house.

Kane joined me in the car and within minutes we were back on the highway headed to the Pointe.

"Did we take a wrong turn?" I eyed the rough neighborhood, taking in the decaying homes. One was being overtaken by vegetation, vines invading it from all sides. Rusted bars covered the windows and the porch sagged, appearing moments from collapsing. I would have thought it abandoned if it hadn't been for the woman standing in the doorway side-eyeing us. She wore gold hot pants, a skin-tight black cami tank top, and black slippers.

We came to a four-way stop behind a late-eighties souped-up Buick low-rider. Kane glanced at the GPS in the dash and shook his head. "No. This road leads us to the Pointe. But maybe we should've taken a different route."

I glanced back at the woman taking a long drag of a cigarette. She pulled a phone from her back pocket and hit a button.

A moment later the front door to the house next to her swung open. A large Hispanic man stepped onto his own decaying porch, wearing jeans and a gun belt, complete with a sidearm. No shoes or shirt. Tattoos covered most of his upper body. Oh, crap. We needed to get the hell out of here. Obviously we'd accidentally wandered into gang territory.

I lowered my gaze and took in the obvious luxury of the Lexus Kane drove. This was not good. Magic tingled in my chest and rushed to my fingertips just in case.

"It'll be fine," Kane said. But from the corner of my eye I saw more men pile out of the house, most of them armed. One had some sort of glass pipe he was lighting up.

"Uh, Kane." My nerves made my voice shake slightly.

"I see them." He tightened his grip on the wheel and frowned at the Buick in front of us. The car just sat there, a faint trail of smoke streaming from its tailpipe. No other cars in sight.

"They're waiting to see what we'll do," I said.

He took a look in the rearview mirror and swore when he saw a black SUV coming up behind him. "Time to go." He swerved out from behind the Buick and peeled out.

As we squealed by, the hooded driver raised what appeared to be a gun and aimed.

I flattened my hand to the car window and shouted, *"Tego Texi Tectum!"*

A round of gunfire sounded through the streets, and bullets rained over the car, bouncing off my protection spell. Holy cripes. That was ugly. And for no reason. We'd just been driving, albeit in a car worth three times more than my annual salary. That wasn't saying much. I was a glass artist who also worked at a cafe.

I started to tremble as Kane maneuvered the car through the uneven roads. Wrapping my arms around my torso, I did my best to get myself under control. It wasn't as if I'd never been in a dangerous situation before, but those times had usually involved demons, ghosts, or evil magic. Since I was a newcomer to New Orleans, straight from the quiet state of Idaho, I'd never been threatened by a random stranger before, much less because I just happened to be driving down the wrong street.

A few minutes later, we turned onto a gorgeous tree-lined street flanked by a sign that said, *Welcome to Coven Pointe, Est. 1719*. The blight and crime had disappeared, replaced by well-kept homes and gardens.

"Whoa," I said. "I've can't believe we went from a war zone to this."

Kane nodded. "I haven't been over here in a long time. Looks like the bad part of town has gotten worse." His house was in the French Quarter. Just a short ferry ride away, but since he worked on the east bank, he wouldn't have much reason to come over here. He glanced at me, worry in his deep brown eyes. "You okay?"

"I will be." I sucked in a breath and willed myself to calm down. "Dealing with evil spirits is one thing. But guns? Yeah, I don't need that. Tell me there's a safer way to get back."

"There has to be." He placed a hand on my knee and, still staring straight ahead, said, "Thank God for you, Jade. That was an impressive bit of magic you used back there."

I covered his hand with mine. "Great driving, too."

His lips turned up into a ghost of a smile. "Thanks. But let's not do that again."

"Deal."

A few blocks down we turned right onto Olivier. The closer we moved toward the river, the nicer the houses got. "Slow down," I said. "I think it's that one on the left."

Kane pulled over in front of a large Victorian home and killed the engine. We both peered across the street. The house was a double shotgun, not unlike Kane's. But this one was set on a double lot and the yard was impeccably maintained. Perfectly trimmed ivy framed the steps leading up to the home, and violas and pansies in purple, yellow, and pink lined the sidewalk.

"Ready?" I asked.

"Sure."

Kane and I crossed the quiet street. The sun was out, and a couple passed us walking a golden retriever and a lab. They smiled and waved. My thoughts jumped to Duke, my ghost dog. I was going to have to find a way to move him to our place in the French Quarter. It would be nice to have a dog around. One who didn't shed or make a mess.

"This is a great neighborhood," I said as Kane and I climbed the ivy-framed steps.

"It's nicer than I remember." He pressed the doorbell.

I glanced around at the neighboring houses. They were mostly shotgun doubles or camelbacks, but there were a few Victorians and Greek Revivals mixed in. "I like it here."

Kane slipped his arms around me, holding me from behind. I leaned into him and then stepped away. This was a business call, after all.

The door swung open and an older woman—mid-sixties, maybe—dressed in beige linen pants and a royal blue silk blouse peered at us. "Can I—"

A loud boom rumbled overhead and heavy storm clouds appeared out of nowhere.

"Witch!" the woman cried as her pupils dilated until her irises disappeared. Her hand came up, magic sparking like a fireball.

"Wait!" I tried to grasp the magic in my chest, but it was too late. A blast of magic shot from her outstretched hand, knocking Kane and me off the porch.

"Ouch!" I cried as I landed on my side, holding my hands up ready to attack. But the door was shut and the witch had disappeared. "Shit. What was that for?"

Kane scrambled to his feet and reached a hand down to help me up.

"Are you okay?" I asked him.

He nodded but kept his gaze straight ahead at the house in front of us that now had half a dozen ravens flying around it.

Blood trickled down my arm. I scowled. It hurt. But worse than that, I couldn't leave my blood lying around where another witch might be able to get it. I spun toward the car and then froze. "Uh, Kane?"

"Yeah?"

"Have you seen this?" Holding my injured arm to my body, I jerked my head toward his Lexus.

He turned and swore. "Son of a bitch." The entire car was glowing. We walked tentatively toward it and then around it.

"Oh my God." I clasped a hand over my mouth, my body turning cold as ice. On the passenger's side there were five round spots that glowed brighter than the rest of the car. "That must be where the bullets hit." One of them was right in the middle of the passenger window. If I hadn't been fast enough with my protection spell, it would've likely hit me in the head.

Kane grasped my wrist and jerked me to him, holding me tight against his chest. He was trembling.

I wasn't doing that great myself.

"Jesus fucking Christ," he whispered in my ear.

I nodded against him, hating that we had the evidence of just how close we'd come to a true disaster.

"You should leave," a female voice said from behind us.

Kane tightened his hold on me, but I pushed back gently and turned to find another woman standing with her arms crossed over her chest. I guessed she was in her mid-forties. She wore a long cotton skirt and a formfitting T-shirt. Very bohemian.

"I don't think you really want us to," I said, trying to keep the defensiveness out of my tone. Regardless of being blasted off the porch, I needed to get these people to talk to me. "Chessandra sent me."

The woman's eyes dilated just like the first woman's had. "Chessandra is not welcome here either."

Distrust rippled through the air, and I could sense the magic building in her.

"Please," I said, holding Kane behind me. His agitation bombarded me, causing my skin to prickle. One more magical outburst from these witches and he was going to lose his cool, if not physically then at least verbally. I needed him to dial it down a notch. If any of them were intuitives, they could read his defensive mood, and that wouldn't help.

I gathered a tiny bit of my own calm energy and pressed it into the palm of his hand. He stirred behind me and let out a tiny grunt of displeasure when he realized what I'd done. Still, his rigid body relaxed slightly, and I knew my magic had done what I'd needed it to do.

"We need to talk to Dayla. It's about Matisse," I said to the witch.

Her pupils constricted slightly and the brilliant blue of her irises glowed, similar to Kane's car. Whoa. These witches did have some weird powers.

"You know where Mati is?" There was hope shining through the skepticism swirling around her.

"I spoke with her this afternoon." I clutched my arm to my T-shirt, trying to stop my blood from dripping on the pavement.

I was about to elaborate on where Mati was, but the witch asked, "Where?"

"She's in another dimension."

"Bring her to us immediately. Then we can talk." She started to stride down the street toward the large Victorian house.

"Wait!" I let go of Kane and ran to catch up with her, wincing at the pain shooting down my arm. "I'm here for information and to help if that's at all possible."

She stilled and then turned slowly. Magic crackled around her. She pressed her hands together as if to keep her power contained.

I stopped and held my hands up. "We mean no harm. Honestly."

She glanced at Kane's car. "Your magic is strong."

Was that a question? I assumed it was. "Yes. I'm a white witch. That—" I gestured to the car "—is because we ran into some trouble on the way here. I was only trying to protect us." I frowned. "I don't know why it's glowing all of a sudden. It didn't happen until after we were tossed off the porch."

She studied me for a moment. Her eyes narrowed as she muttered under her breath and moved carefully past me to the Lexus. Placing a hand on the hood, she closed her eyes and said, *"Release."*

The glow around the car shimmered brighter, flickered twice, and then rushed into her fingertips. She let out a loud gasp and clutched her chest with her other hand.

Unwelcome tendrils of energy crawled up my arms and grabbed on. I stepped back, clutching at my arms. "What the hell is happening?" I cried as the tendrils pinched and something vital was sucked right out of me. "Stop! Stop it!" I tried to call up my magic, but it only made it worse. Every bit of power I manifested was sucked away by the hold this witch seemed to have on me.

"Jade!" Kane called my name, but I couldn't see him. My vision narrowed to the witch in front of me.

Her long, pale blond hair fanned out with what appeared to be static electricity. When the glow was gone, she pulled her hand away from the car and the hold on me evaporated.

My knees weakened as my head spun. If it hadn't been for Kane, I could've collapsed right there in the street.

The other witch stared at me with wonder, her electric-blue eyes piercing me through the storm cloud shadows. "Wow. You weren't exaggerating."

I blinked, rapidly trying to focus.

"What did you do to her?" Kane demanded, anger streaming from him. It wrapped around me and made it hard to breathe.

"Kane," I said weakly. "I need you to calm down."

Guilt and frustration mixed with his anger and my vision started to fade to black.

"Please," I said.

Reluctantly he let go of me. The relief was instant, and I sucked in air as if I'd been trapped under water. The witch came back into focus. She stood there in front of me with her hand held out. I eyed it but made no move to bridge the distance. "Answer him," I said, putting force behind the words. A sputter of magic sparked through me and spread, fortifying my energy just enough that I didn't feel like I was going to collapse.

"Impressive," she said.

I scowled. "What? Giving me a magical smackdown?"

She laughed. "Oh no, honey. If that were to happen, you wouldn't be conscious right now."

I glared at her, acutely aware if we got into it, she'd kick my ass. Obnoxious witch. "What. Did. You. Do?"

"What you should have done." She stalked forward until we were inches apart and with lightning speed, her hand darted forward, catching my neck in a death grip. Then she unleashed her power.

Chapter 6

"Jade!" I heard Kane call and knew he must've leaped forward, but the witch held up a hand, creating a barrier of magic he couldn't penetrate.

My entire body seized. I couldn't do anything except scream silently in fear and anger. Vibrant colors flared around me and then everything faded, and all I saw was white.

Sweet, cool relief rushed into my veins, filling me with my magic, the magic the witch had stolen from me. But still I couldn't move. Whatever she was doing, she had me trapped in my own body. Flashes of being possessed by the ghost Camille took over my mind, leaving me almost broken with despair. Not this again. I couldn't deal with having my will completely taken away. Not like this. With my own magic being used against me.

When the rush stopped, she leaned in, made eye contact, and said, "Don't ever leave your magic behind. Any one of us can use it to control you." Her hand relaxed and my body tingled back to life.

I stumbled backward and landed in Kane's arms. He steadied me, holding me close to his solid frame. Sudden relief swept through me, making my eyes sting with unshed tears. The urge to climb back in the car and head back to Summer

House was overwhelming. I didn't want to do this. Not today. Not anymore.

The witch took off down the street. "Follow me," she called over her shoulder.

I stared after her, fighting the instinct to flee. I wasn't that weak. Something had to be done about Matisse. I turned my head and glanced up at Kane. "You okay?"

His stormy eyes searched mine. "No. What she did…"

I reached up and placed a hand on his cheek. And in that moment, I realized my bloodied arm had been healed. Had she done it? Had the magic transfer caused rapid healing? How strange. That had never happened before.

"Jade?" Kane asked.

"I'm fine. She didn't hurt me." Not physically, anyway. In reality, she'd done nothing but help me. It didn't make the pill any easier to swallow.

"But she could have," he said with a growl.

Another boom reverberated overhead and sunlight shone down between the parting clouds. I glanced up just in time to see the ravens scatter and literally disappear into the atmosphere. Holy cow. What the heck kind of witches were these chicks?

Across the street, both of the witches stood on the porch, staring at us. They were an odd pair. The older one was refined and elegant, the younger one relaxed and dressed as if she belonged in the seventies. The older one in the royal blue silk blouse made eye contact and said, "Come. Both of you."

I sensed the magic behind her words and felt a small tug. But it wasn't enough to force me into following her orders. Kane was a different story. His eyes glazed slightly and without speaking, he wrapped his large hand around mine and followed her command.

"Was that necessary?" I glared at the older witch. How dare she force her will on Kane?

She raised one thin eyebrow before turning and disappearing inside the house.

The blond witch smiled at me. A true, welcoming smile. "That was a formal invitation for witches. Our apologies that it affected your friend."

The moment we stepped through the front door, Kane's eyes cleared and he shook his head as if trying to clear the cobwebs.

The older witch turned to him. "The will of magic is extended to all witches so they can identify the type of magic we use. Witches can resist the force and make their own decision. Others usually have issues. Though she could have stopped you if she wanted to."

Kane crossed his arms over his chest and glared. I couldn't say I blamed him. We came here to help save one of their own and we'd gotten nothing but trouble.

The younger witch just grinned at Kane and then slowly raked her gaze over him, her smile turning wolfish.

"Whoa, there," I said, holding up a hand. "Back off, honey. This one is mine."

Kane turned and raised one quizzical eyebrow in my direction.

"What?" I whispered. "Did you see her mentally seducing you?"

He shook his head, clearly having lost all patience. Turning back to the other witches, he held his hand out. "We haven't been introduced. I'm Kane Rouquette, and this is my fiancée, Jade Calhoun."

The pair shared a glance. The older one nodded. "I've heard of you both." Taking Kane's hand, she added, "I'm Dayla Brinn, the Coven Pointe leader, and this—" she gestured to the blonde "—is Fiona Westin."

I held my hand out to Fiona. When she grabbed it, I said, "I wish I could say it was my pleasure, but that remains to be seen."

Her eyes sparkled as she laughed. "Understandable."

"This way." Dayla swept from the formal sitting room into the adjoining dining room.

Fiona waved a hand, indicating for us to follow. Dayla took us through the modern kitchen and then into a large great room. There were four wing-backed chairs and a loveseat positioned around a small coffee table. "Please have a seat," Dayla said. The request was once again backed by a twinge of magic.

I held tight to Kane's hand so he wouldn't be forced to do anything against his will. I, however, embraced the magic. She'd said they issued an invitation so outside witches could sample it and gain knowledge of who they might be. I'd never heard of that before. And other than white witches and earth witches, I had no idea what witches with other talents might be like. The magic was warm, inviting. Nothing at all sinister about it.

Definitely no black magic. I'd have to ask Bea why our coven never did this when we encountered strange witches. Or did we?

I tugged on Kane's hand and led him to the loveseat. When Fiona and Dayla were seated, Fiona perched on the edge of her seat and clasped her hands. "So tell me, Jade. What does my dear cousin expect you to do?"

"Chessandra?"

Dayla nodded. "Yes, Chessa is my sister's daughter. It's her fault Matisse is missing." Her eyes clouded over and her irises flashed red the same way Chessandra's had. But they faded back to pale ice blue almost instantly.

Kane and I shared a quick glance. He'd noticed as well. Did that mean Matisse was that much closer to death? A tiny shiver ran through me. "Kane and I are shadow walkers."

Dayla eyed Kane, scrutinizing him. "And you're a dream-walker. Interesting."

Kane scooted forward on the loveseat, resting his elbows on his knees. "How do you know that?"

She leaned over, mimicking his pose, and placed her palm on his cheek. Her gaze was intense as if she was trying to read him. Then she sat back, saying nothing.

Fiona shook her head almost apologetically. "Mama can taste magic in the air. Her assessments are correct ninety-nine percent of the time."

"Magic?" I asked. "But Kane isn't a witch."

"Of course he isn't," Dayla said dismissively and rose from her chair. She paced across the wood floors, then stopped and faced us. "You've seen Matisse."

It wasn't a question but a statement. I nodded. "I did. She's stuck in another dimension, caught somewhere between the shadows and this world. It's all gray mist and no one else is there." Guilt and helplessness grabbed hold of me. Why hadn't I been able to help her? "I'm so sorry, but I wasn't strong enough to bring her back."

"But she's all right?" Fiona asked, her face pinched in worry.

"She is not all right," Dayla snapped. Her eyes flashed red again. She blinked once and a single pink tear rolled down her cheek. Wiping it away, she said, "If she was all right, this wouldn't keep happening."

"She's okay for now," I said. "But she's very thin and I don't know how long she can last there. It's as if the atmosphere is leeching her energy."

Fiona jumped to her feet. "You need to take us to her."

"Sit down, Fiona," Dayla barked.

Fiona stared at her and clenched her fists. An angry steam cloud shot from her, aimed directly at Dayla.

Dayla raised her hand and the anger cloud dissipated into vapor.

Whoa. These witches were very different than the witches in my coven. They seemed much more powerful, working from will, not spells.

They glared at each other, but then with an unspoken understanding they both sat. I glanced between them and in my calmest tone, said, "I can't take you to her. I couldn't take Kane. For whatever reason, none of the other shadow walkers can cross over."

Dayla picked a daisy out of a nearby vase and twisted it between her fingers. She raised an eyebrow in Kane's direction. "You can cross. All you need is a nudge."

Kane frowned, and I tensed, sensing something was off, but I couldn't put my finger on it. "What does that mean?" I asked.

"You're a dreamwalker, right?" Fiona asked, smoothing her skirt.

"Yes," he said hesitantly, foreboding clinging to him. "What's that got to do with anything?"

Dayla rose, her skin almost glowing with some sort of magical current. She placed a graceful hand on Fiona's forearm. She frowned but raised one eyebrow in curious understanding. "They don't know."

"Know what?" I jumped to my feet, almost stumbling over a coffee table. "Seriously, someone needs to tell me what the hell is going on here."

Dayla eyed me and gave me a look of impatience, then she turned and moved to the ceiling-to-floor window and gazed out.

I turned to Fiona, intending to demand answers, but she watched her mother with concerned eyes. Worry clung to her.

Well, son of a bitch. Now what? I turned to Kane. He sat, his back rigid and his jaw jutting out. Our eyes met and I knew he was thinking the same thing. *Something is very off here.*

"Jade," Dayla said, still facing the window. "You obviously know you have angel blood."

"Yes." Fear took up residence in my chest. My whole life I'd been different. As a kid, being an empath had royally sucked. Not having the tools to shut off other people's emotions had been a nightmare. Then finding out I was a powerful witch who attracted darkness wasn't exactly a load of fun, either. And now the angel thing had doomed me to being a shadow walker—something I hadn't wanted and had been forced to accept in order to keep my soul safe. If I found out one more life-altering secret about what and who I was, I was going to go postal on someone's ass.

She turned around, focusing on the pair of us. "And you know it's because you're a witch with angel blood that you can shadow walk, correct?"

I glanced at Kane, but he was scrutinizing Dayla, no doubt trying to figure her out. "Yes."

"And what about your dreamwalker here? How is it that he's able to shadow walk?"

Kane's arm slipped around my waist, his large hand resting possessively on my hip. His touch settled me.

"Chessandra said it's because he's a dreamwalker and is my mate," I said.

She let out a low, chuckle. "Well, that's true enough. The dreamwalker part, anyway. I'm not sure him being your mate has much to do with it, other than he probably stores some of your power."

"I'm not magical," Kane said, his eyes narrowed as he studied her. "I can't siphon her powers."

"Not in a way that you'd recognize, you don't." Dayla walked back to us and once again perched on her chair, still holding the daisy. "Take a seat, Fiona. It's time to educate these two."

Fiona refreshed Dayla's tea and her own and then sat back, saying nothing.

Kane and I glanced at each other before settling into the loveseat once more.

Dayla took a sip of tea before asking Kane, "Are you aware of the history of dreamwalkers?"

"No. Not really. I only know that I can and do dreamwalk those I'm close to. It's not unlike those who can travel while dreaming, except I'm able to slip into the conscious mind of those I dream with."

"Yes, that's how it works," she agreed. "But do you know why?"

He shrugged. "No. I don't know any other dreamwalkers."

"I see. There are only two possibilities as to why an individual has supernatural gifts such as yours. One is to be descended from angels like your fiancée here."

Kane stilled and shifted his penetrating gaze between both Fiona and Dayla. "And the other? I'm guessing my family tree doesn't include angels."

She shook her head. "Definitely not angels. But a witch? You would have to. Not a white witch or earth witch. No, it's likely she'd be a sex witch."

My eyes all but popped out of my head. I'd recently been possessed by a ghost who'd been a sex witch. She'd even once lived at Kane's family home, Summer House. They very likely were related. It had been one of the most awful experiences of my life, one I was still recovering from.

Dayla took a long sip of her drink. Then she tilted her head and said, "And she'd had to have attracted the attention of a demon."

The blood in my veins turned to ice. Camille had been trying to get away from an evil entity. Had he been a demon? He'd had no humanity at all. And his presence had been chilling.

"Yes, it's almost impossible to even think about," Dayla said quietly, no doubt reading the horror in my expression. "But it happens. Though not as much as it used to." She turned kind eyes on Kane. "I'm afraid you are indeed a descendant of a sex witch and a demon. The reason you can shadow walk is because of your demon ancestry."

Kane's face went white with shock. Revulsion mixed with betrayal and the primal need for revenge rumbled through his emotions, pouring into me through our joined hands.

"Kane." I caressed his palm with my thumb, trying to soothe him. "It's all right. You're not a demon." Then I snapped my head up and met Dayla's eyes. "Right?"

"That's absolutely correct, but dreamwalking is a trait of a demon and it's the only way it's possible. So Chessandra was technically telling the truth when she said he could shadow walk because he's a dreamwalker. She just didn't tell the whole truth."

It was my turn to stand and pace. I walked the length of the room, trying to contain my frustration at being left in the dark. Why hadn't she told us? I spun to ask just that but stopped when I saw Kane. He was standing next to Dayla, and she had both hands on his cheeks as if she was going to move in for a kiss.

"What the—" I started.

Fiona waved a hand and silenced me. I worked my mouth, trying desperately to get the words out. They wouldn't come. Red spitfire consumed me and power built in my chest. How dare she spell me into silence? Danger or no, something snapped inside me and power crackled at my fingertips. If they'd silenced me, what had they done to Kane?

I tried to move forward, but my feet were cemented to the dark hardwood floor. I was one hundred percent trapped, mind and body, in this witch's house and could do nothing. Again! My magic burned uselessly through my veins. Goddamned son of a witch! How *dare* she?

My gaze locked on Kane's as Dayla leaned in and brushed her lips over his, not a kiss but a soft, loving caress. My stomach turned and more magic burned through me. I was going to fucking kill that dirty old witch. *Get your hands off my man!*

And then, just as I thought my magic was going to combust and rip me apart right there in her living room, a shimmer of red-tinged light outlined Dayla's body and spread, encompassing Kane until they were locked together in a magical cocoon.

Fiona waved a hand, releasing me, and somehow took all my built-up magic with her. I slumped forward, totally spent and unable to even reach the faintest spark of magic.

"Hey!" I cried and ran forward but was so weak my feet didn't obey. I flailed forward and crashed into the loveseat headfirst. "Shit!"

"Settle down, Jade," Fiona said in a soft tone that was full of calming energy and a twinge of magic. The combination filtered into me, achieving exactly what she'd commanded. I could have staved it off if she hadn't just wiped all my energy from me. Instead, I was at her mercy. And dammit, that was unacceptable.

"What the hell is going on here?" I demanded. "What is she doing to Kane? And why did you attack me?"

Fiona held out a hand to help me up. "My apologies, sister witch. It wasn't my intention to overpower you. Dayla and your Kane are in an energy bond right now. If you'd interfered, it would have been dangerous for both of them."

Her eyes were apologetic, and through her touch, I felt the heavy weight of her regret. She hadn't wanted to spell me, but she'd done what she thought was best for everyone.

"Don't ever do that again," I said, not caring that she was remorseful. Kane was still snared in Dayla's hold, certainly against his will. "We came here to help, not to be assaulted."

"My sincere apologies, Ms. Calhoun." Fiona's tone and intent were sincere. I struggled to get past my fear and outrage in order to understand what was going on.

"What is she doing to him?" I asked, fear lacing my voice. I swallowed it down. Now wasn't the time.

"She's giving him the tool he needs to bring Matisse home."

"What?"

But she didn't answer. She only turned and raised her arms high over her head and chanted, "Lilith, Goddess of the night, hear our call. We give you one of your sons. Awaken the gift within."

The lights flickered once and then went out, leaving us in the dim glow of the red cocoon still holding Dayla and Kane together.

I wanted to run to him. To scream at these witches. To drag him away and break their hold on him. But they'd just called up a demon Goddess. And she'd responded. To interrupt now would have far greater consequences than whatever they were trying to accomplish. One did not tempt the wrath of Lilith.

I bit down hard on my cheek, keeping quiet, and forced myself to stay still. The red outline grew brighter and then the magic started to shift from Dayla to Kane, pulsing over him in the double rhythm of a heartbeat.

Tears burned my eyes. What were they doing to him? "Kane?" I said so quietly, I was certain no one heard me. But as soon as the words were out of my mouth, he turned and pierced me with a red gaze, all the molten chocolate gone from his gorgeous eyes.

I stood there in Dayla's parlor, horrified. His face was contorted in an evil sneer and pure hatred stared back at me.

My breath left me in one long whoosh as the horror of what he'd become sucker-punched me in the gut. "You turned him into a demon!" I cried and ran forward toward Dayla, small shocks of magic finally sputtering through me.

But just as I was about to reach her, Kane's arms came around me and pulled me to him, my back against his chest. He leaned down, his breath sending a tantalizing sensation straight to my toes. "No, Jade," he said in his sexiest voice, the one he usually reserved for the bedroom. "Not a demon. An incubus."

Chapter 7

The world stopped. Blood rushed to my ears and everything went hot, then cold. Kane's warm breath sent shivers down my spine. I closed my eyes and fought against the unwanted and untimely desire claiming me. Kane's touch was too much and my response entirely too inappropriate.

"Let her go, Kane," the older witch commanded.

Kane's grip tightened around me, and Lord help me, I could feel his arousal at my back.

"Let go," I said in a harsh whisper, twisting my head to stare up at him.

His irises flashed from that crimson back to deep chocolate and then shock flashed through his wide eyes. He released me and jumped back, rubbing a hand down his face. "What the hell just happened?"

I gaped at him, totally at a loss for words. Had he really said incubus?

"You're here to figure out how to rescue Matisse, are you not?" Dayla said coolly.

"I…" Damn if I couldn't get any words out.

Kane straightened. "Why did I say I'm an incubus?" His tone was clipped, dangerous. And deeper than usual.

A tremor of fear took up residence in my gut. His eyes had gone back to their normal color, but there was something…

different about him. He seemed taller somehow. More alluring in a way that made me want to reach out and touch him.
Almost as if I craved the feel of his skin. My neck started to
tingle where I'd felt his breath.

"It was not my wish to force this on you," Dayla continued
in her pleasant tone. "I was afraid if you'd been given a choice,
you would've walked out, and I couldn't let that happen.
Matisse is my niece. Losing her is not an option."

"Wait just a goddamned minute," I yelled, totally losing
my cool. "We came to you because we want to help her. Not
so you could put a dangerous spell on Kane and treat us with
zero respect. How dare you do this? I demand you reverse it
right this instant!"

"Zero respect?" Dayla got to her feet and stalked over to me,
stopping only when she was invading my personal space. "I just
unlocked a very powerful gift in your mate that will likely be
the only thing that will help you bring Matisse home. And if
I've been less than welcoming, it's because your kind generally
do not care for our form of magic."

Unlocked a gift. She'd used magic, but it wasn't a spell. It
was permanent. My mouth went dry. Kane was an incubus.
What would that mean for us? I crossed my arms over my
chest, trying to ignore the fact that I was painfully aware of
Kane's proximity. It was as if his physical presence called to me.
I cleared my throat, focusing on the other bit of information
she'd just given me. "What kind of magic is that?"

She glanced once at Fiona. Her daughter nodded, answering
the unspoken question. Dayla fixed me with an unapologetic
stare. "We are sex witches."

I raised an eyebrow as if to say *so what?*

She pursed her lips. "That doesn't bother you?"

I shrugged. No wonder they knew about dreamwalkers.
Being sex witches and all. This type of lore would be strong in
their family line.

Kane wrapped his hand around mine. A tingle started in
my fingertips and crawled lazily up my arm. Warmth spread

through me and I shifted uncomfortably, embarrassed that Kane's presence was having such an effect on me.

Dayla lifted one shoulder in a half shrug. "Most witches think using sex to gain power is wrong."

She'd said it as a statement, but the way she was looking at me, it was clear she wanted to know what I thought. "Who am I to say if it's wrong? As long as your sex partners are—" I cleared my throat in an effort to keep my emotions in check. "As long as your partners are willing and are aware of any consequences, I don't see how it's any of my business."

Dayla studied me and then slowly her lips turned up into a friendly smile. But I wasn't yet ready to let bygones be bygones.

"However. This—" I pointed at Kane "—changing him against his will…that's a hell no. And if you ever touch my fiancé again, you'll have me and the entire New Orleans coven to contend with."

Dayla folded her hands into her lap and met my eyes with an impassive stare. "I didn't change him. This is who he is. All I did was transfer a bit of magic to him in order to ignite the dormant incubus slumbering inside him."

"You did change me. Without your magic, I wouldn't be an incubus," Kane said, steel in his tone.

I shifted, logging all of Kane's gorgeous features. Smoldering eyes, full lips, fuller than they had been. Slim waist, broad shoulders, angular jaw, and the sexy dark eyes. He took my breath away. And even though I hadn't known it was possible, I wanted him more than ever. I was drawn to him in some mystical way that had my neck tingling again and I longed to touch him…everywhere.

I shook my head. What the hell was wrong with me? I was sitting in a stranger's living room—a woman old enough to be my grandmother—and here I was getting worked up about how much I wanted Kane. It was sick.

"It would've happened sooner or later, Kane. Dreamwalkers have an inner incubus that lies dormant unless tapped. It's a lot like Jade's powers. From what I understand, she didn't know she was a white witch until recently. It was only a matter of time before your gift was unlocked. I just helped it along."

I tightened my grip on his hand, a silent request for him to remain calm. I clamped my mouth shut. This argument wasn't going to change anything anyway.

"Let me start again." Dayla took one of my hands and one of Kane's and led us into the kitchen. "Have a seat."

We sat at the bar and waited while she filled two glasses of ice water. Unfortunately the stools were so close together our thighs touched, making my entire body ignite with want and need. I shifted quickly, doing my best to put a tiny bit of distance between us. "Don't touch me right now," I whispered to him.

He stared down at me and took a deep breath.

I licked my lips and hated myself for it when his expression turned to one of pure hunger. I twisted and clasped my hands in my lap, refusing to look at him.

"I know this is frustrating," Dayla said with a knowing laugh as she set the water glasses in front of us.

I narrowed my eyes at her and glared.

Totally unfazed, she took a sip of her own water. "Matisse is a sex witch. About a month ago she got involved with a young man, Vaughn Paxton. Only it turns out he wasn't quite what he seemed on the surface. And when he got what he wanted, he left, leaving her so depleted of magic, she spent weeks on medical leave."

"Not what he appeared to be?" I echoed. "Was he a witch? He'd pretty much have to be in order to steal her magic."

Kane shook his head. "No. He was an incubus."

"Yes," Dayla confirmed. "He was."

I twisted to eye Kane, not at all sure what to say. "How did you know that?"

"I don't know," Kane said, frowning. "When Dayla said his name, something in my mind clicked, like a veil lifted, and I just knew it to be truth." He got up and paced.

As I watched him, I couldn't shake the image of his eyes glowing red and the evil on his face when Dayla had unlocked his power. My body went cold and I shivered.

He stopped and faced me. "What's wrong?"

I cleared my throat and whispered, "You've been turned into an incubus. A sex demon."

His expression tightened with frustration. "Incubi aren't sex demons. We aren't demons at all."

"He's right," Dayla confirmed. "Just like you aren't an angel. Incubi can take power that's harnessed from someone else through sexual energy. And they can dreamwalk and jump the planes from world to world without too much trouble."

She'd given him the power to harness magic. More specifically, my magic. Because who else was he going to get power from? Irritation filtered through me, but a knot in my gut eased. At least he wasn't a demon. Still, she'd overstepped her bounds. "You should have discussed this with us first."

Dayla ignored my hostile gaze and walked to Kane's side. She scanned his body, studying him. Glancing back at Fiona, she said, "It worked."

Fiona crossed her arms over her chest. "Jade's right. You could've asked him first."

The older woman appraised her daughter with skepticism. "Is that what you would've done?"

Fiona flinched at her mother's words. But when she spoke, there was conviction in her tone. "Yes. It would've been the right thing to do."

Dayla tsked. "And this is why you'll never be the leader of this coven." The older witch turned to Kane. Her voice took on the authoritative tone of one who was used to being in charge. "I've given you the gift of the incubi. You will gain power through sexual energy. And with this power you are connected to all the other incubi in existence. That is how you'll find Vaughn Paxton, the incubus who raped Matisse of her power."

"Raped?" I gasped and sank to the couch, horrified. An incubus had raped that lovely girl.

"It's not what you're thinking." Fiona walked across the room and touched a black-and-white picture hanging on the wall. "My mother is being melodramatic." She plucked the framed photo from the wall and held it out so we could see it. A tall, light-haired woman with quiet elegance stood with a tall, dark-haired man. His intense eyes and hint of a smile gave him an air of mystery. The absolute passion in the way they were looking at each other was enough to bring my temperature up a few degrees.

"Whoa." I glanced at Dayla, realizing the woman was a much younger version of her. "You two look like you had quite the romance."

"None of this is relevant." Dayla scowled and tried to take the picture, but Fiona pulled it out of her reach.

"It is." The younger witch put the picture on the counter and turned to me and Kane. "The man in the photo was my father. He and my mother had a whirlwind romance. One for the record books. They were even married. But a week after the wedding, he disappeared. With most of Mom's power."

"He was an incubus," I guessed, putting two and two together.

"Yeah," Fiona said quietly. "He didn't even know. But after they…uh, consummated the marriage, his incubus side awakened and he was called into service."

"Service?" Kane asked. "To do what?"

The image of a brothel or a bath house flashed through my mind. I shook my head, trying to dislodge the ridiculous thought.

"Hunt demons," Dayla said, cutting Fiona off before she could speak again. "The incubi spend their lives protecting this world from demon invasions. The only complication is they need a sex witch to awaken their power before they're pressed into service. Max didn't know about his calling. And after we…well, after he was with me, he was called." She perched on the edge of her chair. "Neither of us knew what happened. I was left almost broken. It took years for my power to restore itself because we were kept apart. And that's what happened to

Matisse. Your job is to find Paxton and take him to her. He's the only one who can help her get her power back."

"And that's why you did this to me?" Kane demanded. "You turned me into a demon hunter? Jesus. We have other ways to find people these days."

Dayla leaned against the counter and regarded him. "Incubi walk in the shadows, Mr. Rouquette. Hiring a private detective or running an Internet search isn't likely to help you. Incubi are notorious for slipping in and out of this world. Even if you did track him the traditional way, he'd likely disappear before you caught up with him. With what I've given you, you'll be a part of the inner circle and will be able to track him from within."

Kane didn't say anything. He just studied Dayla.

I stood and held my hand out to him. We'd learned a shit ton of information in a very short time. It was no wonder he seemed to be at a loss for words. I almost was. But I sucked in a breath and asked, "What does this mean for Kane? And is this curse permanent?" I assumed so. She said she'd unlocked his power, but I had to ask.

"Oh, honey." Fiona laughed. "It most certainly isn't a curse for you as long as he doesn't drain your power." She gave me a sly smile. "You're a white witch, so I imagine you can hold some back. But the more magic you can share with him, the better off he'll be as a demon hunter."

Was she seriously sitting there telling me my sex life was about to get explosive? Judging by the effect he'd been having on me since Dayla had tagged him with the spell, she probably wasn't wrong. But I sure as hell didn't want these strangers talking about it. "Umm, okay. Thanks for the warning."

Kane placed a hand on my knee, sending tingles everywhere. "You didn't answer her other question. Is this permanent? Is there a way to change me back to who I used to be?"

"That all depends," Dayla said and waved for us to follow her. When she got to the front door, she pulled it open. "Once Matisse is back home and whole again, we'll see what we can do."

"Mother!" Fiona admonished, her expression truly horrified. She turned to me. "I'm so sorry, Jade. This isn't how we normally do things."

I ignored Fiona and focused on Dayla. "Blackmail? Is that how you want to play this?" My magic stirred in my chest and I had to fight to keep from throwing a bolt at the older witch. "No wonder Bea doesn't trust you."

"Beatrice can go to Hell," Dayla said. "And don't forget to tell her I said so."

"Jade." Kane touched my arm. "It's time to go."

His dark gaze was serious, focused, and when his fingers curled around my wrist, hot electricity shot straight to my center, almost bringing me to my knees. I closed my eyes, trying to get a hold of myself. His effect on me was damned inconvenient.

"We have what we came for," he said.

"Looks like we got a lot more than that," I muttered. Turning back around, I met Dayla's hardened stare head on. "Stay out of our way, and if you ever touch Kane again, it really is going to be full-out war. Got it?"

Dayla's lips curved into a self-satisfied smile. "I wouldn't have it any other way." And before I could say another word, the door slammed closed, rattling the old windows.

"Holy fuck," Kane said.

I turned to him, noting the hard lines of frustration creasing his forehead and his determined stance. "We'll be okay," I said softly and cupped his cheek with my palm.

Sparks shot from his skin into my fingertips, almost bringing me to my knees.

His eyes blazed with molten fire while his pulse quickened. But all of that was minor compared to the raw desire streaming off him. It wrapped around me, caressing me with coaxing fingers, sending shivers everywhere.

I wasn't sure he knew exactly what he was doing to me, but his body was mirroring the trembling lust claiming mine. I wrapped my hand in his and dug my fingernails into his palm. "Take me home," I said in a husky tone.

His gaze shifted to my lips, and for a moment I thought he was going to devour me right there on the porch. But then he gave my hand a quick tug and pulled me toward the car. Once strapped in, he stared straight ahead and said, "Forget the house. It'll take too long. I can't wait."

"Hotel?" I asked and couldn't keep the excitement from my tone, even though I knew we had more pressing matters.

Kane didn't say a word. He just put the car in gear and peeled away from the curb, leaving a trail of rubber on the asphalt.

Chapter 8

Kane sped through the streets of Coven Pointe. Instead of getting on the bridge to head back over to his house in the French Quarter, he headed west on US 90. He kept one hand on my knee. His touch sent a sensual spark straight to my center, and I struggled to not squirm in my seat.

"Hurry," I whispered.

He kept silent, but his hand tightened and the car shot forward with a tiny burst of speed. At the second exit, he swerved and cut off two cars. Less than a minute later we were parked in front of a chain hotel that advertised free cable and continental breakfast.

Kane cut the ignition but didn't move to get out of the car. He pulled his hand away and gripped the steering wheel as if he was struggling to regain control.

"Kane?"

He hung his head but answered, "Yes, love?"

"Take me inside before I combust right here in your car."

His head snapped up and damn, those eyes. They were so full of the desire and conflict he was trying to keep contained. But he should know better than to try and keep his emotions from me. They were almost an extension of mine.

"Please. I want you to."

"But…" He took a deep breath. "It feels wrong. I don't want—"

I pressed my fingertips to his lips, stopping him from whatever he was going to say. "It's not wrong. It's you and me. And right now, you need me, babe. I can feel how much you need the physical outlet. Let me do this for you. I want you. This thing… it's affecting me too, you know. It's not wrong. With us, it's never wrong."

"Jade," he started, but when his lips brushed against my fingers, a groan came from the back of his throat. His tongue darted out, tasting, and then he wrapped his lips around my fingertip and sucked. A dart of pleasure hit me hard, and this time I moaned.

My response only made him suck harder, and my entire body lit with fire. I needed to feel his hands, his lips, his skin. I needed it like I needed to breathe. His fingers inched their way over my thigh and slid upward. I wanted to beg for more, beg him to take me right there in the car, but we weren't going to be able to get close enough. Good God, I wanted all of him and I wanted him everywhere. "Hotel, now," I forced out.

But my demand went unanswered. Kane's hand moved higher between my thighs and his expert fingers pressed against my most sensitive spot. Pleasure burst through me and my hips bucked against him.

"Oh Goddess," I cried as I threw my head back against the seat. Breathing heavily, I grabbed at his shirt and pulled him close, our mouths barely an inch apart. "If you don't get me inside that room in less than five minutes, we're going to be breaking a few laws."

His eyes dilated and he pressed forward, crushing my mouth with his. Our tongues tangled, warring with each other, and then just as abruptly, he pulled away and jumped out of the car.

I sat, clutching the edge of the leather seat, trying to come back to myself. Even though he was striding through the sliding glass doors, his touch was still everywhere. My neck, my thigh, my sex. He'd branded me and I couldn't think. Couldn't even move from the trembling desire consuming me.

A knock on the window came out of nowhere and I jumped, hitting my head on the car roof. "Crap."

A young man in his early twenties smiled at me and gestured toward the hotel.

I opened the door. "Can I help you?"

"Hello, ma'am. Mr. Rouquette has asked me to escort you to your room." He smiled again, his eyes kind.

"Uh, where is Mr. Rouquette?"

"He's inside. He says he'll meet you in your room momentarily."

"Okay." This was highly unusual. I mean, the hotel wasn't a roadside motel, but it wasn't the Ritz, either. Still, Kane had gone in and this guy was wearing a hotel uniform. Who knew what Kane was up to? I grabbed my handbag and slammed the car door.

"Do you need help with any luggage today?"

I was about to shake my head no when I remembered I still had my wedding night bag in the trunk. And although I had a feeling my sexy lingerie would be pretty much a waste, considering the electricity already sparking between us, I fished the spare key out of my purse and popped the trunk. "Yes, thank you."

The bellman grabbed my bag and together we headed into the hotel. He escorted me to the top floor, and when we reached room twenty-eight ten, he knocked once before sliding the plastic key into the slot.

Once inside, I tipped him and then stood alone in the middle of the room. There was a king-sized bed, plenty of down pillows, and a print of the New Orleans skyline on the wall. Nothing special, but nice enough.

Where the heck was Kane? With nothing else to do, I pulled my sexiest Victoria's Secret outfit out of my bag and disappeared into the bathroom.

A few minutes later, I heard the hotel room door open.

"Jade?" Kane called.

"Just a minute." I slid on my strappy black heels, the same ones I'd worn on our very first date, and then slipped back into the room.

Kane stood at the end of the bed, his shirt off, holding two champagne flutes. The moment he saw me, his gaze traveled the length of my body from head to toe and back up again. When our eyes met, I felt a blush work its way up from somewhere around my belly button.

"Nice corset," he said.

"I thought you might like it." I smiled sweetly.

"Take it off."

I raised one questioning eyebrow. "That's pretty demanding. I thought you might like the pleasure."

His gaze dropped to my generous cleavage. He licked his lips. "I'd very much like the pleasure. But if I take it off you, there won't be anything left of it."

My smile widened with anxious anticipation. "In that case…" I crooked a finger at him. "Come closer."

He shook his head, the muscle in his neck pulsing with barely constrained control.

"Okay then." I trailed a finger down my neck and over the swell of my breast. His eyes tracked my progress as I moved lower to the front silk ties. I fingered the silk, watching him. And when I saw him swallow hard, I tugged.

"Off," he commanded again.

"You're sure?"

"Jade," he all but growled.

I brought my other hand down and loosened the ties just enough to slip the corset down. It slid over my hips easily and landed with a soft swoosh at my feet.

"You are so damned beautiful," he said breathlessly.

"Your turn," I said, standing before him in nothing but my heels and red lace panties.

His gaze dropped to the V between my legs and once again he licked his lips. Heaven help me if I didn't almost orgasm right then and there.

"Kane," I said, my voice hoarse.

He raised his eyes to mine and clenched his fists at his sides. "Your jeans," I commanded.

Something close to sheer desperation flashed over his face, but the expression disappeared just as fast. And in one swift movement he had his fly open and jeans off. Then he was on me, hands sliding up my thighs and over my hips. "This isn't what I imagined for tonight," he whispered into my ear.

"It's not far off from what I was imagining," I teased and pressed my breasts against his hard chest.

He shivered against me. "God, Jade." Then that magical spark was back, dancing across my skin everywhere he touched me, bringing every nerve ending to life. His left hand came up my side, sliding over my breast, and kept moving up the length of my neck almost as if he was claiming every inch of me with his touch.

I tilted my head back, arching into his touch, wanting that delicious rush to take over my entire body.

And Kane didn't disappoint. His lips touched the sensitive spot just below my ear, and he trailed hot, needy kisses to my collarbone, scraping and nipping with little darts of pain and pleasure. I grabbed at his shoulders, digging my nails into his skin.

The fire burning inside me was more intense, more consuming than anything I'd ever experienced before. I couldn't get close enough. I wanted Kane everywhere, over me, inside me.

"Tease me," I breathed and arched my chest up, bringing my nipple inches from his mouth.

He smiled against my skin and nipped the swell of my breast harder. Then without warning he twisted me around so I was facing the wall. Both of his hands came up, cupping my breasts. His thumbs and forefingers closed around each nipple, squeezing until that glorious pleasurable pain shot straight to my center. I ached with intense need.

"Kane," I moaned and pressed my backside to him, needing to feel him.

His length pulsed against me as he bit the nape of my neck. "I'm going to take you right here," he said, his voice strained with need.

I whimpered and answered by yanking my red lace down. Spreading my legs slightly, I bent and arched my back, giving him all the access he needed. "Do it. Now."

A deep, possessive growl erupted from Kane as he gripped my hip with one hand and ran a firm but gentle hand down the length of my spine. And then he was pressing into me, his fullness invading me in the best possible way. I rocked into his intrusion, my eyes rolling back in my head at the sheer bliss of having him inside me.

Magic pulsed and swirled in my chest, making me come alive. The sensation was so new, so overwhelming that my head began to swim in a sea of pleasure and pure sensation.

Then Kane's hands moved, one teasing my right nipple, the other inching toward the V between my legs. My magic pooled and as he pumped into me, my power built and concentrated everywhere he touched and teased. The magic intensified with each tantalizing caress. Excitement consumed me and my body became tight with certain release until my magic spiraled into a crescendo of unwieldy power.

Kane shifted, leaning forward, and slowed his pace. His breath was hot on my neck as he said in that sexy, hoarse voice of his, "Let go, Jade. I want to feel you lose control."

Then he slammed into me, over and over again. My muscles tightened, and powerful magic burst and shattered through me. Pleasure I'd never known gripped my body and crashed through me in never-ending waves. All the while Kane continued to thrust into me, letting me ride out my release.

Finally I cried out and went limp against the wall with Kane still filling me from behind. He buried his face in my neck and kissed me softly, trailing whispered promises of more to come.

"That was..." He paused to rain kisses on the other side of my neck.

"Fucking crazy," I whispered, leaning into the wall to hold myself up. I was so weak I could barely stand. And all the magic I'd built up had burst forth and seemed to evaporate into nothing.

"Jade?" Kane asked, sudden concern in his voice.

"Hmm?"

"Are you all right?"

I nodded and rested my head against the wall. "Just spent, I guess." But as I shifted, I realized he was still anchored inside me, hard as if we'd just started. My eyes popped open and I pressed back into him. "Hey, you're not done."

He chuckled into my ear and then pulled away, slipping out of me. The shock of his retreat left me shivering with loss. I wrapped my arms around myself, trying to control the trembling.

"Babe." Kane wrapped his arms around me. "Come here."

I twisted in his arms, certain his incubus status was responsible for my current state. Yes, incredible orgasms tended to take something out of a girl, but this was more than that. Still, this was Kane, and despite my vulnerability, I felt loved, safe.

He pressed a kiss to my temple. "Let's move to the bed." He lifted me up, and I instinctively wrapped my legs around his waist, holding on while he carried me.

Pulling the covers back, he smiled down at me and laid me on the bed. As his gaze swept over my naked body, he trailed those tantalizing fingers of his down my leg and gently freed my feet from the heels I'd so carefully selected. He smiled at me and the tenderness in his eyes told me he'd remembered. I'd worn these on our first date. The night I'd twisted my ankle and Kane had carried me home.

He climbed in beside me and tucked the blankets around us.

"I don't know why I'm so cold," I said. The chill would not leave.

"I bet I can warm you up."

"I'm sure you can." I snuggled into him. Heat instantly warmed me from the inside out. "Wow. What just happened?"

He shook his head and nibbled once again just below my ear, his hands roaming seductively over my bare skin. "It's the incubus connection, I think."

Right. He was full of my magic now. "How are you feeling?"

His smile turned lopsided. "Good, except I'm still going out of my mind wanting you."

Of course he was. He'd brought me to orgasm before he let himself go, like he always did. I ran a gentle hand over his cheek and gazed up at him with undisguised love. He was everything I ever wanted and, in this moment, I felt like we were true partners. He wasn't standing by while I dealt with the crisis of the week. We were in this together, and if my magic helped him to do what he needed to do, I would continue to give it to him. I lifted my head up, bringing my lips to his. "I want to give myself to you."

"You already did, pretty witch."

I shook my head. "No. Not really. Or not totally." Our lips met and the kiss started slowly, tentatively, as if he was trying to gauge how far I wanted to take this. But when my hands curled in his hair and I draped one leg over his hip, his tongue darted hard and fast against mine in a war of friction. Then he was on top of me, pressing his weight against me.

That magic spark we'd shared earlier came roaring back, and although I'd expected the effect to be weaker, it was stronger. Much stronger.

Kane pulled back, his eyes wide with both wonder and fear. "I don't think we should—"

I pressed my fingers to his lips. "Don't think, Kane. Not now. I have something to give you. Please let me."

The look in his eyes changed and suddenly all my hesitation was gone. That live wire came to life inside me and with each caress, each touch, it only built. And when I spread my legs for him, he pressed into me in one smooth thrust, filling me so achingly deliciously that I let go of all control. My magic spilled from me to him and formed a shell around us. We moved together in a perfect harmony of love, lust, and desire.

Then when he brought me once again to the edge of release, I tightened myself around him and cried, "Now."

Kane stared down into my eyes, his dark ones lidded with lust, and thrust once more, hard and deep inside me.

My body spasmed and wave after wave of magic-filled pleasure crashed over me. But this time Kane didn't wait me out. He thrust once, twice, and again a third time. Then he groaned into my ear. Our bodies shuddered together, but as Kane spilled into me, something else took over.

My magic. And the intoxicating tendrils of power that lived deep in my chest rose and fell and then burst from me like a breach in a dam. As Kane absorbed the release, I could feel his wonder, excitement, and pure elation. It was a raw craving that was finally being filled.

Still locked together, his body arched above me as if my magic rushing into him was too much for him to handle. All I could do was watch in equal parts awe and horror. This was my magic we were talking about.

The realization brought me back to myself, and although I knew Kane hadn't taken anything from me I hadn't willingly given, I suddenly felt helpless. Empty.

"That's enough," I cried and pushed him off me. I scrambled out from underneath him and clutched the covers to my chest.

Kane rolled over and stared at the ceiling, seemingly unaware of my outburst.

"Kane?" I asked tentatively.

He turned his head and blinked a few times. Then he sat up and faced me. "Jade?"

"Yes?"

He reached out and ran his fingers lightly over my lips. The familiar signature of my magic tingled over me with his touch. "You gave me something precious. I intend to use it wisely."

"You'd better," I said, still feeling hollow from my loss.

"But right now, I need to give some of this back."

I glanced up at him, startled. He just smiled and leaned in to kiss me.

Chapter 9

"But—"

His kiss cut off my protest. I automatically opened my mouth, welcoming him, but all the passion we'd built between us was gone. It wasn't that I didn't want Kane to touch me. It was that the all-burning need had been satisfied.

"Kane," I said and pushed him back gently.

"Yes, love?" He gazed down at me with tender eyes.

"I don't think… I mean, I just need a moment to myself."

His sweet expression turned concerned and he sat up. "What's wrong?"

I turned my head to the side, wanting to cry. But I held the tears back. "I don't know. I'm having a hard time being touched." Not wanting to admit the truth even to myself, the words came out in a whisper. This was Kane. I couldn't remember a time I hadn't wanted to be close to him. Not even after Camille had taken over my body and I'd felt so incredibly violated.

"Look at me." Kane's quiet voice was like a soft caress over my bare skin.

I turned and met his gaze.

"You're okay. We'll be okay." His fingers curled into mine, and he pulled my hand close to his heart. The slightly elevated beat beneath my fingers settled me, grounded me to him. "This thing, this incubus spell caused what you're feeling here." He moved his other hand and caressed the left side of my chest right over my heart. "Let me hold you. I can fix this."

I wanted him to hold me. But at the same time I wanted to curl into myself and disappear into my own world, where I wouldn't have to deal with the emptiness inside me. "How do you know?"

He shook his head. "I don't *know* anything. But there's an instinct in here." He pointed to his chest. "It's telling me what to do."

"And what is that?" I whispered, feeling more broken than ever.

Kane scooted down next to me and wrapped his arms around my body. "Just let me hold you for a while."

I sensed the sheer desperation churning in him to fix me. To bring me back to myself. And I wanted to let him do it. I didn't want to feel this way, but I just couldn't. Not yet. Crossing my arms over my chest, I rolled away from him, facing the wall, and let the tears fall.

"Oh, Jade." The words came out strangled, full of emotion, and in that moment his love slammed into me, thick and warm, filling all those empty crevices.

Still facing the wall, I reached one hand behind me. "Take it."

His fingers tentatively slid over mine.

I tightened my hold and pulled his arm around me. "I think this is okay for now."

He let out a long, slow sigh, scooted down onto the bed, and tucked me close to him, my back to his chest. His warm breath tickled my neck as he buried his face against my hair. "Jesus, Jade. I feel like such a dick right now."

"No." I pulled his arm tighter around me. "Those witches did this to us. We'll be okay." I said the words but wasn't quite sure I believed them. My only saving grace was that I could sense his emotions and how much he needed me and ached to be near me. My heart swelled with love. Yet my body still felt distanced from him. Like our last joining had taken every ounce of physical pleasure from me, leaving me with nothing left to hold on to. It was terrifying. "Kane?"

"Yeah?"

"Do you feel powerful now?" I couldn't help but wonder what kind of effect my magic was having on him.

He laughed, but it was humorless. "I feel incredibly helpless. All I want is for you to be whole again. But I can't…won't force myself on you. And this power inside me is worth nothing if it breaks you."

I heard what he'd said, appreciated the sentiment more than he could know, but I really wanted to focus on what our joining had done to him. I rolled over and placed my palm on his cheek. "I love you, Kane."

"I know, pretty witch." He closed his eyes. Pain lanced across his features and shot like a jolt through my hand.

"Stop," I said gently. "Don't blame yourself."

"How can I not? I stole a part of you."

"I gave it to you," I said with a smile.

He raised a skeptical eyebrow. "Not exactly. But thank you for trying to make me feel better."

The longer we held each other, the more balanced I started to feel. My magic was weak and I could barely call on it, but as long as we were here, safely locked away from the rest of the world, it didn't seem to matter that much. But as soon as I started to think about leaving, or rejoining the rest of the world, panic set in. I caught my breath and let it out very slowly.

Kane didn't say anything. He seemed to understand my struggle, and instead of trying to calm me with words, he caressed my bare back, running his fingers along my spine.

"That feels nice," I said.

"You sure?"

I nodded. "Yes, this is okay."

Kane continued his gentle exploration and when my body started to relax against him, he increased the pressure, kneading my knotted muscles.

"Keep doing that," I murmured against his chest.

He responded by brushing his lips over my temple. The kiss was soft, tender, loving, and a whisper of a spark manifested from the connection.

I sucked in a breath and tilted my head up. "Kiss me again."

He regarded me with hopeful reluctance. "You're sure?"

"Yes," I said with force.

His lips twitched and curled into a tiny smile. "If you say so."

Slowly he leaned in and brushed his warm lips over mine, giving me plenty of time to change my mind. But when I opened my mouth and flicked my tongue over his lips, he followed my lead and opened his mouth, welcoming me.

The magic connection flared to life and my body became alive once more. The sweet rush of my power flowed from him into me like a quick shot of adrenaline. "More," I demanded, desperate to take back what was rightfully mine.

His kiss turned frenzied and I matched him with fervor. Our bodies pressed together, and I swung my leg over his hip, ready to be joined with him once again. To feel that power sparking all over my tongue and skin, to pool between my legs.

"Jade," he said breathlessly.

"I want you. Need you." Clutching at him, I jerked my hips against his and moaned when the sweet relief of his hardness pressed against me. "Yes. Make love to me, Kane."

I was fully aware I'd gone from zero to sixty in ten seconds flat, but I couldn't control the desperation consuming me.

Kane pressed me down on the bed and rolled on top of me, his weight welcome and enticing. I spread my legs, more than ready. But he pulled back and looked down at my naked body, his expression tortured. "I can't, love."

"What?" I placed a hand on his chest, anxious to keep our connection. If he let go, I'd be lost again.

"If I make love to you, I'll only drain you again."

"But I—"

"Shh," he whispered. "Just lie back and let me restore your magic."

"How?"

He answered by kissing my neck. His hot, shocking kisses made my body come alive under his mouth. I could feel my magic coating my skin, but I wasn't absorbing it. It was as if I had it at my fingertips but couldn't quite grasp it.

Then his hands roamed, bringing heat and pleasure everywhere they touched. I could have gladly stayed in the moment for the rest of my days if he'd just keep touching and teasing me with the sensual blend of my power and his incubus caress.

Heat, fire, pleasure, and pain. It was all present, all fused with the intoxicating spark of my magic. My body was taut, consumed by pure need and desire. I almost whimpered with it. And just when I thought I couldn't take anymore, Kane's lips brushed over my nipple. I arched my back, begging for more. And then his hand slid lower, leaving a tantalizing trail of magic in its wake. My body started to tremble uncontrollably.

And this time when I spread my legs for him, his fingers dipped between my folds and plunged into me.

"Yes, Kane. Yes," I cried and bucked against him.

My excitement overtook me as he pleasured me, taking nothing for himself. The pressure built quickly and when the waves of release gripped me, he pressed deeper. Then it happened. Power rushed from him to me on a stream of pure bliss. The orgasm hit me hard, harder than any other, making my world spin. I wasn't sure if I'd passed out or if I was just lost in a cloud of magical energy.

When I came back to myself, lying still and spent beside Kane, I stared up at him and focused on my magic pulsing peacefully beneath my breastbone the way it usually did. I felt more alive, more ready to take on the world than I had in months.

"Hey there." Kane brushed a lock of my hair off my forehead.

I smiled up at him. "Hi."

"Better?"

"The best." I couldn't keep my smile from blossoming into a grin. Then concern hit me. My magic was back completely. "Did I take it all back?"

"Your magic?"

I nodded, afraid we hadn't found the balance we needed to maintain this new partnership.

"No, love. I have what I need."

"You're sure?" I sat up.

"Positive." His brow furrowed. "I'm not sure yet how this works. But to me it feels like there's a give and take. When I get pleasure from you, your power transfers to me, and when I give you pleasure, it transfers back. And if I take too much, that's when we get into trouble."

So that was why he wouldn't make love to me. He'd get too caught up and I would've been left empty again. I tilted my head at him and asked again, "How do you know this?"

He frowned. "I don't know. It's instinct. Not only that, but the joining of our connection comes from me. To some extent, I'm the one with the control over the magic transfer."

As in, he could siphon my magic and I wouldn't have any control. Or would I? I eyed him. "Are you willfully taking my magic when we're together?"

"Not exactly. But I feel the pull come from deep inside me."

Hmm. Was it possible I could stop him from taking everything? If I didn't give myself to him completely, I should be able to control how much he took. I smiled a little devilishly. "Next time we'll try a little test."

"A test?"

"Yeah. To see if we can't have a little magical tug-of-war." The idea sent a new shot of desire through me. The addition of that incredible rush of power while we pleasured each other was an added bonus I might have to thank the Coven Pointe witches for. But only if we could keep the connection from draining me.

Kane gathered me in his arms and held me to his chest. "I'm willing to try anything you want, just as long as you don't get hurt. I won't let that happen to you again. I swear it."

The love in his eyes brought fresh tears to mine. "We'll figure it out."

"We always do."

Chapter 10

An hour later, after we'd showered, we sat on the bed with a tray of room service between us. I tucked my feet under me and grabbed a croissant. "Any luck?"

Kane shook his head. Dayla had said he'd be able to track Vaughn with his new incubus status. "No. The only person I can sense is you. It's almost as if your magic wants to rejoin with you, and now not only do I have our personal connection, but there's the magical one as well."

"That's kind of…I don't know, nice?"

He smiled. "Yes. It is. But it's not helping us at the moment."

"Maybe we should try a locator spell?" I suggested.

"Can you do that? I thought you needed DNA or the coven behind you for that."

I nodded. "Yeah. Probably. But we could try to round up enough witches to give it a shot. I was thinking if we can do a locator spell for angels, we might be able to do one for incubi."

Kane tore apart a bear claw. "It's worth a shot, but we have no idea if this Vaughn guy is even anywhere near New Orleans."

I pulled my iPhone out and did a quick Internet search. As suspected, nothing came up outside of a few mismatched social networking hits.

"If he's a demon hunter, he'll cover his tracks better than that," Kane said.

"I suspected as much." I set the phone on the bedside table and sat back. "Had to try, though."

"Do you want to call Lailah? Or Bea?"

Neither was a bad suggestion, but for some reason I was reluctant to share Kane's incubus status. It just seemed so... personal. Like I was inviting them into our bedroom. Still, I couldn't leave Matisse in that other dimension just because of my modesty. I grabbed the phone once more. Just as I started to scroll through my contacts, the electric lights we'd left off flickered while the air seemed to get thicker with magic. Then suddenly the door burst open and a tall, black-haired man wearing jeans, boots, and a form-fitting black T-shirt burst into the room. In his left hand he held an ornate medieval-type dagger. He had it half raised as if he was ready to use it, but not really on attack.

I jumped up, my magic collected at my fingertips. Without even thinking, I let out a blast of power enclosing Kane and me in a protective circle. "Who the hell are you and what are you doing in our hotel room?"

The man ignored me and focused on Kane. "Hello, brother. Sorry I'm late. I would've been here as soon as the witch shared her power, but there was a situation."

"Hello." Kane's voice seemed to be far away, not right in front of me. I tore my gaze from our guest and looked at Kane. I gasped. His eyes had turned black and he was standing at attention as if he were a military recruit. "Kane?"

He didn't acknowledge me. I didn't think he'd even heard me.

Black T-shirt tried to hold his hand out to Kane, but the circle was still active and his hand bounced off the wall. That got his attention. He turned to me. "You can lose the circle now."

I shook my head. "We have some negotiating to do first."

He snorted. "I don't think so. Now drop the circle before things get ugly."

It was my turn to snort. "No doubt, but I'm willing to risk it. What did you mean 'as soon as the witch shared her power'?"

He squinted as he raised an eyebrow in irritation. "Your power. Once you shared it with him, he was ready to join our organization. Don't make this harder than it has to be. I can't leave here without this man. It's too dangerous. Now step aside—"

"No," I said. "You don't seem to understand. I'm not letting him go anywhere without me."

"Witches aren't welcome. Especially sex witches."

Anger flared deep in my gut and rose to the back of my throat. "First of all, *incubus*, I am not a sex witch. Not that the title should cause such disdain. But I am a white witch and his fiancée. And due to circumstances beyond our control, our wedding was interrupted in favor of this." I waved a hand at him. "So if you think I'm leaving his side now, you've lost your mind."

He opened his mouth to speak, but I cut him off. "And furthermore, I have experience in fighting demons and winning. I've even shared a soul with a demon. I think I have some knowledge you might be interested in."

"You…uh, shared a soul with a demon?"

I nodded. Sort of, but he didn't need to know the gritty details. "It's been resolved."

"I can tell." He eyed me hungrily, as if he wanted to study every inch of me.

"Really? How?"

"I'd be able to smell demon on you a mile away."

"Oh, lovely." That was disturbing, to say the least. I glanced at Kane, but he still stood at attention, focusing entirely on our guest. I waved a hand in front of his face. "Kane?"

"He'll be nonresponsive until initiation."

"What?" I cried. "When will that be? And why is he like this?"

He cocked his head and side-eyed me. "That's to combat resistance as we bring them into the fold."

My anger ratcheted up to the point of boiling. "New incubi aren't given a choice?"

"No." He widened his stance in a show of dominance. "They are who they are and they either join or they fall."

My heart dropped to my feet. "Fall? As in turn into a full-blown demon?" I knew angels could fall if they abused their power, but witches couldn't. If we succumbed to black magic, it could destroy us, but we couldn't fall. "Does this mean Kane could turn demon?"

"Afraid so. Not at first, but eventually they all lose the battle. Going it alone never lasts long. Will you remove the barrier now?"

My body went cold as ice. Dayla had done this to him—put his soul in danger to save her niece without even explaining the consequences to us. Son of a bitch! I waved my arms and dropped the circle. "I'm going with you. And if you try to stop me, we're going to have one hell of a fight."

"No worries, white witch," he said. "Anyone who can fight off a demon possession is someone Maximus is going to want to meet." With one wave of his hand, the world tilted, and when it righted again, we stood in front of a large white antebellum home.

I glanced around at the lush greenery and concluded we were somewhere in the Garden District. No one else was on the street, which was odd, considering I could hear the roar of the crowd and the music from the parades a few blocks away. But as I took a step forward, I felt a small resistance. The nudge to turn around and go somewhere else. It was a repellent spell designed to keep those uninvited from invading this private sanctuary. I fought the urge and trailed after Kane and his recruiter.

The black wrought iron gate swung open with a light squeak, and although every instinct inside me demanded I turn around and go somewhere else—hell, anywhere else—I kept putting one foot in front of the other.

That was, until the front door opened and half a dozen incubi spilled out, their ornate knives raised and ready to attack.

"Whoa." I held up my hands.

"Witch," one of them said in a hushed whisper.

They moved closer, tightening around us, and I was sure from the tension sparking between them if I made one wrong move, one of those knives was going to find a home in my chest. For some reason they really did not want me here.

I inched my hands up in a surrender motion. "I'm not here to hurt anyone, or even to intrude. I'm only here for my fiancé." I pointed to Kane. "I want to make sure he's safe before I go."

My excuse sounded lame to even me, and the incubi glanced at each other, then zeroed in on Kane's recruiter.

"She survived a demon attack," he said.

Immediately they all stood at ease.

I tilted my head curiously. Everyone was silent, watching me. The older gentleman slipped through the threshold of the door and said, "Ms. Calhoun, it's a pleasure to meet you."

I glanced up at him, startled, and then gasped as I realized I recognized him. He was the same man in the photo at Dayla's house. Fiona's father.

Chapter 11

We were quickly shuffled inside to a massive foyer. The seven incubi formed a semicircle behind us. The leader stood at the entrance to a grand room, facing us. "Ms. Calhoun, please join me," he said.

I eyed the leader. "How do you know who I am?"

His lips turned up into a cocky smile. "I make it a point to know as much as I can about those living in my city who wield considerable power."

I wanted to delve into exactly how long he'd been keeping tabs on me, but I held my tongue. Now wasn't the time.

"Ms. Calhoun?" he said again. "Will you join me?"

I glanced at Kane, not wanting to leave his side.

"He'll be watched over. We have a few things to discuss first."

"I'd rather do that when Kane is himself again." I slipped my hand around Kane's possessively.

The leader pressed his lips into a straight line, clearly irritated. "You will submit to my request or you will leave, Ms. Calhoun. This is not a negotiation."

The incubus clan took a step forward, closing in around me. The attempt to dominate me had my magic straining to burst forth. Considering I was surrounded by armed demon hunters, that didn't seem like a good idea. Reluctantly I let go of Kane's hand. He stood still, staring straight ahead, and didn't seem to notice. "What's wrong with him?"

"Nothing. He's waiting for the induction. Depending on how our conversation goes, I may let you stay for that. If you do not cooperate, I will send you back to where you came from."

What exactly did that mean? The hotel? The house I shared with Kane? Idaho? I didn't really want to find out. "Fine. But he'd better be in one piece when we get done or there's going to be hell to pay."

That made him laugh. "Ms. Calhoun, Hell does not scare us."

Of course it didn't. Stupid demon hunters. I took a deep breath and followed him into the next room. The meeting hall was open to the second story and was empty except for a raised platform with a line of chairs at the far end of the room.

"This way." He strode past me to the platform and climbed the steps. Behind the chairs was a red drape embellished with intricate black embroidery of the same swirls that decorated the knives each of the incubi carried. He pulled a rope and the drape swung open, revealing a round table with seven chairs on the far side, facing toward the room. "Have a seat."

I waited for him to take the chair in the middle and then sat two seats down from him.

He gave me a wry smile. "This is just an interview, Ms. Calhoun. There is no need to be concerned."

I gave him a skeptical look. "Really? My fiancé was turned into an incubus without his permission. Now he appears to be zombified and I'm being interrogated. Seems like there are a few reasons to be *concerned.*"

"Turned against his will, you say?" There was surprise in his tone. He scrutinized Kane. A small bit of power shot from his dagger, circled Kane and returned. He furrowed his brow. "Kane was not born a natural incubus even though he has demon blood. This was not naturally occurring. How did it happen?"

Shit! I probably shouldn't have said that. "Well, not turned so much as spelled." Might as well be honest since I'd already let the cat out of the bag, so to speak.

His eyebrows rose to almost the top of his hairline. "By you? But you're not a sex witch."

"Oh, Goddess no. On both counts." I sat back. "Look, Kane and I have been tasked with a mission from the High Angel Council, and that mission took us to another witch who's responsible for this. Kane doesn't want to be an incubus—"

"You're sure about that?" The leader flashed one of those devilish half smiles and his dark eyes glittered, shifting him from serious by-the-book dude to sexy-older-gentleman dude.

"I assume you're implying he might enjoy the added perks of incubus status. And you might be right. But he certainly doesn't want to be a demon hunter. And I can guarantee he doesn't want to be zombified like he is right now."

He leaned in. "You know, with your fiancé a powerful incubus, that helps you as well. Your powers will grow over time."

"I don't need more power, Mr….?"

He held out a hand. "Pardon me. I'm Maximus Brock. Leader of the New Orleans demon hunters. And you're Jade Calhoun, white witch of the New Orleans coven."

"How come I've never heard of you?" Despite what Lucien said, surely Bea had to know about a whole gang of demon hunters.

"We like to stay out of the spotlight. Our existence…" He paused and glanced around as if to check if anyone was listening. "Our existence is sort of dependent on flying under the radar. Let's just say our power source is controversial."

"You mean that you use sex to feed your power." I knew my statement to be true, but I wanted to see if he would admit it.

He sat back in his chair and eyed me. "Yes. It's a curse we each have to deal with privately. But I think it's safe to say we do our best to make up for our shortcomings."

His tone implied he was regretful about his fate but that he'd accepted it a long time ago.

"But your Kane, now that is unusual. Only a witch who held a piece of an incubus could have worked that sort of spell. Who was it?"

I crossed my arms over my chest, not sure if I should say. "We'll find out sooner or later."

"How?" I asked, really curious about how their powers worked.

"Each incubus has a power signature. Everyone else will be able to sense it. If he shares his power source with another, it'll be obvious."

"What does that mean, exactly?"

"Only that all incubi are aware of their brothers' existence by their power signature."

That was what Dayla had meant about Kane being able to find Vaughn. "Ah." No point in hiding who spelled Kane then. "It was Dayla, the Coven Pointe leader."

He nodded, not seeming surprised.

I cleared my throat, still wanting answers. "Are you saying if an incubus is happy or experiencing joy and other private emotions that everyone else will know?"

Maximus nodded. "Yes. But that's only true at first. Once a new hunter starts to settle in, that fades and he'll only have the connection we all do."

"And what connection is that?"

He narrowed his eyes at me. "You have a lot of questions."

"So do you."

"I have an operation to run and I've suddenly been given an incubus who wasn't necessarily destined for this life. I think I have a right to ask a few questions."

"As do I. He didn't ask for this, remember? Look, we've fought a demon before. We've fought angels and black magic and evil spirits. We're not strangers to the supernatural world. But we know nothing of this. I hadn't even heard of demon hunters until today. All I want to do is keep my fiancé safe."

"And I bet you can, too."

"You'd better believe it. Now, what is it you want from me? I assume that's why you brought me in here. To ask me something?"

He stood up and paced the platform. Then he pulled out his chair once more but turned it around and straddled it. "You've shared the soul of a demon and survived."

"Not exactly," I said cautiously.

"An ex-demon."

"Yes." Where the heck was he going with this?

"I want access to the former demon. That's what I want from you."

"Why? She's an angel now. And I bet it's safe to say she'll never consider venturing to Hell again. So she isn't likely to fall ever again either. Not that she could at the moment anyway."

"No? And why is that?"

"Don't you know?"

He furrowed his brow. "Know what?"

"Oh, come on." I slapped a hand down on the table. "You have to know the veil to Hell has been blocked. And by a local witch, too."

Maximus didn't look surprised in any way. He had known. But satisfaction rippled over his skin, making me uber suspicious.

"What do you really want from me?" I asked him.

"A meeting with Dayla."

"Wait. What?" I stood. "Why can't you just go to her house? I did."

"And had she wanted to, she could've killed you. No doubt she didn't welcome you with open arms. It's frankly a true miracle you're here at all. She's not open to strangers."

"She is if they're searching for a missing member of her coven." Not really. She'd pretty much locked us out. And had it not been for Fiona, we wouldn't have seen her at all. But then, we wouldn't be in this incubus mess, either.

"Someone's missing?"

I clamped my mouth shut. This was private angel business. "You'll have to ask her."

He scoffed. "Trust me, I would if I could."

"What's that supposed to mean?"

"You really don't know, do you?" He scratched his angled chin. "Sex witches never consort with incubi. It's too dangerous. The power gets out of hand. And more often than not, someone gets hurt."

He was Fiona's father. Dayla had history with him. Couldn't he just call her? "Then why do you want me to set up a meeting with her?"

"She has something of mine. And I want it back." He stood up and crossed his arms over his chest. "Now, will you help?"

"I can try," I said, feeling uneasy about this whole situation. How hard was it for him to get in his car and go see her?

"Good." He pulled on another rope, and this time when he did, the doors across the room opened and Kane and the demon hunters walked in. They stayed in the same semicircle formation around Kane. "Stay here," Maximus said and got up to face them.

I did as I was told but moved my chair so I could get a better view of Kane. He was still zombified, and it pissed me off. What the hell was with their magic that it put someone in a state where the person had no free will? *Think of Matisse.* Kane wanted to help her just as much as I did. Not that we had a choice in the matter anymore.

As soon as Maximus took his position in front of the hunters, he raised his dagger in the air. Each one of them mimicked his movement. "Today marks the day of a new warrior." He glanced at each of the hunters. "We welcome our brother into the fold."

The group chanted the ritual back in unison.

"Do you swear to accept Kane Rouquette into the brotherhood of demon hunters from now until the end of this life?"

"We do," they said.

"And to teach him the way of the dagger?"

More acceptance.

"And to follow him into Hell, to save his soul, should a demon take hold of him?"

"Yes, Maximus, we swear."

The leader smiled at his troupe and then narrowed his focus on Kane. With a quick slice of his dagger over his arm, a small line of blood welled as he said, "Kane Rouquette, do you hear the call of our blood?"

Kane blinked once. Then twice. His vision cleared, and then he looked from me to Maximus, clarity shining in that deep gaze. He was himself again, though I didn't know how much he remembered. "I do."

"Do you swear to protect the world from demons and to commit your life to your brothers?"

I held my breath. This was a serious binding ritual. One that would be sealed in blood.

But Kane didn't hesitate. "I do," he said again.

"By the binding of blood, you are now a protector of souls. A demon hunter of highest order."

Kane held his hand out without being asked, and in one swift movement, Maximus sliced Kane's palm.

He didn't even wince. He just looked at me with wide, pleading eyes, begging me to understand his decision.

Chapter 12

"Wait!" I threw my hands up and ran toward Kane, but Maximus grabbed me around the waist, holding me back.

"Do not interrupt, white witch."

"He can't do this. He can't make such a binding promise without all the facts." My voice rose to hysterical levels. He wouldn't have done such a thing if he hadn't been under their control. Clearly whatever had happened to him to cause that trance state had left him confused. This was not the plan.

"I can," Kane said quietly.

I twisted to face him. His determined expression took the fire out of my protest. "Kane?"

He shook his head. "I have to do this. The images. They're unbearable."

"Let go," I said to Maximus. Kane nodded, and the leader released me. I bit back a snarky comment and jumped off the platform, heading for Kane. But he stepped back, keeping a bit of distance between us. I froze, shock filling me. Why was he backing away from me? I took a deep breath, trying to calm the panic. "Images?"

"The horror. What those people went through. I can't sit back and let it happen."

The demon hunters behind him nodded solemnly.

"What people?" I held out a hand, hoping he'd take it, but he didn't seem to notice.

"The ones the demons take." His face contorted with a mixture of pity and pain. He closed his eyes and when he opened them, he met my stare. "Do you remember when we were in Hell and you felt the awful emotions of the souls trapped in those stone sculptures?"

"Yes," I said carefully. "I wanted to free them, but you said we didn't know why they were there and that maybe they belonged there."

"They do," Maximus said. "But they didn't always."

I spun to face their leader. "How did the souls get there?"

"Demon possession. Most of them were regular people when it happened. Then once the demon takes over, their souls become corrupted forever. When the demon has used up all the victims' resources, their tainted souls are stored in Hell. There they are forced to live through the horrible things they did forever. Usually the crimes are against their loved ones. It is by far the worst existence a soul is subject to."

Chills overtook my body as I processed the horror of what he'd just said. "Worse than being a demon?"

"Yes." Maximus climbed down off the platform and joined his hunters. "Demons have no remorse. They live in a world of zero consequences. Once the demon is done with a soul, he moves on, leaving the soul broken. Haunted. The soul exists in a world of torture and despair. Our mission is to keep the demons from possessing anyone not already corrupted. We want to save as many people as we can."

"I can't walk away from that," Kane said.

I glanced from him to Maximus, torn between fear and pride. If Kane did this, his soul would likely always be in danger. If he didn't, he'd regret it for the rest of his life. "Okay. So what does that mean?"

"Kane has a few days of initiation and training to go through, then he'll be called to serve." Maximus nodded to one of the hunters. "Take him to the office."

"No!" Uncontrollable magic flared to life and sparked at my fingertips.

"Ms. Calhoun, control yourself or you will be neutralized." Maximus crossed his arms over his chest and sent me a warning glare.

I hadn't meant to call up my magic. I couldn't help it, though. It happened sometimes when I was stressed and scared. It wasn't like I wanted to fight seven demon hunters. All I wanted was to be near Kane and work with him to save Matisse, so we could get on with our lives. Him joining a secret society of demon hunters wasn't the plan.

"Kane, please," I begged. "We need to talk."

Kane blinked and something shifted in his expression. Recognition? Understanding, maybe? Then he looked at Maximus. "Is there a place we can talk privately for a moment?"

Maximus frowned and furrowed his black eyebrows. Pursing his lips, he started to shake his head, but I intervened. "I'll consider that meeting if you give us ten minutes."

He stared at me with a blank expression. Then he jerked his head toward the hunter who'd burst into our hotel room. "Derke, take them to my private study. Give them the privacy she asked for."

Surprise filled Derke's eyes but he bent his head in acquiescence. He strode past me and said, "This way."

I reached my hand out to Kane once more and sighed in relief when he took it. His fingers wrapped around mine and squeezed lightly. I squeezed back, relief streaming through me. He wasn't completely lost in this new role of his.

We followed Derke down a cream-colored hallway filled with pretentious portraits of former demon hunters. They were all dressed in a black button-up uniform that reminded me of a Marine's dress blues. High color, crisp lines, gold buttons. Only there weren't any ribbons or patches. The uniforms were plain. And one lone symbol graced the right shoulder. The embroidered scrollwork was the same as on the drapes. The scroll pattern must be their symbol.

"Here." Derke opened a door and waved us into a large study. Books lined every square inch of the walls. One large desk sat in the middle of the room. Across from it was a row of wooden chairs. Most of the room was practical, full of reference and research materials. But under the window was a sweet built-in bench. The cushions were covered in red gerbera daisies and it was quite literally the only thing in the study that appeared to have any life in it at all.

Hadn't I seen daisies at Dayla's house?

I shook my head. None of that was important. I needed to talk to Kane. I waved my fingers at Derke. "Thanks. We've got it from here."

He glanced once at Kane. "You sure you want to do this, man? Women can really fuck with your head when you need to make these kinds of decisions."

Kane frowned and shook his head in irritation. "I'm fine. I'll be ready in ten minutes."

A breath I hadn't known I'd been holding came out in a soft sigh.

As soon as the door clicked shut, Kane pulled me into his arms and hugged me tight. "I'm so sorry, Jade. This isn't what I asked for, but since I've been exposed to what demons can do to innocents, I can't walk away. I hope you can understand."

"I suppose I do," I said on the verge of tears, only this time they were in relief. He was himself. He wasn't zombified anymore. He was a man making a decision he had to make. I could live with that. "I was scared for you."

He pulled back and caressed my shoulders. "I'll be fine. Listen, we can't waste any time. I haven't forgotten about Matisse. And Dayla was right. The only way I'm going to find out about this Vaughn guy is by becoming one of them. When I was in that trance, their history flashed through my mind. They're a persecuted race. It's not pretty. But that's why they keep who they are secret."

I nodded solemnly and clutched at his T-shirt. "Okay. But what am I supposed to do? I can't just leave you here."

"You can. It's safe enough in this house. I'll come to you tonight and let you know what I find out. Then we can go from there."

I clung to him, reluctant to let go. A knock sounded on the door. Kane slipped from my grasp and went to open it.

Maximus stood in the doorway. "Everything all right?"

"It's fine. Jade and I were discussing this change of plans. I'm sure you understand. Today was supposed to be our wedding day, not the day I turned into a demon hunter."

Maximus nodded. "Yes, I do understand. My sincerest apologies your plans were interrupted."

"Thank you," I said with more sarcasm than I intended. It wasn't his fault any of this had happened. But I still didn't like that they'd put Kane in a weird trance that had convinced him he needed to do this. Any man with decent character wouldn't turn his back on such a terrible injustice.

I gave Kane one more hug, holding on as if it were the last time I'd see him.

He whispered in my ear, "I'll see you in a few hours, love."

Standing on my tiptoes, I kissed his cheek, then sprang loose and headed for the door. If I didn't make a clean break, I'd never leave.

Maximus cleared his throat. "Ms. Calhoun, I believe we have some more business to attend to."

I turned and placed my hands on my hips. "Your meeting with Dayla?"

He inclined his head. "Yes."

"After we find her niece. That's when I'll see her again. That will be your chance."

"Her niece is the one missing?"

This time worry spilled from him, which surprised me. So far he'd been really good at keeping his emotions contained. "Yes. Matisse. That's why we went to see Dayla."

"Matisse is the one trapped between worlds?" The genuine shock on his face was interesting. He'd known someone was trapped but hadn't known who. Did he know about Matisse's connection to Vaughn? I couldn't tell. But maybe this was a good thing. If he was emotionally invested, maybe he'd help.

I nodded. "She's the one trapped. It's my job to get her home safe before she wastes away."

He ran a hand through his hair, glanced once at Kane and then back to me. "If there is any way I can be of service, please let me know."

"We will," Kane said but didn't elaborate.

I sent him a questioning glance. He shook his head ever so slightly. No. He didn't want me to say anything about Vaughn. Okay. I turned my attention to Maximus. "When can I see my fiancé again?"

He shrugged. "A few days. Maybe a week. It depends on what comes up."

I clenched my teeth to keep from saying anything I'd regret. A week? He was out of his mind. I sent Kane one last glance, trying to memorize his stoic expression. I hadn't seen him like this before. Everything about him appeared amplified. His looks, his determination, his compassion. I memorized the sincerity shining back at me in his eyes and then bolted for the door.

When I was halfway down the hall, Maximus caught up with me and touched my elbow.

I stopped mid-step and barked, "What?"

"He'll be safe here, you know." His voice was tender, meant to calm me.

"For now."

"Yes, but we'll give him the tools he needs not only to survive but to thrive."

"If you say so." I wasn't interested in any of this. All I wanted to do was leave, to crawl into our bed back at the French Quarter house and wait for Kane to find me.

"Trust me." There was sincerity spilling from him, but it wasn't that I didn't trust him. It was the life. What would be expected of Kane now that he'd sworn with a blood oath? It appeared to me that he was a part of this for the rest of his life. One couldn't just break a blood bond.

"I need to go," I said.

"Of course. I'll escort you out."

Neither of us said anything more as we walked through the massive house. When we got outside, I swore. "Dammit. I have no way to get home."

Maximus squinted into the night and cocked his head toward the sounds of Mardi Gras still filling the streets. "It's going to be hard to get a cab."

"Never mind." I waved an impatient hand. "I've got somewhere I can go."

"You're sure?"

"Yes." I took off down the walk, trying to acclimate myself to my surroundings. If I could find Magazine Street, I'd know where I was.

"Ms. Calhoun?" Maximus called.

I stopped and glanced back. "Yes?"

"Don't forget. I still want to meet the ex-demon. I think she could be really useful to our cause."

"I'll ask her, but no promises." And without waiting for his response, I took off down the street.

Chapter 13

Luckily the Garden District wasn't really that big a neighborhood, and in no time at all, I had my bearings. In less than ten minutes, I was standing on Bea's front step, grateful for the light shining through the front window. She was home, and I wouldn't be stuck penniless trying to find a way back to the French Quarter.

I knocked twice and waited. What a shit day. I was actually looking forward to taking one of Bea's calming herbs and curling up on her sunflower-print couch. It was a far cry from my original plans, but when in Rome…

The door swung open and my bad mood lifted.

"Jade?" my best friend Kat cried, throwing her arms around me. "What are you doing here? Where's Kane?"

Her red curls tickled my nose, and I pulled back, trying not to sneeze. "Can we go inside? There's a lot to tell."

"Sure." She backed up into the small carriage house. Lucien was inside, sitting on Bea's loveseat. I gave my second-in-command a halfhearted wave. Well, he'd once been my second. Currently both of us were benched from the coven. Lucien until we figured out his black heart curse, and me until I got back from my honeymoon. I sighed. Maybe it was time to take over again anyway.

I scanned the room and the adjoining kitchen. "Where's Bea?"

"Working," Lucien said and stood. "So is everyone else as near as we can tell. Lailah is at the shop with Bea. Pyper went to work the club. Ian is assisting her."

I raised my eyebrows. "And you're both here because…?"

Kat chuckled. "Bea offered the house so we could 'do' Mardi Gras without being forced to deal with the Quarter."

"That was nice of her." I sat down on the couch, kicked off my shoes, and rested my feet on Bea's coffee table. "But that doesn't explain why you're here and not watching the parades."

"We came back for dinner. Then we were planning on going out again, but after a while we got to talking and…" A blush crept over Kat's face as she glanced at Lucien.

"And?" I asked with a warning tone. Lucien was in love with her and he was tainted with a black heart curse. Even though Bea had in effect disabled his magic, the spell wasn't foolproof. Witch power could be very unpredictable. If he managed to do any bit of magic around her or lost control in any way, she could be compromised again. A few weeks ago she'd almost died. We were lucky—with Bea's help, I'd been able to bring her back, but it had been damned difficult. If it happened again…I didn't even want to think about it.

"Oh, Jade." Kat waved a hand. "A little kissing isn't going to hurt anyone."

I stepped back and glanced between them. Kat's button-down shirt was misaligned, leaving one side longer than the other. Her red curls were mussed as if someone had been running his hands through them, and there wasn't a speck of lipstick on her lips, despite the fact that she never went anywhere without it. Lucien's shirt was wrinkled, his shoes were off, and he had smeared lipstick on his jaw. "Just a little kissing, eh? Looks like I walked in on a serious make-out session."

"Jade—" Lucien started.

I held up a hand. "Stop. You're both adults. I can't make you stay away from each other, no matter how much I want to." I felt the tension drain from my face. "I love you both. I just want you to be safe. And I'm not talking about contraception, either."

Kat laughed.

I gave her a weak smile. "We just don't know what other harm the black heart curse can cause."

Lucien stood. "I should go."

"What? No." Kat moved to his side and took his hand in hers. "You have to stay."

He gave her a pained look. "Jade's right. You could get hurt and we're… Well, letting things get out of control."

Irritation shot from Kat and brushed against me as it flew around the room. "Your magic has been neutralized. Bea did it herself. So unless anyone thinks you still have access to your power, I think we're just fine. And quite frankly, I'm getting sick of everyone else deciding what I should and shouldn't do. So, no. As much as I love Jade, she doesn't have a say over what I do. Or you either."

Lucien stared at her, open mouthed. I coughed to hide a chuckle. Kat and I had been best friends since we were fifteen. I'd seen her temper in action numerous times. But Lucien hadn't. In her adult life, she was pretty reasonable and it took a lot to get her worked up. But when she did, whoa, watch out.

"Kat." Lucien rubbed his jaw thoughtfully. "The thing is, even though Bea neutralized my magic, that doesn't mean it's gone. I *want* to think nothing bad can happen because, well, dammit. I want you." He continued to stare at her while her blush deepened.

"I'll be in the kitchen," I said and took a step backward, not wanting to be in the middle of this conversation. The place was so small, though, I'd still hear every word they said. At least I wouldn't be right in the middle of it.

"Lucien," Kat said softly. "I want you, too."

"But I don't want to hurt you." He reached over and tucked a stray curl behind her ear. "Jade's right. If something goes wrong with Bea's spell, my magic will be right there again. Plus we don't even know what the black curse is doing to me. If I lose control around you, the consequences could be devastating."

Their situation was heartbreaking. The curse was only a problem for the one Lucien loved—Kat. And I was supposed to be helping Lucien figure out how to reverse it. That had been first on the list for when Kane and I got back from Italy. Now here I was in the middle of something else.

I pressed my head against the cool refrigerator, trying to calm the ache above my eyes. I didn't know yet how to help Matisse and I sure as hell didn't know how to help two of the people I loved most. What was the point in being a white witch if I didn't know anything?

"Jade?" Kat called.

"Yeah."

"Can you come in here?"

"Sure." I opened the fridge and pulled out a diet soda before joining the lovebirds back in the cheery yellow living room.

Kat sat on the couch, and Lucien was in one of the chairs across from her.

I sat next to Kat and twisted the cap on my soda. "What's up?"

"We could really use something else to focus on right now." She glanced down at her clutched hands. "Do you think you could tell us what happened after you left Summer House?"

"You sure you want to talk about that right now?" I glanced at Lucien. His jaw was set at a stubborn slant.

Kat took a deep breath. "Yes. We seem to have come to an impasse on the previous topic of discussion." Her words came out clipped, the bit of irritation aimed at Lucien.

I took a moment to study him and then sent a tiny energy probe in his direction. Regret. Sadness. But there was also joy. Probably from just being in the same room as Kat. A small crack formed in my heart for him. I leaned into Kat and whispered, "Give him a break, maybe? This is hard for both of you."

She whipped her head around, ready to blast me, but then she took a good look at me and stopped. "You're exhausted."

"It's been a day," I said, slumping against the cushions.

She clamped her mouth shut and took my hand. Her worry touched me.

I squeezed her fingers. "I'm okay. I think."

"What happened?" Lucien leaned forward, his green eyes locked on mine.

I took a sip of my soda and started with the meeting with Dayla and Fiona. Then I talked about Kane's transformation to an incubus/demon hunter and how he needed my power to stay strong.

"Oh my God, Jade." Kat stared at me in horror.

"Incubus?" Lucien said.

"Yeah." I closed my eyes, knowing I sounded insane.

"They're pretty rare," he said.

My eyes popped open. "You knew they existed?"

He nodded. "Well, sure. A lot of supernatural beings exist. But we're unlikely to come in contact with most of them during our lifetimes."

I sat up and placed my feet on the floor. "Do you know any incubi?"

He shook his head. "No. But I had a friend whose stepbrother was called."

I didn't know why, but I had a feeling that what he was telling me might be significant. "What do you mean called?"

"You know. To the demon hunters."

My eyebrows shot up. "You knew about demon hunters?"

He shrugged. "Sort of. I heard about them from Chez, and outside of his brother, Wren, I've never met any of them. And I knew Wren only before he joined. Like you said, they're really secretive. I'm not even sure Bea knows any of the demon hunters."

I found that hard to believe, considering their headquarters was just blocks away. I'd suspected they'd had some sort of agreement. But then, wouldn't Bea have called on them for help when we'd had issues with Meri? It didn't quite make sense. Maybe she wasn't involved with them.

"Anyway," I plucked at my jeans. "We need to find this Vaughn guy. That's Kane's mission while he's with the demon hunters."

Kat tilted her head. "But didn't you say he wanted to be one of them? Did he mean, like, permanently?"

I shook my head. "I have no idea. And he has no hope of losing the incubus curse until we free Matisse anyway. So that's my focus. We'll take everything else one day at a time."

The three of us fell silent. After a few minutes, Kat got up.

"Where are you going?" I asked.

"To make you a sandwich, then after that I think it's time to go home."

Home. My eyes stung with tears of sheer exhaustion. What I wouldn't give to be tucked away in the bed I shared with Kane. At least then I'd have his familiar fresh-rain scent.

"Um, you think we're going to be able to get into the French Quarter?" Lucien asked.

"Not all of the streets are blocked off," Kat said testily.

"No, but that last parade is going to run until at least midnight or one a.m., and the party on Bourbon Street isn't going to wind down until the wee hours of the morning. I'm just trying to decide what might be the most practical solution."

"Summer House?" I said hopefully. Mom and Gwen were there. Of course, so were Kane's parents. That thought took the wind out of the idea. But if I went straight to bed, I wouldn't have to deal with Hurricane Shelia. Probably. Hopefully.

"Oh, Jade. You don't really want to drive all the way out there tonight, do you?" Kat said.

"All the way? It's only thirty minutes."

"Once we get on the freeway. And think of the drunk drivers. I'm just concerned, that's all."

"Well. Both of our places are out." She lived in the French Quarter as well. "So unless we go to Lucien's, we're pretty much out of options."

Kat glanced at him with one eyebrow raised in question.

"That's fine, but I only have one bed," Lucien said.

I'd crashed at Lucien's house once before. He lived in a meticulously decorated single shotgun house. It was plenty big for one or two people who shared a bed, but add in visitors and things tended to get tight really fast.

I waved a hand. "Why don't you two go? I'll stay here. I'm sure Bea won't mind." Bea had a guest room I'd utilized before.

Kat stood abruptly. "I'm staying, too."

"Why?" But as soon as the word flew from my mouth I knew the answer. She didn't trust herself to be alone with Lucien. "Never mind. I'm sure Bea won't mind having both of us."

"You'd better call her."

"Right." I grabbed Bea's cordless landline and silently thanked her for her old-school technology. I'd been taken from the hotel room without my purse, and my phone was still on the nightstand. It sucked.

Bea answered on the fifth ring. "Hello, dear. How is everything?"

I gave her a vague rundown of what had happened and then blurted, "Bea, I need a place to stay for the night. Is it okay if I crash here?"

She didn't even hesitate. "Of course it's fine. The guest room is already made up. I had a feeling it might be needed. Call it intuition."

Whatever she wanted to call it, I was grateful. "Thank you. Kat might stay over as well. Is that okay?"

"Of course." A bell rang behind her and then she said in a rushed voice. "Gotta run! Talk to you later."

I turned to Kat and Lucien. "We're all set."

Kat smiled halfheartedly and I wondered what that was about. Lucien? The fact that I'd interrupted them? That her night was coming to an end?

"You two spend some time together. I'll just go on upstairs. I could use a few minutes to myself." I gave Lucien a hug and whispered, "We'll figure this out. I haven't forgotten."

He didn't say anything as he hugged me back and then stuffed his hands in his jeans pockets when I let him go.

I gave them both a little wave and took off, feeling more and more uncomfortable by the minute. No one liked being the third wheel.

Chapter 14

Bea's house was as familiar to me as my own. At the top of the stairs I turned right and headed to the hallway bathroom. After washing up, I crossed the hall to the spare bedroom. She'd changed it since I was last there. The sunflower bedspread was replaced with a rich velvet purple one. The edges were piped in gold satin. No doubt this was her nod to Mardi Gras.

I sat in the middle and held my head in my hands for a moment. The day's events hit me hard. I hadn't spent a night away from Kane since I'd been trapped in the angel realm. And for it to be tonight of all nights, it was too much. I stripped out of my jeans and climbed into the bed, burying my head under the covers. The sooner I fell asleep, the sooner I'd find Kane.

As I lay in my cocoon, I heard the soft murmurs of Lucien and Kat downstairs. My heart ached for their situation. To be in love with someone and to know he loved you back but to not be able to be with him was awful.

My thoughts did nothing to settle me, and I drifted in and out of consciousness. At some point, the front door opened and I heard Bea and Lailah's voices, but I never left my cocoon. If only I'd had some booze or one of my mother's sleeping herbs, I might have drifted into oblivion. After tossing and turning for what seemed like hours, I finally fell into a fitful sleep.

And there was Kane. My heart fluttered with anticipation as he opened his arms to me. "Hey, pretty witch. Where have you been?"

I stepped into his embrace and tilted my head up to look at him. "At Bea's. I had a hell of a time getting to sleep. How long have you been waiting?"

"Forever." He kissed the top of my head. "But you're here now."

We held each other in silence for a while. Finally I pulled back and glanced around. We were in his living room in the French Quarter home. "Sit with me?"

He smiled and moved to the couch, pulling me down beside him.

"This is much nicer than sleeping alone in Bea's guest room," I said into his chest.

"You didn't go home?"

"No car. No money. No keys. Plus the crowds. It was easier to just stay there."

"Right." He stroked my hair and tightened his hold on me. "I think I might owe you an apology."

I glanced up, noting the tightening of his jaw. "Why?"

He frowned. "I made a pretty major life decision without even discussing it with you. That's not exactly how I wanted to start our lives together."

I shifted and clasped my hands around his. I'd been frustrated earlier, but not exactly angry. "I can imagine what those images must have done to you. I felt them once, remember?"

He nodded, but the tension in his face didn't ease.

"I agree it's a major life decision and not one either of us was ready for. But I get it. I don't know that I could've walked away. I haven't, actually. I've got a coven to look after. You've never once asked me to step back or refuse to help anyone who needed it."

He brought one hand up and caressed my jaw. "How could I ask you not to? It's who you are."

Brushing my lips against his, I whispered, "And it's who you are, too."

His lips parted and his tongue slipped between mine, the kiss hot and needy, a sensual desperation on both of our parts to just feel each other.

When we broke apart, I eyed him. "Interesting."

"What?"

"Your incubus allure is gone. I don't feel that magical tug I did earlier."

He cocked one eyebrow. "Are you trying to say you don't find me sexy anymore?"

I laughed. "Hardly. No, that's not it. Your new incubus status has a physical effect on me…and, I'm certain, other females. It's uncontrollable and primal at its core. But what we have together right now? It's mostly emotional. And I'm sure if things went further, the heat would ratchet up, but it's not the same as what happened earlier today."

He held my gaze but didn't say anything.

"Isn't that odd, considering the legend of incubi is that they visit their conquests in their dreams?"

He pulled me back against his chest. "Is there anything about this that isn't odd?"

I chuckled. "No. Not at all."

"All I know is that I'm not interested in subjecting anyone else to this incubus charm."

"Well, that's good," I said a little sarcastically. Then I sobered at the serious expression on his face. "What is it? Something's up."

He extracted himself from my arms and got to his feet. Pacing the living room, he started to talk. "I don't know when I'm going to be able to get away from the brotherhood. There are rituals and training classes for procedures and weapons. I already took the blood oath, so it's not like I can just up and leave. Or maybe I could, but they'd track me down pretty quickly."

"But what about Vaughn?" I jumped to my feet.

He stopped and faced me. "I need you to hunt him down on your own. I've got some personal information on him that might help. And I'll keep trying to get a lead on him, but so far I'm not finding him."

"What does that mean? I thought you were supposed to have a connection with everyone."

"I do." He let out a breath. "But mostly it's with Maximus."

Of course it was. "It was his energy that Dayla used to spell you, right?"

He nodded. "And now I always know where he is and I assume he always knows where I am. I can sense other incubi, but it's vague. I suspect because I'm not a natural incubus, that part of the gift is a little muddy for me."

Just perfect. The whole reason he'd been turned into an incubus hadn't even worked. I scowled.

"Yeah. I agree," he said in response to my frustration. "But I did manage to get some background information on him."

"Really?" I glanced around, looking for a piece of paper, but then realized we were in a dreamwalk. That wouldn't be helpful. "Lay it on me."

Kane sat across from me on his coffee table and clasped his hands together. "He grew up in Baton Rouge, so he has family fairly close by. It's likely he's at least in touch with them. The demon hunters don't go completely underground. He's young. Twenty-two, twenty-three maybe. He used to attend Tulane University, but he dropped out a year ago."

"I'll see what I can do." I held a hand out to him. He took it but didn't get up from the table. "I'm going back to see Mati tomorrow morning."

That got his attention. His head snapped up. "Jade, no."

"Yes. I'm going to try to bring her some food and ask her if she knows where to find him."

He tensed and narrowed his eyes in resistance.

I put a hand on his arm. "Kane, I went in before and came right back out. I have to try. I can't leave her there."

He visibly calmed himself. "Do me a favor and take someone with you. Like Bea or Lailah."

"That's not a bad idea."

His skin started to shimmer, and I knew he'd be gone soon. "Come here," I said.

He swept me into his arms and kissed my temple. "Be safe."

"You, too."

And then he was gone. My eyes popped open and the pale predawn light filtered through the blinds. Kat was curled up next to me, sleeping peacefully. I slipped from the bed, grabbed my clothes, and tiptoed to the bathroom.

A few minutes later, I was standing in Bea's kitchen, making coffee. The quiet of the early hour was almost too much to bear. I wanted to turn her radio or TV on for background noise but didn't want to wake anyone up. Instead, I went about making breakfast.

I rummaged through Bea's cabinets and came up with pancakes and bacon. Before long, a skillet was sizzling and I had a stack of pancakes ready to go. I was setting the table when I heard light footsteps on the stairs.

"Jade," Bea said hesitantly.

"Morning, Bea. Breakfast is ready."

She clutched her robe tighter around herself and shuffled to the table. "Were you expecting more company?"

"No, I had a few things to work out in my head."

She nodded. "I see."

"I hope I didn't wake you." I grimaced. It was still before seven and she must have gotten home really late.

She sat at the table and poured herself a cup of coffee from the carafe. "The bacon is responsible for that, but I can't think of a better way to wake up." She held the coffee carafe over another cup and nodded to it, silently asking me if I wanted any.

"Yes, please," I said and turned the stove off.

Once I was seated across from her, she propped her elbows on the table and leaned forward. "Do you want to talk about it?"

"Not really." I smiled apologetically. "But I did want to ask a favor."

She took a small bite of bacon and nodded for me to continue. "I'll help in any way I can, you know that."

More footsteps on the stairs interrupted us, and Kat rounded the corner. She stopped when she noticed both of us staring at her. "Am I interrupting?"

"Not at all. Have a seat." I poured another cup of coffee.

She sat next to Bea and sipped. "Thanks. I needed that."

"I hope I didn't wake you."

She shook her head. "No, I set my alarm. I wanted to get home before the traffic gets crazy again."

"Oh, good. Can I catch a ride?"

"Of course."

"What's going on, Jade?" Bea asked, concern radiating from her. "What happened yesterday?"

I spent the next half hour explaining everything that had happened after Kane and I were transported to the demon hunters' headquarters and then relayed my plan.

"That sounds reasonable. I'm happy to go with you."

"And I'll work on tracking Vaughn and his family," Kat said.

"Thank you," I said to both of them. "I just feel so helpless, like there isn't anything I can really do."

"You're already doing it," Kat said as she grabbed my hand. "Both you and Kane are doing as much as you can."

"She's right," Bea agreed. "And after you meet with Matisse, you'll have more to go on."

We spent some time brainstorming possible spells that might free Matisse, but Bea wasn't confident in any of them. Finally we called Lailah and asked her to meet us at the club. "Give us an hour," I told her.

"Sure," she said. "See you then."

I honestly didn't think either of them could help, but it sure made me feel better knowing I might have backup.

Chapter 15

It was Monday, the day known as Lundi Gras, the day before Fat Tuesday. And at eight in the morning, the city streets were mostly deserted. Trash and broken plastic beads lined Saint Charles along the parade route. In a few hours, the crowds would convene again and traffic would be impossible to manage as everyone lined up for another evening of parades.

It was not the best time of year to be on a search for someone in the city. Not to mention I didn't have a car. I could borrow Kane's, but it was still at the hotel on the west bank. I glanced at Kat in the driver's seat of her Mini Cooper. She'd drive me wherever I needed to go, but I hated taking her on supernatural missions. With no magic to call on, she was the most vulnerable of all of us.

"Stop it," she said.

"What?"

"You're giving me that go-home-and-lock-the-door look. Just forget it, all right? I'm helping, and there's nothing you can do about it. Got it?"

Busted. I gave her a sheepish smile, but my heart sank a little. If anything happened to her again—

She hit the brakes just a little too hard at the light and we jerked forward. "Don't make me go all apeshit on your ass. You can't do everything alone, you know."

I twisted in my seat. "I'm not. You're here. I called Lailah. Bea is helping. We've even got Lucien doing some research."

The light turned green and she eased through the intersection. "Yeah, but I know what you're thinking. You don't want to call your mom or Gwen or Meri and you definitely don't want to tell Pyper about Kane because you're too afraid they're all going to want to get involved."

"Well…" She wasn't too far off. I didn't want to call any of them, but it was because I wasn't sure what they could do. I wasn't in any immediate danger. Neither was Kane as far as I knew. "I do need to call Meri. The leader of the demon hunters wants to meet with her."

"Why?"

I shrugged. "I suspect he wants information on what it was like to be a demon. I don't really know exactly."

"Makes sense." She double-parked in front of Kane's house. The street was already packed. "I'll drop my car off at my house and will meet you at the club in, what…twenty minutes?"

"Yeah. If I'm not there yet, just go through the café. I'm sure Charlie will already be there." The club usually didn't open until around four in the afternoon, but because this week was the busiest of the year, they were running extended hours. Hopefully we could get in and out before they opened for business. It would be easier since I'd have Bea, Lailah, and Kat. It wasn't like any of them could shadow walk. They'd be a little conspicuous.

Kat sped off toward her apartment a few blocks over. I ran up the steps and stood on the porch, realizing I didn't have my key. No problem. Clutching the knob, I touched the power pulsing quietly in my chest. Then I imagined the door unlocked. The power tingled through my veins, and a second later the lock clicked.

I smiled. That was one perk of being a witch. The house felt big. Empty. And the sudden loss of Kane not being by my side hit me hard. I sank down on the couch we'd sat on the night before in the dreamwalk. The ache in my heart widened and tears stung the back of my eyes.

I jumped up and blinked them back. What the hell was wrong with me? It hadn't even been twenty-four hours since I'd seen him. Just a few since we'd last talked. I wasn't one of those needy girls who had to have her man by her side at all times. I never had been. I shook my head and stalked into the kitchen. I wasn't hungry but opened the fridge anyway. I needed something to fill the void eating me up inside.

Unfortunately the fridge was all but empty. We were supposed to be on our way to Italy. "Shit!" I slammed the door shut and ran to the bedroom to change.

Ten minutes later, dressed in fresh jeans and a sweater, I walked into the Grind.

Holly, Pyper's assistant, greeted me. "Jade! I'm so sorry about the wedding. It's awful the minister had an emergency and you had to cancel. I hope you can reschedule soon."

So that was the story of record. Okay, I could live with that. No one needed to know angels came down and ruined my wedding day. I gave her a tight smile. "Thanks. I'm sure we'll work it out."

"Oh, Jade." Her sympathetic expression shifted to one of pity. "Don't worry. I'm sure Kane won't change his mind."

"What? This had nothing to—"

"Good morning," Pyper said as she burst through the back door. "Holly, can you make Jade a chai latte please?"

"Sure." She flipped her blond hair over her shoulder and went to work steaming soy milk. She knew my typical order.

"We'll be next door when it's ready." Pyper slipped her arm through mine and tugged me into the back. When the door closed, she gave me a horrified expression. "God. I'm so sorry. There's a rumor going around that Kane called off the wedding."

My mouth fell open in shock.

"But don't worry. I've been putting a stop to it. Or trying to at least. It doesn't help that he's not here. Where is he, by the way?"

"Oh, son of…"

"Jade? What's going on?"

"Let's go next door. Is Lailah here already?"

"Yes." She tugged on a lock of her bright pink hair. She must have put a fresh strip in her dark hair the night before. No doubt it was for the Mardi Gras party she was attending tomorrow night. The one where she'd be body painting a bunch of celebrities.

"Okay, let's only do this once then."

Bea, Kat, and Lailah were sitting at the bar chatting with Charlie, who was busy restocking the liquor bottles.

I waved at Charlie.

"Hey, gorgeous." She sent me an air kiss and winked, flashing me that genuine smile she reserved for her friends.

"Morning. Looks like a long day ahead of you."

She shrugged. "Yeah, but I wouldn't want to be anywhere else." She pumped her eyebrows suggestively.

Everyone laughed. But when I plopped into one of the blue velvet chairs, all eyes landed on me again. "Okay, here's what's going on." I went through the entire story one more time, pausing only to answer a couple of questions. When I was done, no one said anything. I stared at Pyper. Her face was white and she looked like she might either pass out or hit something. "You okay?" I asked her.

She got off the stool, walked around the bar, and poured herself a shot of bourbon. After she downed it, she pierced me with a stare and said, "No."

Kane was Pyper's best friend and business partner. They'd known each other since college and he was in many ways a brother to her. "What can I do to help?" I asked.

She shook her head and poured another shot. She held it in her palm for a moment but then put it back down and pushed it toward Charlie. Turning back around, she asked, "Are we going to see him today?"

"I doubt it. He has demon hunter stuff. That's as much as I know." She was taking this harder than I thought she would.

Kane wasn't in any real danger. Not if they were just training. But then, I didn't know anything about her family. Or even if she had any nearby. Kane was likely the only person she'd ever truly relied on.

"When you see him, tell him to dreamwalk me." She took off toward the office. Before disappearing through the door, she said, "Y'all don't need me for this, right? There isn't anything I can do even if I wanted to."

Bea shook her head. "No, dear. I think we've got it covered."

Pyper met my eyes, waiting for a signal, I supposed.

I nodded my agreement to Bea's statement. "You'll be right inside if we need you."

"Okay," she said quietly and slipped into the office Kane shared with Charlie.

"She'll be all right," Lailah said as she stood.

I eyed the angel, wondering if she knew that from Pyper's aura or if she was just trying to make everyone feel better. But I didn't ask. Pyper *would* be fine. She was tougher than anyone else I'd ever known.

"Let's get this going," Bea said as she stood and made her way to the area where the portal would appear. When I joined her, she handed me a small bag. Inside were a few bottles of water, a tin of herbal supplements, and a homemade sandwich.

"That's all?" I asked, glancing around.

"Put the tin in your pocket. I doubt the rest of this will make the trip, but it's good to try."

"But the tin should?"

Nodding, she waved at the bag. "The food items are likely too organic. But the pills are spelled with powerful magic and so is the tin. Cross your fingers they both make it."

I thought back to the day before when I'd jumped through the portal. Had I lost anything? Was there anything to lose? Not that I could remember. But a paper bag and a bottle of water? Bea had a point. When Kane and I had jumped into Hell, I'd lost some notes I'd handwritten. I took a deep breath. "Okay.

I'm going in. Any advice before I go? A spell that might help should I get stuck? Or something to leave with Mati?"

Lailah and Bea shared a skeptical glance.

"There are the ones we talked about earlier, but as I said before, I doubt they'd work in this situation," Bea said. "Almost everyone is locked out except a few special shadow walkers. Spells aren't going to change that."

"That's what I thought." Stepping up to the edge of the circle, I closed my eyes, ready to call up the shadows.

"You could try leaving something of yours there," Bea said, gently touching my arm.

My eyes flew open. "Like what?"

"Anything that's important to you. It might give Matisse a connection back to this world. Likewise, if she has anything she can give you, you'll both be linked. Then if we do come across a spell, it should help. At the very least, a connection to you will help her maintain whatever strength she has left."

I stared into Bea's worried face. "Have you done this before?"

She shook her head, her stylish auburn hair bouncing around her shoulders. "Not this exactly. But I have dealt with individuals trapped in other realms. Any anchor to where they truly belong helps more than anyone really knows."

Lailah nodded. "It's like how when you were in the angel world and you gained strength from the bead you made for your mother. Connections matter. That's what Bea's suggesting."

I felt around in my pockets but came up empty. I had nothing of importance on me. Frowning, I shook my head. "I don't— Wait. I have something upstairs. I'll be right back."

"Jade," Kat called, but I was already out the door and rounding the corner to fly up the stairs. I had just the thing. A few minutes later I was back in the club with a small smile on my face. "I'm ready."

Lailah held her hand out. "Give me your ring."

"What?" I clenched my hand into a fist. No effing way. "I don't think so."

Lailah stared me down. "We need to anchor you here. If you have trouble getting back, you'll need something. And I can't think of anything more significant to you than your engagement ring."

I glanced at Bea and Kat. Both nodded.

Oh, crap on toast. I hated when they ganged up on me. With extreme reluctance, I pulled the diamond off my finger for the first time since Kane had slipped it on me. But instead of giving it to Lailah, I handed it to Kat. She was my best friend, after all.

She pushed it onto her middle finger and squeezed my hand. Then she undid her silver necklace that had a tree of life pendant attached to it and clasped it around my neck. "This is to anchor you to us."

I fingered the pendant, letting my fingers graze over the etched tree. It was silky smooth and felt just as wonderful as it looked. Suddenly Kat's emotions burst through like a dam, filling me completely with worry, pride, and even a little resentment. Resentment? That she had to be here doing this again? But her eyes flickered to the diamond I'd just given her. No doubt this was about her not being able to be with Lucien.

I crushed her into a hug. And then let her go without saying a word. I didn't need to. She knew what that was about.

"I'm going now. If I don't come back out…" I gave them all a cheeky smile. "I'm sure you'll find a way to drag me back here one way or another."

"Positive thinking, Jade," Bea said harshly. "Always assume the best possible outcome."

"And prepare for the worst," I quipped.

Out of the corner of my eye, I saw Lailah shake her head, and for the first time in weeks, I missed hearing whatever snarky remark she had going on in her head. She rarely said them out loud, but for a while there I'd had a front-row seat to her humdingers.

Once more, I took a deep, calming breath and let my vision blur. Instantly the portal opened to a bright light of calm. I could still see everyone else, but they were looking around as if I'd disappeared. Of course I had. I was in the shadow world already. Just as well. I didn't need tear-filled goodbyes or any of them trying to follow me.

"Here I go," I muttered to no one and jumped.

The world spun around me in a blanket of gray and once again my backside slammed into the hard ground. I stared up into the mist and shivered. It was colder here than it had been last time.

I sat up and tried to peer through the fog, but I saw nothing. What was that spell Matisse gave me last time? I couldn't remember exactly. Magic was about intention. I formed a picture of the fog parting in my mind. The grayness faded a tiny bit. Not the best outcome. Time for my sixth sense. Opening my emotional barriers, I sent my probe out. Nothing. A trickle of my own panic filtered through me. "Matisse?" I called. Was I in the wrong place? Had I jumped to some other dimension? Was anyone here? I probed further, desperately reaching to latch on to anyone.

Nothing still. Standing, I focused once again on banishing the fog and yelled, "Matisse!"

The gray wall of fog parted slightly, letting a tiny ray of sunshine through. I stepped forward. "Matisse?" This time I said it tentatively, afraid of what I might find.

But the fog parted again and more sun shone down, leaving a trail on the brick pathway. I followed it. A few steps later, despair prickled against my skin. It was her. I recognized the emotional signature. Running now, I ignored the cold, the fog, and everything about the desolate place except Matisse.

I found her lying shivering on the bank of the river, her eyes closed and her body almost blue from chill. Only it wasn't *that* cold here. Not enough to freeze to death. Falling to my knees, I stripped my sweater off and laid it over her.

She didn't open her eyes. She didn't even move.

"Oh my Goddess," I said and glanced around me for my bag and water bottle. It was gone. Damn, Bea had been right. They hadn't made the trip.

The tin.

I shoved my hand in my back pocket and nearly cried in relief when my fingers hit the cool metal. As I pulled it out, the pills rattled around on the inside.

"Thank you," I whispered and popped the top. The compartments were labeled. Energy, Nutrition, Hydration, Strength. I pressed the energy pill to her lips first and said, "Matisse, open your mouth. Come on." When she didn't respond, I put a tiny bit of will behind my words. Reluctantly she did as I said. "That's good. There you go. Swallow now."

I waited until I saw her throat work and then fed the other three pills to her one by one.

After a few minutes, she rolled over and stared up at me. She blinked. "Jade?"

I smoothed the dark hair off her forehead. "Hey there."

She glanced around and grimaced. "Damn. I thought it was all a nightmare."

"I'm afraid not." I scanned her body, taking in her tattered pants and fraying T-shirt. "What happened?"

Mati shook her head. "Nothing. Everything just seems to be deteriorating here. I do nothing but sit and wait. And all the while I get weaker and my clothes start to fray. I feel like I'm in a wasteland."

Wasteland. That was exactly what this was. And if we didn't get her out, she wouldn't die, exactly. She'd just fade away. "We're working on a plan to get you home. I spoke to your Aunt Dayla."

Her eyes lit with a spark of hope. "Is she here?" She glanced around, and then the spark dimmed. "She can't enter, can she?"

I shook my head. "I'm afraid not. But we think someone else you know might be able to. Vaughn?"

She bolted upright, coming perilously close to knocking her head against mine.

I jerked back just in time. "Whoa."

"No. You can't bring Paxton here. Absolutely not." She scooted away as if I were suddenly dangerous.

I sat back and regarded her. "Is there something I should know about this guy? Your aunt said—"

"I don't care what she said. You cannot bring him here. Got it? The last time I saw him, he almost killed me." Her voice wavered on the word "saw." She averted her gaze. "That's just not an option."

I gave her a moment to collect herself. When she finally looked at me again, I asked, "What if he's the key to bringing you home?"

Her mouth pursed with tension and she narrowed her eyes. "Then I will die here."

Chapter 16

Matisse's words were full of so much conviction, I wasn't sure what to say. And when she turned her back on me, I decided it was best to just drop the subject. If we determined Vaughn was the only person who could save her, I knew I'd bring him here regardless of what she'd said. Letting the vibrant young woman perish because of some perceived wrong was unthinkable. But I wouldn't give her anything else to worry about while she was stuck in such an awful place all by herself, either.

Instead, I unclasped the necklace from around my neck and held it out to her.

She didn't take it. She watched the glass bead pendant dangle from the chain and then her gaze met mine. "What's that for?"

"It's an anchor to our world. We're hoping that if we can ground you to one of us—and in this case, me—we might be able to work a spell to bring you back to our world." I quickly scanned her body for any sort of jewelry but didn't see anything obvious. No necklaces, bracelets, or rings of any sort. Not even an earring. "Do you have anything on you I could take back with me? It's a bonding thing."

She chewed on her bottom lip.

After a few moments, I said, "Matisse, please. Even if you don't have anything for me, this will help. Or at the very least, it can't hurt."

Finally her big brown eyes met mine. She reached up with both hands and undid an earring at the top of her left ear that had been obscured by her long hair. "It doesn't look like much, but it was given to me by someone who was important to me once."

Her words radiated melancholy and touched me to my core. It was as if she was giving me the only important thing she had left—memory of a loved one. I held my hand out, and she placed it gently in my palm. "It's perfect, then," I said softly and handed her my necklace. Not wanting to lose the earring, I pulled Bea's tin out of my pocket and dropped it into one of the empty pill slots. "I'll keep it safe for you."

She nodded and secured my necklace around her neck.

A soft glow of magic radiated from the bead at the same time I experienced a small shock right in my breastbone, where my magic resided. Good, we'd definitely formed a connection. "I made that a while ago."

"Really." She tightened her hand around the bead. "It has positive energy."

I smiled. "I was practicing trapping my magic into glass. I'm glad you can sense it. That means you're strong. Not everyone can."

"Well..." Matisse stared at her feet. "I used to be a lot stronger."

I placed a soothing hand on her arm and was gratified when she didn't jerk back. She was beginning to trust me. "You'll be strong again."

She let out a skeptical laugh. "Yeah, sure. But only if you keep feeding me those pills."

"You can bet your life I'll bring them every damn day until you're home safe."

She sighed wearily. "I don't know what's worse, sitting here waiting endlessly or just fading away."

She seemed so dejected, so hopeless, I wanted to cry for her. But that was the last thing she needed. I gently grabbed her by both arms. "Listen to me. I will not let you rot here. Not like this. Whatever I have to do, I'll do it. Understand?"

Her eyes misted and as she nodded, two tears spilled down her cheeks. A pain slashed through my heart for her. How easily this could have been me at her age if my circumstances had been different. How dare Chessandra task her to complete such a dangerous activity on her own? Why had it been so important to get the veil closed now? And by someone who was so inexperienced. Was Matisse that strong? Or was Chessandra just out of her mind? I was guessing somewhere in the middle.

"I need to get back so we can keep working on how to get you out of here. But I'd really like it if you'd try to merge your magic with mine to see if you can cross over with me."

"It didn't work last time," she said.

"I know. But we have a bond now." I smiled and touched the glass bead around her neck. "I'm going to focus on my friend, Kat. She has a talisman of mine. I'd like to see how well this might work."

She waved at the fog closing in on us. "Anything's better than this."

I held out my hand, and when she clasped hers in mine, I was overwhelmed with a rush of gratitude and anxiety. She was thankful I was here to help. But also very skeptical that I could be of any use at all. She didn't really expect to ever get home. The crack in my heart widened. It was awful to see her lose hope. I squeezed her hand. "Just focus on me, or, if it's easier, my necklace."

"I'll try." Her voice seemed far away already.

I peered at her, my eyesight already blurring, and the world started to tilt. I clasped her hand tighter and yelled, "Hang on!"

But when I landed once again in the club, my hand was empty and the only people I saw were Bea and Lailah hovering over me.

"How is she doing?" Bea asked, clutching the hem of her coral silk shirt.

I glanced around, trying to orient myself again. Kat and Charlie stood near the bar, gaping at me. Besides Lailah and

Bea, the place was empty. Disappointment consumed me. "Crap. It didn't work."

"What didn't? The pills?" Bea held her hand out to help me up.

I took it and stumbled to my feet. "Oh, no. Those did the trick. Thank you very much. If it hadn't been for you..." I didn't finish, couldn't finish. Poor Mati. I cleared my throat. "I left my necklace with her and she gave me an earring. I was hoping the connection might be useful enough to bring her back. No go, though I guess I suspected as much. Seems stupid to think that would work."

"It's not stupid, Jade," Bea said gently. "Things carry energy. You know that."

Boy, did I ever.

"It could've worked, but I suspect your power is strong enough that if it was possible for her to cross at all, you could've done it on your own."

"So what was this about?" I pointed to Kat's tree-of-life necklace secured around my neck.

She shrugged. "Like I said, it doesn't hurt."

I flopped into a chair, totally frustrated. "Now what?"

Kat stepped forward and handed me my engagement ring. I slipped it on my finger and clutched my hand, grateful to have a piece of Kane. "Here," I said, reaching up to give her the necklace back.

She shook her head. "Keep it. I like knowing you have something of mine with you just in case." Then she held her phone out. "I got a text from Lucien. He says he thinks he knows where to find Vaughn's brother."

I let my vision slip to the shadow world one more time and stared at the white light shining from the portal. I hated leaving Matisse there. How long would Bea's pills last?

"Jade?" Kat called, startling me from my trance.

My vision cleared and I shook my head. "Yeah?"

"Did you hear that? We need to meet Lucien."

"Right. Sorry. Let's go."

Kat and I pulled to a stop in front of Lucien's house in Mid-City. Bea and Lailah were a few minutes behind us. As soon as we climbed out of Kat's Mini, Lucien strode across his porch and waved for us to meet him at his car. "He's there now. We have to go."

I changed course mid-step and climbed into the backseat of his Jeep. Finding Vaughn was priority number one.

Kat cast me a questioning glance as she held the front passenger-side door handle. I waved for her to get in. I wasn't going to make her sit in the backseat of her boyfriend's car… even if they weren't officially dating. Whatever they were doing, they were obviously together.

After we jumped in the car, Lucien peeled out of the driveway, and a few minutes later we were on Interstate 10, heading east away from New Orleans. Cars were stacked up miles deep trying to get into the city, and I had heart palpations thinking about getting back home later. Traffic was going to be a bitch.

"Where are we headed?" I asked Lucien.

"Six Flags." He shifted lanes, cutting someone off.

My stomach dropped to my feet and I grabbed a door handle. "Whoa, what's the hurry?"

"I don't want to miss him."

I glanced at Kat. "Six Flags?"

She shrugged and pulled her phone out. "I'll text Lailah and tell her and Bea to meet us there."

"But I thought it was closed. Why would anyone be there?" After Hurricane Katrina, the theme park had never opened again. As far as I knew it was abandoned.

"There's a film shooting there today, and Mitch is a production assistant. If we hurry, we can catch him before they wrap for the day."

"Ah." The line of cars on the interstate trying to get into the city was not thinning. Damn. "Have you spoken to him?"

Lucien shook his head. "No, but I got a hold of his mom. She told me where he'd be."

Kat's phone buzzed, indicating an incoming text. Her fingers flew across the screen as she sent a reply.

I caught Lucien's green gaze in the rearview mirror. "And she gave up the information just like that?"

The back of Lucien's neck turned red, and that was when I knew he was holding something back.

"Lucien? What's going on?"

He met my eyes in the mirror once more and grimaced.

Kat caught his look and raised curious eyebrows at him. "Lucien?" she asked quietly.

He let out a long breath. "Sorry. When I heard the name Vaughn Paxton, it sounded so incredibly familiar but I couldn't place why. I mean, the guy is ten years younger than I am. It's not like I run in the same circles as he does. But when I started researching, I found his half-brother Mitch."

I scooted forward, waiting for him to continue. When he didn't, I said, "And?"

Kat reached over and turned the radio off. The road noise filled the Jeep.

Lucien's knuckles went white as he clutched the steering wheel. "I went to high school with Mitch. And we were at the same college for a few years before he dropped out. We weren't friends. More like acquaintances, really. But I did spend a lot of time with him. We were on the basketball team together. It's hard to avoid a guy in that situation. It gave me credibility when I asked about Mitch. When I casually inquired about Vaughn she was pretty vague. I'm hoping we can get more out of Mitch."

Lucien's expression turned troubled as he focused on the road. Kat touched his knee and when he glanced at her, she sent him an encouraging smile.

"What do you know about him?" I asked. "Whatever it is, you need to tell me before we get there."

"He's a witch." Lucien glanced over his shoulder and gave me an apologetic look. "But he's not really discerning about how he uses his magic."

My mind immediately jumped to black magic, and fear mixed with anger coiled in my gut.

Lucien must have sensed my unease, because he didn't even glance at me before he started speaking again. "It's not what you're thinking. He uses it to manipulate people to do what he wants. Small things like getting a girl to kiss him when it's pretty obvious she isn't into him. Nudging professors to give him a better grade. Taking every opportunity to better his situation, even at the expense of others. He also crosses lines, and I don't trust him. Never have."

"And no one ever called him on it?" I asked, feeling sick to my stomach. It might not have been black magic, but it sure as hell wasn't ethical.

"A few of us tried, but we could never prove it to anyone who mattered." He shook his head. "I despise the guy."

"I already do and I haven't even met him." Entitled bastard. "You said he was a production assistant. If he's so determined to get ahead, why wouldn't he use his magic to run the show? Or hell, even star in the movie?"

Lucien shrugged. "Probably because he likes to stay under the radar. That kind of thing would shine too big of a spotlight on him. I wouldn't be surprised if he was hired as an intern and forced a promotion within hours."

If Mitch was still up to his old tricks, then that made sense. "And you say this Vaughn guy is his half-brother?"

"Yes. But I don't know him at all, other than I'd seen him around some of the basketball games. But he'd been a kid then. Like seven or eight? I have no idea what he'd look like now. Not like Mitch, that's for sure. Mitch's mom married Vaughn's dad, and Mr. Paxton adopted him. Mitch never talked about his real dad. Not once."

I sat back and took a deep breath, trying to get a grip on

my anger. "How long has it been since you've seen him? Ten years? Maybe he's changed."

Lucien glanced over his shoulder and then shifted lanes to take the exit to five-ten. "I doubt it. His tendencies were getting worse the older he got. There was a rumor he roofied a girl. Only she tested negative for any traces of drugs."

That got my attention. As a witch, if he had any skill at all, he wouldn't need narcotics to alter a girl's cognitive state. "Do you think he assaulted her?"

Kat's lips formed a thin angry line. We'd been put in a position when we were fifteen that had our friend Dan not stepped in, one or both of us surely would have been attacked. I knew that day was running through her mind, just as it was mine.

"I honestly don't know. But I wouldn't want either of you left alone with him. He's just one of those people I've never trusted."

"Noted," I said and blew out a breath. I wasn't so much worried for myself. I could hold my own in a magical battle, but Kat? That was a different story. "Kat?"

"Yeah?"

"When we meet him, do me a favor and stay close to me."

She frowned, her eyes squinting with annoyance. "I'm not a five-year-old. I think I've already figured out I should stick close to one of you."

Lucien glanced at her. "No, babe. Not close to me. If there's a magical duel, I'm useless. My power is neutralized, remember? Not to mention if I were to cast anything…well, it's just not going to happen. Stick with Jade, Bea, or Lailah for now."

Her expression went blank, but she couldn't hide what was going on from me. She was suppressing a very healthy dose of frustration and fear. I reached across the seat and squeezed her shoulder. "We'll stick together like we always do, right? You'll keep me balanced, and I'll send a magical sucker punch to anyone who dares get in your way."

Her lips twitched and then she grinned. "Yeah. I can hang with that."

Lucien's shoulders relaxed and relief swirled around him.

It was on the tip of my tongue to tell him not to get too comfortable, but I didn't want to ruin the moment. "Did Lailah text back?" I asked Kat. "Are they on their way?"

"Yes, but they're about twenty minutes behind us now. They had to stop for gas."

That wasn't exactly what I wanted to hear. With those two along, we could handle just about anything. Still, I was strong enough that I could probably handle Mitch on my own, even if he was an ass. And who knew? Maybe he'd grown up since college. One could hope.

We pulled into the weed-infested parking lot of Six Flags and parked under a defunct lamppost. There weren't any cars in sight. "Are you sure this is where they're filming?"

"That's what his mom said." Lucien pushed his door open and jumped out. Kat and I followed. We made our way to the chained entrance.

I sent Lucien a questioning glance. "You still want to go in?" Trespassing wasn't exactly something I made a habit of doing.

"Do you feel any emotional energy?"

I made a face. In general, I tried not to let my barriers down in heavily trafficked areas. Especially ones like an abandoned park. The emotions that lingered were usually the unpleasant ones. But if no one was there, I didn't want to waste time exploring a deserted location. "Give me a second."

"I'll be right here if you need me," Kat said.

"Thanks." She was really good at calming me after an emotional overload. I hated to do that to her, though, since it left her a little weaker. And that was the last thing I wanted for her or any of my other friends right then. I paced in front of the gate for a few moments, and after I gathered my courage, I sent out an energy probe.

An onslaught of every emotion imaginable slammed into me. The most prominent, terror and despair, collided in a tornado of chaos. My stomach lurched as I stumbled forward, clutching the chain-link gate. Bile rose from the back of my throat and I coughed, trying not to gag. There was a trace of excitement and joy as well, but the emotions were so faint they had zero effect on me.

"Jade," Kat said softly from behind me.

If I reached back and touched her, it would all go away. I'd find peace. But if I did that, we wouldn't find out if Mitch or anyone else was around. "I'm okay," I said, though I wasn't. Not really.

You can do this.

I had before and I would again. Pushing all the stale emotions aside, I let my gift take over and searched for those active emotions. The ones that belonged to a specific signature and were always changing. It took a few moments, but then a trickle of annoyance, mixed with greed, filtered through the noise. Faint traces of other active emotions brushed my psyche, but I couldn't quite place them. We were too far away.

I slammed my walls into place and stepped away from the gate. "There are people here. But they must be a ways away. I can barely feel them through the echoes."

"Echoes?" Lucien asked.

"Emotions left by people who were here before," Kat told him. She held her hand out to me.

I shook my head. "I'm okay."

"For now. But what about when we get closer to them? You look a little pale. Come on, Jade. This is what I'm good at. Let me do it." She stretched her arm farther, waiting for me to accept her touch.

I couldn't help but smile. That was what best friends were for. Taking her hand in mine, I let her calm energy give me the boost I needed to feel whole again. I squeezed her fingers gently and let go. "Thanks. Are you okay?"

She wrapped her arms around herself. "Jeez. That was sort of intense." Before I could apologize, she held her hand up. "I meant all those echoes. That was something else."

"You felt that?" Normally she just got a little tired. It was rare for her to feel what I did.

"Yeah. Weird. Anyway. Let's do this." She glanced at both of us and then slipped through a hole in the fence.

Lucien and I looked at each other. I shrugged. "You heard the lady."

Chapter 17

The amusement park was a ghost town of creepy despair. We entered what must have been a quaint main street of shops at one time. Now the buildings were deserted, the windows broken, and debris lined the streets.

"It looks like a zombie apocalypse," Kat said, clutching Lucien's hand.

I had to agree. We walked in silence past each deserted and rusting ride, past the decimated building of what used to be Gotham City, and when we got to what used to be a Mardi Gras ride, I shivered at the giant, grinning, broken mask that had fallen and was propped against the wall. It was almost worse than the beheaded clown that stared at us from the asphalt.

"Now that's creepy," I said, pointing at it.

"I'll never sleep again," Kat added.

"It's just plaster," Lucien said, but he quickened his pace, and I had to stifle a laugh.

He was right. It was just plaster. But most of the buildings were covered with graffiti that depicted hopeful messages such as *NoLa Rising*. Eight and a half years later, there wasn't anything hopeful about it. The destruction was just sad.

I led our little group to the back of the park, where a small film crew was set up in an open lot. Lucien left us to talk to a production assistant with a clipboard. Kat and I stayed back far enough to not be in the way. After a few moments, Lucien returned. "She says he's probably at the production trailer." He pointed behind a building that used to be the center of a food court. "This way."

We wound our way through broken plastic tables and eventually came to a gate with a rusted turnstile. The gate was closed, and instead of trying to open it, I jumped over the rusty metal bar.

Kat laughed at me and went through a section of the fence that had been cut away.

I shook my head. "Showoff. I didn't see that."

"Obviously."

Lucien ignored us as he stared straight ahead. I followed his gaze and locked eyes on a black-haired man in his early thirties. He was tall, maybe six-two, with a narrow waist. His chest and shoulder muscles bulged against his white T-shirt. There was no mistaking he spent a lot of time at the gym.

Lucien strode forward, his hand stretched out. "Mitch, it's been a long time."

They were a mixed pair. Lucien had blond hair, was a few inches taller, and was long and lean with corded muscles. But the biggest difference was that Lucien had kind eyes and exuded goodwill. Mitch had suspicion swimming in his piercing gaze.

Great. This would go well.

"Boulard, what are you doing here?" Mitch, holding a coil of cable over his shoulder, took a step back.

"Actually, we came to talk to you if you have a moment." Lucien smiled pleasantly, seeming totally at ease. But the tension spiraling off him was making me dizzy. He didn't trust this guy at all. This wasn't a matter of a few nudges of will. Something had happened between the two of them that Lucien hadn't told us about. I was sure of it. Because the emotional vibe I was getting from Lucien made me certain he would spell Mitch's ass into Hell given half a chance.

Mitch glanced over his shoulder. "Dude, I'm working here." But then his gaze landed on me and Kat and his entire demeanor changed. The scowl disappeared and he stood up straighter, interest replacing the suspicion in his eyes. "Who do we have here?" he said with a charming, dimpled smile.

Wow. That was some transformation. He went from creepy loner dude to cutie-pie dude in two seconds flat. However, seeing the way he reacted to Lucien before he realized he had an audience meant I didn't buy his act for one damn second. Not to mention his emotions were locked down tight. It was almost as if he knew someone might be able to read him, and he was actively keeping his energy to himself. That didn't usually happen unless the other person was an intuitive. And he wasn't. His aura would've been tinged purple. His was a dark shade of maroon, suggesting his normal aura color was red, but right now it was tinged black, making it appear darker than it should.

Tinged black? That could mean he was dabbling in black magic. It could also mean he was sick or severely depressed. After what Lucien had told us, my heart sank. All signs pointed to black magic. *Please let Bea and Lailah show up soon.*

Was that why he had his energy locked down? Was he afraid another witch would sense it?

A tickle of magic crept over my skin and made me want to recoil from the sheer sliminess of it. But Kat smiled and tugged me forward. "Lucien, aren't you going to introduce us to your friend?"

Lucien gave her an odd look and then turned to me with a question in his eyes. I shook my head. I couldn't say it out loud, but I knew exactly what had happened. Mitch had used his magic on us. Lucien hadn't been able to feel it because his power was benched. But I had, and he'd clearly had an effect on Kat.

Magic surged through my limbs as I imagined unleashing a magical takedown on Mitch's ass, but that wasn't going to help us find Vaughn or rescue Matisse.

Lucien cleared his throat. "Mitch, these two lovely ladies are friends of mine." He pointed to me. "Jade Calhoun. She's our current…well, soon-to-be current New Orleans coven leader. Bea's holding down the fort until Jade…uh, never mind. She'll be back in charge soon enough. And this—" he draped an arm around Kat possessively, "—is my girl, Kat."

Girl? Had he just publicly claimed Kat in front of this psycho? Idiot! He could've just put her in danger. I glanced at Kat to find her beaming, and I suspected this was the first public declaration that they were indeed a couple.

Damn Lucien. Obviously he was marking his territory. But she didn't seem to mind in the least. I struggled to keep from reaching over and smacking the back of his head.

"Hello." I held my hand out. "It's nice to meet you."

Mitch stared at my hand as if I'd just offered him a flaming bag of dog shit.

"Something wrong?" I asked, not backing down.

"No, no." He quickly shook my hand. "Just in a bit of a hurry. The crew is waiting."

I let my arm fall to my side and actively forced myself to not wipe my hand on my jeans. It was itching with unease. There was something seriously off about him. If Vaughn was anything like this guy, Matisse was right. We wouldn't want him anywhere near her. I prayed he wasn't.

Kat held her hand out to him, and he smiled, taking her hand and holding it in both of his. Interesting. He was definitely hiding something from me, either because I was an empath or because I was a witch. But he knew Kat was neither. I'd guess he was trying to spell her, but I couldn't sense any magic.

"It's lovely to meet you, Kat." Mitch flashed her a thousand-watt smile. She smiled shyly and didn't seem to notice he hadn't let go of her hand yet. I glanced at Lucien, who was scowling.

I tugged on Kat's other arm, gently pulling her away from him. "You don't want to hold him up." I gave Mitch a fake smile. "If you don't mind, can we wait here for you? There's something we need to ask you about."

The alluring charm he embodied so well slipped, and irritation flashed over his features for a second. Then it cleared just as fast. "I don't know how long I'm going to be. It might be better if—"

"We only need a few minutes, Mitch," Kat said with that flirty smile of hers. "If you don't mind, maybe we could walk back with you and we could chat on the way."

He regarded her with what appeared to be genuine interest, and although I couldn't sense anything he was feeling, I got the impression he was calculating something. But what? And why? He had no idea what we were going to ask about. Or did he? "Sure, sugar. You can walk back with me. I think that'll be just fine."

Lucien stepped forward, and I thought he was going to burst a few blood vessels, judging by the veins trying to pop out of his forehead.

I put my hand on his arm, holding him back. Leaning in, I whispered, "Let her schmooze him."

Lucien gave me an incredulous look. "You're joking, right?"

Kat fell in step beside Mitch, and the pair slipped through the fence back into the amusement park.

"No," I said to Lucien as we trailed behind him. "He's clearly not pleased to see you and he's suspicious of me. But Kat? He's interested." I took a breath, gathering courage. Letting her deal with a snake like him put me on edge, too, especially if he was a black magic user. But I was right behind her. I could step in at the first sign of any trouble. "And this gives her the opportunity to help us. You know how hard it is for her, always being on the fringe of the supernatural world."

A thick fog of jealousy clouded around him as he shot eye daggers at the back of Mitch's head.

"Deep breath," I said. He turned his murderous gaze on me, and I held my hands up in defense. "Hey, I'm on your side."

"Just watch him. He's bad news."

"Oh, I am." We quickened our pace, catching up with Mitch and Kat. We walked behind them, listening in on their conversation.

"I understand you're an assistant producer on this movie," Kat said to him. "What does that entail on a daily basis?"

Mitch awarded her attention with a smug smile. "Why don't you spend the day with me and find out?"

Lucien ground his teeth together but said nothing.

Kat laughed and playfully touched his arm. "Oh, I doubt your boss would be too thrilled about that."

He gave her a mock frown. "A gorgeous girl like you? The boss wouldn't mind. Not at all. Now that guy—" Mitch jerked his thumb over his shoulder at Lucien "—his ugly mug wouldn't be welcome for long." He laughed and shot Lucien a smirk.

Lucien didn't take the bait, but Kat was going to need to do some major sucking up to coax him out of his shitty mood after we left.

Kat's emotional energy was a whirlwind of disgust and irritation, but she did a fantastic job masking her body language. She tossed her hair over her shoulder and smiled at Mitch as if he was oh so amusing. "Do you get to bring guests to the set often?"

"Nah. Most days it's not that exciting. Like today, we're just filming scenery shots." Mitch waved at the cameras.

Kat pushed her lip out in a mock pouty expression. "That's too bad." Then she flashed him another smile. "I'd love to learn more about the process. Maybe we could come back another day when there's more action?"

"Sure, gorgeous."

"Where is she going with this?" Lucien hissed in my ear.

I shrugged, not sure myself.

But then Kat did a double take and eyed one of the other workers. He had dark hair and was sort of the same build as Mitch. She glanced between the two. "Wow, that guy kinda looks like you. Brother, maybe?"

Mitch scoffed. "Heck no. My brother builds motorcycles for a living and spends his time trolling bars. If it's not something that's going to get him laid, he's not interested."

Motorcycles? That was interesting. I made a mental note to check the city's shops.

"I see." Kat bit her lip and glanced around. "You said they're just filming scenery? So no actors or actresses are here?"

"Not today."

She glanced around the park and focused on the film crew. "That's disappointing."

"But you're here." He inched closer to her.

"Mitch," I said, my senses on high alert. He was invading way too much of her personal space.

He turned and his smile fell.

"Sorry to interrupt, but did you just say your brother builds motorcycles for a living?"

"Yeah. So?"

"Oh, good. Is there a way I can get in touch with him?"

Mitch pursed his lips and narrowed his eyes in suspicion. Oops. Too obvious. He shifted, appearing agitated, but I still couldn't sense one emotion from him.

"It's just that my fiancé has been talking about a custom bike for months now, and I'd love to surprise him, but I don't even know where to start. If I had someone I could—"

He held his hand up. "NoLa Custom Choppers. His name is Vaughn. But I don't know his hours. We don't talk much."

I reached out and touched his arm. Still no emotions. This guy was like a stone. "Thank you. I really appreciate it."

Mitch draped an arm around Kat and tugged her toward a trailer.

Magic shot to my fingertips as Lucien growled and moved to follow, but Mitch stopped mid-step and twisted, throwing an ugly gray ball of magic right at us.

"Watch out!" I cried, throwing up a protective shield, and then tackled Lucien just in case. We hit the asphalt and pain shot through my knees on impact just as Mitch's ball slammed against my magical barrier. The invisible wall flashed a putrid shade of yellow green and sizzled as it shattered to the ground.

"Kat!" Lucien scrambled to his feet, a thin sheen of magic pulsing around him.

It shouldn't have been possible. Bea had neutralized his magic, but he was pulling it from somewhere.

Kat let out a yelp as Mitch pushed her forward into an abandoned souvenir shop.

"Lucien!" I jumped up and ran after him. "No!"

He took off in a sprint, magic rapidly gathering around him. And then suddenly darkness crept over him, tainting his magic.

I stopped mid-run, a cry caught in my throat. Lucien was consumed by black magic.

Chapter 18

My heart stuttered and nearly broke in two. My best friend was being kidnapped by a psycho, and Lucien's soul was being claimed by black magic right before my eyes. If I didn't stop it, he'd be lost to us. The kind, powerful witch would be a force of evil we'd have to contain, and he wasn't likely to survive it. There was no way to save them both.

With tears in my eyes, I said a silent prayer that Kat could find a way to escape and called up my magic from the depths of my being. The magic burned white hot as it seared through my veins. When it hit my palms, a cry ripped from my throat and a bolt of my energy zapped across the park.

The magical energy coated Lucien, clinging to the black energy consuming him. A hollow feeling took up residence in my chest. A second later, I fell to one knee, too weak to keep standing.

Lucien writhed, his arms flailing as if my magic was burning him alive.

"Oh my God." Horror filled my soul. I barely noticed the tears spilling down my cheeks. This couldn't be happening. It was too awful to even contemplate. But it was real, and there wasn't anything I could do about it. I wanted to reach out to him, to somehow siphon the magic off him, to take it into myself and make it go away. But I couldn't. I couldn't even stand up. I grabbed a nearby table and tried to get my feet under me, but shadows clustered around me as I slipped into the shadow world.

I whipped my head to the side to find a hooded man inching toward me. My heart sped up and I blinked. Everything shifted again. Both of us were in the amusement park, the man covered in the same black magic. The energy pulsed and moved as if it were alive.

"What do you want?" I demanded, shaking with the effort to focus. I'd spent all my magic trying to save Lucien from whatever had come over him. I glanced in his direction. He was lying on the ground, his body twitching and his eyes unfocused.

Desperate, I crawled forward, trying to get to Lucien, but I only got a few feet when the man reached for me. My vision became fuzzy and my head started to spin. Then I felt a tug. Invisible hooks had clasped onto my remaining energy, and the little bit I had left was slowly being leeched from my reserves.

"No," I forced out and curled into a ball, trying to cut off the intrusion.

"Jade!" Bea's sharp voice cut through my haze.

I opened my eyes to find her and Lailah with their arms raised and magic bursting around them. My attacker hissed and turned his attention to Bea and Lailah, his dark magic growing around him.

"Get up." Bea's magical signature washed over me, and coven magic filled that place below my heart. I scrambled to my feet, fortified by the coven connection.

"Now!" Lailah cried and without conscious thought, I joined them in the focusing of unwieldy power. Our light slammed into the man, his back arching from the onslaught of power funneling into his chest. His mouth opened and out came a roar. Where black magic met white, a fireball erupted and the connection was broken.

"Again!" Bea demanded, and I felt her tap the magic that connected us. But before we could continue our attack, the figure turned and ran. After a few steps, he disappeared entirely.

I blinked twice, not sure I was comprehending what had happened. But as I stared at the empty pavement in front of me, I couldn't deny he was gone.

"Lucien!" I said to no one and ran to his side, panic making me tremble.

"What happened?" Bea asked, kneeling beside me.

"Kat." My voice broke on her name and I glanced in the direction I'd last seen her with Mitch. I swallowed hard. "Mitch kidnapped Kat, and when Lucien tried to stop him, he called forth black magic."

"Goddess above," Bea whispered. "It's the black heart curse." She glanced over her shoulder at Lailah. "I could use your help."

Lailah didn't hesitate. The pair went to work on pumping Lucien full of their magic.

"Jade?" Lailah asked when I didn't join them.

"I'm sorry. I have to go after Kat."

I'd already started running when Bea called, "Go. Do what you have to."

With the strange man gone and Bea and Lailah working on Lucien, I sprinted across the park, sending my emotional energy out as far as I could. A faint trace of Kat's signature brushed against my psyche, but I couldn't tell if it was left over from our walk through the park or if it was her active energy.

I sped up, gasping from the sob clogged in my throat. I'd failed her. I'd brought her into this and hadn't done anything to help when that bastard Mitch had taken her. Kat didn't have any way to fight back. She was a jewelry silversmith, for God's sake. Her only power was to help stabilize my energy when I overdid it. And even that was because we'd known each other for so long, she knew me better than anyone else, not because she had a special gift. Outside of a few self-defense classes in college, she was helpless.

I rounded the corner, and the trailer where we'd first found Mitch loomed in front of me. Kat's energy was stronger there. A healthy dose of fear and anger made my arms itch. *Kat.* She was just ahead. Without knocking, I barged into the small trailer and came to a full stop.

There was no one there. Just a mountain of cables, lights, filters, and tools. "Kat!" I called, climbing over the cables toward the back of the trailer.

Nothing. Not one little sound. Then I heard the roar of an engine. I twisted, slamming my hands against a window. A small black truck shot by. And the only thing I could focus on was Kat's horror-stricken face, staring out of the passenger side window.

"Shit!" I burst out of the trailer and ran into the parking lot just as the truck's taillights disappeared around a corner. Goddamned son of a… I hadn't even been able to get a read on the license plate. Lucien's Jeep was on the other side of the park. There was no way I could catch up.

I stared at the spot I'd last seen the truck, praying they would materialize again. But I knew it wouldn't. They were gone. Slowly, I turned around and then took off running back to Lucien.

When I got to his side, Lucien was sitting up, holding his head in his hands. The rest of the film crew was standing around asking questions. They wanted to know what had happened and if Lucien was all right. Holy shit. Had they seen everything that had gone on? If so, they should be a lot more surprised than they seemed to be at the moment.

"Lucien?" I asked as I kneeled beside him. "What happened?"

"He fainted," said a young woman wearing torn-up jeans. "He was just standing there and then…whoosh. He fell over. Could be an inner-ear thing."

I raised a curious eyebrow at Lailah.

She shot a look at Bea and mouthed *spell*.

Right. A suggestion spell.

"Let's get you up," Bea said to Lucien and wrapped an arm around him as he staggered to his feet.

He turned to me. "Kat?"

I shook my head sadly and willed myself not to cry again.

"We'll find her," Bea said firmly. "We need to go."

"Better get him to a doctor," said one of the spectators.

"We'll take care of him," Lailah said and grabbed Lucien's hand. She whispered something under her breath and a moment later, Lucien stood up a little bit straighter.

He met her gaze and gave her a small grateful nod. She nodded back, her eyes full of sadness.

No one said anything on the way back to the cars. When we got to Lucien's Jeep, I held my hand out for the keys. "Let me drive."

He fished them out of his pocket and dropped them in my hand.

"Follow me," I said to Bea and Lailah, my tone all business.

"Where are we going, Jade?" Bea asked gently.

"Kat's. We're going to do a finding spell." Without another word, I jumped into the Jeep and shoved the key into the ignition.

The drive back to the French Quarter was hell on earth. The traffic was bumper to bumper and it took over two hours to go ten miles. By the time I pulled in behind a dented up green car in front of Kat's apartment, my nerves were so frazzled I accidentally bumped the bumper.

"Shit." I grimaced and turned to Lucien to apologize, but he was already out of the Jeep and headed up to her apartment. I bolted, taking the stairs two at a time.

When I caught up to him, he was standing on her porch, staring at the doorknob, a scowl on his face. I nudged him. "I got it."

He ran a frustrated hand through his hair and stepped aside without saying anything.

With one zap of magic, I had the door open, and Lucien followed me inside. He strode to her kitchen and pulled out a small white dish and some herbs.

"Kat has the herbs for a finding spell?" I asked, eyeing the items on the counter. We could've made do with some more basic ingredients, but the herbs were preferable.

He nodded. "I've been stocking her cabinets with basics just in case."

In case what? In case he needed to do any spells while he was here?

Before I could ask, he said, "That was before…the incident."

The incident. Right. That would be the day he'd used a minor spell and Kat had almost died. The day we'd found out about his black heart curse. And the last day he'd cast any magic until today. I placed a supportive hand on his arm.

He shrugged it off, gut-wrenching pain radiating from him as he put a little distance between us.

"Lucien." I met his eyes. "It's not your fault."

He shook his head, pulled out a knife, and went to work on chopping the herbs.

A few minutes later, Bea and Lailah appeared. Bea nodded to me and went straight to Lucien's side. Lailah came to a stop beside me. "Jade?"

"Yeah?"

"We need to talk." She motioned for me to follow her into Kat's living room.

I sat beside her on the couch and waited.

"I'm worried about him," she said, keeping her gaze on the kitchen.

"His soul?" I guessed. "The black magic?"

She piled her honey-blond hair onto the top of her head and nodded. "That shouldn't have happened. Not when Bea had already neutralized his magic. It means the curse is spreading. If we don't find a cure soon, he's going to be in real danger."

My emotions were so raw I had no choice but to slam the doors on the turmoil raging through me. I closed my eyes and shut down until everything was numb. I couldn't help anyone if I couldn't focus. "What can we do?"

"We have to find out who put the curse on him. It's the only way to reverse it."

My mind whirled. Kat was missing. Lucien was getting worse. Matisse was still stuck in the void. Kane was off with demon hunters doing God knew what, and the weight of the world was on my shoulders. I wanted more than anything to lean on him, to hear him tell me we'd get through this. Instead, I had an angel laying more responsibility at my feet. "How are we supposed to do that?"

She stared at her hands. "I don't know. Maybe do a reading on Lucien. A memory spell. You did one with me before."

"I don't know how that would help. He remembers walking into the spell. He just doesn't know who cast it. Your situation was a lot different. You had blacked out."

She sat back and crossed her arms over her chest. "I don't know. I'm just trying to help. What happened to him today... it was scary. He could have died. He could have joined ranks with that demon and suffered a fate worse than death."

"Demon?" I gasped, and a ball of fear burst through my protective walls. "That being was a demon?"

Her brow furrowed. "What did you think he was?"

"I don't know. A black magic user?" I'd seen demons in Hell before, but they'd been a lot more animated. And their energy was different. This guy had been more like a shadow.

She must have clued in to what I was thinking because she said, "It's because the veil to Hell is closed. He needs black magic to sustain him. No doubt that's why he showed up when Lucien tapped his curse."

I slumped back. "Holy jeez. Could this day get any worse?"

"Don't say that," she said sharply. "Things can *always* get worse."

Chapter 19

Famous last words. *It can always get worse.*

Lucien and Bea emerged from the kitchen, both of them with grim expressions. Lucien bypassed the table and sat in a chenille chair across from me. He hunched forward and closed his eyes. A muscle in his right arm pulsed as he squeezed the armrest.

Bea took a seat at the table and motioned for us to join her. "Jade, you conduct the spell, since you know her best."

Tears prickled my eyes again, but I forced them back. There was no time to grieve. And I refused to believe there was reason to. We would find her. That bastard Mitch would pay. I sat at the end of the table, and Lailah took the chair across from Bea. The three of us clasped hands as I focused on the herb-filled bowl. *"Ignite,"* I whispered.

The herbs went up in flames, and I cleared my mind of everything except Kat. The fire turned green as the smoke twisted and turned, morphing into a woman's shape. Kat. Her face came into focus. We'd found her.

A gut-deep ache filled my core and my breath caught in my throat. Her eyes were squeezed shut, pain lining her face. The image started to fade. I couldn't see her through my turmoil.

Focus, Jade!

Her image instantly came into sharp view.

Bea squeezed my hand. "Follow her trail."

I wasn't exactly sure what she meant by that, but spells were mostly about intention. So I concentrated and said, "Show me where you are."

Lailah and Bea repeated my mantra.

The green fire brightened and the image vanished. Lailah let out a frustrated gasp. But I ignored her and let the spell wind through my mind. Kat's essence was there. I could feel her with me. The flames twisted one more time and when the scene came back into view, Kat was lying on a floor. A hardwood floor. There was nothing else in the room. Just Kat, the wood floor, and an old brick fireplace.

"Show me more." My voice was trance-like, and I barely heard Bea and Lailah repeat my words.

The scene shifted, zoomed out, and a house came into view, a New Orleans-style camelback. No lights lit the old house. No cars were parked in the driveway. No one was around. "More," I said with force.

"There," Lailah said.

The house number came into view and then the New Orleans fairgrounds. I let the magic go, and the fire died, leaving the bowl full of ash. I turned in my chair and caught Lucien's eye. "We've got her."

Without hesitation, he stood and moved toward the door.

Bea rose and placed her hands on the table. "Lucien. You can't go with us."

Green fire blazed from his gaze. "I'm well aware. Since I'm useless to help the one person I'd give my life for, I'm going to track down Paxton. I'll call Lailah if I find anything."

I got up and met him at the door. He gazed down at me, pain consuming him. I sighed and hugged him tight. The connection settled me a tiny bit. Hell, I probably needed this just as much as or more than he did. After a few beats, he returned my embrace and let out a strangled breath.

He pulled back abruptly. "I have to go."

"Thanks for checking on Vaughn. We'll call you as soon as we know anything."

With one last nod, he disappeared out the front door.

"Ready?" Bea asked.

"Let's go kick some black magic ass," Lailah said.

My resolve hardened, and I knew without a doubt that given half a chance, Mitch was going to wish he'd never met me. No one threatened my friends and got away with it.

The camelback house appeared just as deserted in person as it had in the vision. The three of us stood on the sidewalk, assessing our best plan of action.

"I vote we kick the door in and go in magic blazing," I said.

"Jade." Lailah shook her head. "Someone could be armed. And not just with magic."

"I don't sense anyone besides Kat," I said stubbornly. Never mind that I hadn't been able to feel Mitch's emotions earlier.

"We'll try something a little less risky," Bea said. "Lailah, you knock on the door while Jade and I head to the back. Try to get yourself inside. And don't be afraid to compel anyone. Remember, a life is at stake."

Lailah's mouth dropped open in surprise.

Bea sent her a cold, determined stare.

The angel closed her mouth and gave Bea one solemn nod.

"Compel?" I whispered.

Bea shrugged. "It's not something I condone. Compulsion is a gateway to dark magic. But we have no idea what we're getting ourselves into. I would've called the rest of the coven in, but given we're in the middle of Mardi Gras, rounding everyone up to form a stronger magical circle would have taken too long. We're just going to have to work with what we have."

That was fine with me. I wasn't excited about crossing a line, but I'd do it. For Kat.

The back entrance was protected with a security door. But for two witches, that wasn't an issue. I wrapped my hand around the doorknob and just like it had at Kat's house, the lock shifted and the door opened. With that handy tool, I could be a cat burglar.

The house was dark, almost pitch black. The windows were covered in heavy blackout-shade material. If I hadn't known better, I'd think this was some sort of vampire lair. Only everyone knew vampires didn't exist. Right? But then two days ago, I hadn't realized incubi existed.

My throat tightened with the effort to not call out Kat's name. Instead, I sent out my emotional energy. She was here, but unconscious. I still didn't feel anyone else. That didn't mean Mitch wasn't here, though.

"This way," I whispered to Bea and led her through the kitchen to a short hallway. Then I pointed at a closed door. "In here."

Bea put her hand on the door, and a tingle of her magic spread over the wood in small ripples. I wasn't sure what she was doing. A protection spell? A silencing one? Or maybe she was just assessing who might be on the other side. Whatever it was, I trusted her.

The loud click of the door unlocking made me bristle as the sound echoed through the room, but no one came running. Thank the Goddess.

Then Bea opened the door. Kat lay in the center of the room, her wrists and ankles bound. Her eyes were closed and blood coated her forehead.

"Kat," I gasped and ran to her side, my insides churning with trepidation. Pressing my fingers to her neck, I felt for the steady beat of her pulse. There. I let out a small sigh of relief. Somewhere in the back of my mind, I'd known Kat was alive. That was the only way I could've sensed her emotional signature. But that hadn't stopped me from seeking reassurance. She just looked so broken.

I started to pull at the restraints around her feet, but when I realized they were bound with spelled zip ties, I swore. Nothing was going to get those off except magic. And not just any magic—careful, nuanced magic that wouldn't hurt her further.

Bea smoothed her hair back and checked her head wound. "How is it?" I asked.

"Not great. She'll have a nasty lump and bruise, but she'll live. It's okay to move her."

Good. 'Cause she couldn't stay there. "Just one second." I placed my hand over Kat's ankle restraints and tugged at my magic. It sprang forth, but I barely let any go. A second later the zip tie disintegrated.

"Jade!" Lailah cried. "No!"

I jerked my head up in total confusion and then frantically scanned Kat's ankles for damage. Nothing. Then I felt it. Hot, searing pain shot into my back and my world turned black.

I woke to bickering. "Why her?" a whiny voice asked.

"Because she's the one who neutralized the curse," said another man. "And we're going to see if she can do it again."

I blinked, trying to clear my blurred vision. My hands were bound together in front of me, but my feet weren't. Where was I? I shifted and nearly cried out from the spasm that shot through my back. Flashes of light went off like lightning bolts in my brain. When the pain eased to a dull ache, I panted and blinked again. I was almost certain I was still in the house across from the fairgrounds. But not the same room Kat had been in. This one didn't have a fireplace.

"When's he going to get here?" Whiny asked.

"Shut up."

The door opened and light spilled in, making my eyes water. I wiped the tears away and focused on the asshole standing in the doorway. Mitch. That bastard.

"Good. You're awake."

My magic tingled in my chest, ready to blast his ass to smithereens, but as soon as I reached for it, that bolt of pain seized my back, making my eyes roll into the back of my head.

"Every time you try to use magic in this house, the pain will only get worse. I suggest you submit to my will, or it's going to be a very long night for you."

I let out a low hiss and glared at him. "Where's Kat?"

"She's still here. We need to conduct a few experiments, and she's volunteered." His lips turned up into an evil smile, making it quite clear she hadn't volunteered for anything... unless it was to kick him in the balls.

"And Bea and Lailah?"

His face turned to stone. "The angel has been neutralized. And that witch, that goddamned bitch. She's finding out what it means to pay for your consequences. I suggest you cooperate or you'll be joining her."

Until that point, I'd only really been fearful for Kat. The rest of us had powers we could rely on. But hearing him speak of Bea, my mentor, as if she was suffering at his hand, and the fact that he'd said Lailah had been neutralized, sent a bolt of pure panic through my body. He was only one witch. "How?" I asked.

He grinned a cat-that-ate-the-canary smile and raised his arms. Black magic danced over his skin, stronger and more powerful than anything I'd experienced before. It filled the room, flattening me to the floor as I struggled to even breathe.

Fear silenced me.

"Good," he said, studying my face. His magic subsided, granting me temporary relief. "I can see you've acknowledged the predicament you find yourself in. Think carefully about your next move, Jade."

My next move? It involved ripping his heart out and feeding it to the gators. "What do you want from us?"

He leaned against the doorjamb and crossed his feet casually. "The angel? Nothing. She's just in the way. The rest of you, though? You're going to help me figure out where the spell went wrong."

I shielded my eyes against the artificial light from the next room glowing around him. "What spell?"

"You haven't put two and two together yet. That's…interesting. Disappointing, actually. I was hoping you'd be a little brighter than the average witch. But I see you rely more on your power than your brain, like most."

Well, that was damned rude. But I chose to ignore his taunt for what it was. A way to rattle me. "Put what together? Why did you take Kat?"

"You really have to ask?" His eyebrow rose. "He's in love with her."

Lucien. He'd said he had history with Mitch. Neither liked the other one. Was this revenge for something? Then his words from earlier hit me. *Because she's the one who neutralized the curse.* They'd been talking about me. And the curse was the black heart curse. The one that had almost killed Kat.

"You cursed Lucien." It wasn't a question but a statement.

"Now you're catching on." His grin turned maniacal.

"Why?" This guy had clearly turned to black magic at some point in his life, but he wasn't so far gone that he was lost to it. It was hard to believe it hadn't consumed him after he'd cast a black heart curse.

"Why?" Mitch roared. "You're asking me why? Because that bastard stole the only person who ever cared about me." His face turned a dark shade of red. "As far as I'm concerned, he deserves much worse."

Horror seized my heart. "The girl Lucien was dating, the one who died. That's her, right?"

He regarded me for a long moment, clearly contemplating how much to tell me. Then he looked me dead in the eye and said, "The bitch deserved it. She promised to marry me and three months later she was sleeping with him. They both deserve what they got."

The light went out behind him, and a second later the door slammed, leaving me alone in the darkness.

Chapter 20

I lay on the floor in the dark, going over and over what Mitch had said, trying to make sense of it all. How had he known Kat had almost died? Or that I'd saved her? Had he been keeping tabs on Lucien for the past ten years? And if so, why? Just to feed his sick, twisted need for revenge?

The house remained dark and quiet, but I could sense that Kat, Bea, and Lailah were still there. Whiny Boy, too. But not Mitch. I had no reason to believe he'd left, though. He'd told Whiny Boy they were waiting for someone.

How the hell was I going to get out of this one? My body was almost numb as if I were on a drug. Could I call up any magic at all? Tentatively, I reached for that spark. My back arched and I gasped as a spasm claimed me. Shit, that hurt! No, magic wasn't an option. I took a shallow breath as I let the magic go. The numbness took over again.

I was virtually useless. But two things gave me hope. Bea and Lailah were still there, and if anyone could get us out of this mess, it was them. And second, Mitch had said he wanted me to replicate a spell. In order for that to happen, he was going to have to lift the spasm curse. I'd just have to be ready.

Time seemed to slip by and my heart began to hurt for not only my friends in the other rooms but for Matisse as well.

What if I couldn't get back to her? What if she faded away into the mist? And Kane? How would he ever even know what happened to me? Or my mom, Gwen, and my stepdad Marc? Or all the rest of the people I had in my life now after years of just Gwen and Kat?

All because this witch had once been hurt by his fiancée? The selfish son of a bitch. I wouldn't let this happen. Not on my watch.

After what seemed like hours, the door finally opened again. No light this time. "Get up," Mitch ordered.

I rolled to my side and stifled a groan. "I don't think I can," I said, hoping to get him to lift the curse.

"You can and you will if you want your friends to live. Or at least a few of them," he added with a sick laugh.

The anger that shot through my veins gave me the strength to push myself up into a sitting position, and then I was able to get my feet under me. I held onto the wall with my bound hands. "If you lift the curse, I'd be a lot more cooperative," I lied.

"Why would I do that? Look at you. I don't even have to lift a finger to get you to obey."

Obey? Oh, he was going to pay for that one.

"Move it." He kicked the back of my knee, and I fell against the door, barely holding myself up.

My magic pulsed with the desire to knock him out, but it only resulted in making me clutch the door harder to keep from collapsing. There was too much pain shooting through my torso. The spasm curse was beyond cruel.

"That way." He pointed down the hall, toward the front of the house. I shuffled along, using the walls for support. But when we stepped into the living room, the desperation streaming off Kat made my legs go weak and I slid to the floor, landing lightly on my knees.

"Kat?" I said softly, my gaze landing on her curled form in the corner.

"Jade?" Hope rang clear in her tired voice. "You're here?" Then her tone shifted to panic. "We have to get out of here. He's evil. He's the one who cursed Lucien."

"She knows," Mitch said lightly, clearly amused by her distress. "But I might take issue with being called evil."

Kat flinched and lifted her head to get a good look at him. Steel shone in her determined eyes. "Does 'evil bastard' work for you?"

His amusement faded and he looked like he wanted to slam a fist into something. Maybe Kat herself. He turned to me. "Keep her in line or she'll be dead a lot faster."

Pure hatred. There was no other way to describe what I was feeling right then. "If you touch her again, even breathe on her, your life is over, got it?"

"I doubt that, *white witch*."

"Try me." My voice vibrated with rage.

In answer, he raised his hand and pointed at me. With one swipe to the left, pain exploded through my side and I crumpled to the ground once more. He hadn't even touched me. I writhed silently and focused on shutting out the pain. I could get through this. I just had to stay conscious long enough to wait for my opening.

The front door opened and crashed into the wall. Sunlight poured into the dark house, blinding me. On instinct my emotional radar went off, alerting me to two people. One of them was Lucien.

I jerked my head up, praying he'd brought the cavalry, that he was here to bust us out. But when my eyes focused on him, all hope fled. His hands were in zip ties just as mine were, but his feet were bound as well. He was also gagged.

"Where do you want him?" the new guy asked. His tone was measured as if he were still assessing the situation. Then his eyes landed on me. "What the hell, Mitch? Why do you have a white witch bound like that?"

"You can tell what I am?"

"It's a gift of mine." The tall man kneeled in front of me. He appeared to be in his early twenties, hooded dark eyes, kind of mysterious looking. Very attractive. Well, he would've been if he hadn't just brought Lucien in, all trussed up and ready for Mitch. "Why are you here?"

Mitch scoffed. "She's here because she broke into my house."

The man stood. "What did she want?"

"I'm guessing she was searching for him." Mitch pointed to Lucien. "I bet she thought he was already here."

Lucien? I would have, but no, I was here for Kat and for some reason, Mitch had lied. "I came for—"

Mitch waved his hand again, his magic punching me in the stomach. My breath left me, rendering me momentarily speechless. "She's being difficult." Mitch eyed the man. "How did she know you were bringing the witch? Did you tell anyone you were working for me?"

He cast Mitch a bored expression. "I don't tell anyone about my work." He glanced at me once more and then frowned. "You know she's the coven leader, right?"

"No, she isn't. The old lady is. But I've got this covered. You can go now."

The young man held out his hand. "Payment."

Mitch scowled. "Fuckin' A. You know I'm good for it."

"Payment on delivery. Those were the terms. If you ever expect to use my services again, you'll make good on the deal."

Mitch reluctantly pulled a wad of money from his front pocket and handed a stack of hundreds to the man, who must be a bounty hunter.

"It's good doing business with you." The bounty hunter shoved the bills into his back pocket and turned toward the door.

Clearly he wasn't a key player in this operation. And if he was only a bounty hunter, he might not have any idea what was really going on here. He'd been asked to bring in a witch who was cursed with black magic. If he didn't know Lucien and just searched his magical signature, it certainly would look like he'd been engaging in some evil dealings. And he'd been told I'd broken into the house. Which was true, but the bounty hunter didn't know why.

"Hey!" I cried out, finding my voice. "None of this is what you think. Mitch kidna— Oomph." A boot slammed into my rib, and my vision filled with white spots.

"Shut up," Mitch said. "Lying bitch. She can't seem to separate fact from fiction." His voice was cool, dispassionate, as if today was just another day. "We've got it from here."

The bounty hunter glanced at me, then Lucien, and then Kat. His gaze lingered on her, but the fact that she was beaten and lying on the floor didn't seem to have an effect on him. After a moment, he stepped back toward the door and said, "You know where to find me."

The soft click of the door made me whimper. Would that be our last chance at help?

"Landon, get your ass in here." Mitch moved over to Lucien and stared down at him with a scowl on his face. "Such a fucking idiot. I knew when your girlfriend started pumping me for information about my brother and motorcycles it was really about Vaughn. It always is. So I went ahead and gave her the information she wanted, hoping you'd show up there and make his job easier when I called in the order. I never dreamed you'd show up today. I just paid full price for a fucking job that took him less than two hours."

Lucien glared at him, unable to speak. The hatred streaming from him sent a ripple of fear down my spine. If Lucien ever got free, we were going to have a black magic bloodbath on our hands.

"Here's how it's going to work," Mitch continued. "You're going to spell that little hottie over there again, and we're going to see if this one—" he pointed to me "—can reverse it again. Oh yeah, I heard about that. Don't think I haven't been watching you all these years, Boulard. I was watching to see when you'd break and corrupt her again, but imagine my surprise when the three of you came looking for me."

He shook his head. "How could I pass up such a golden opportunity to see my spell come to fruition once again? And now we're going to see what went wrong a few weeks ago. No

one should be able to break that curse once it's set in motion."
He shifted his attention to me. "No one. Got that, bitch? Today
we're going to find out exactly what makes you so goddamned
special."

Holy...oh my God. This guy was certifiable. He'd been
watching us? Had been waiting for the time when Lucien
would lose control again to see Kat die? And then when we'd
come looking for him, he'd made a snap decision right then
and there to kidnap Kat and put a bounty hunter after Lucien.
Had I been part of the plan as well? Or did he just decide to
study me because I'd broken in, looking for Kat? Probably the
latter. He didn't seem to be terribly organized.

He strode over to the door and locked it, then a bolt of
magic hit the doorknob and it started to glow. "Try to touch
it and you'll lose your hand." He disappeared back into the
depths of the house.

I gritted my teeth against the back pain and forced myself
to my feet again. "Lucien," I said softly as I shuffled toward
him. There wasn't much I could do about his zip ties, but I
could do something about the gag. It took me a minute, due
to my bound wrists, but I was able to loosen the knot enough
to pull the fabric down.

"How's Kat?" he asked, twisting to stare at her crumpled
form.

"I'm okay," she said faintly.

I shook my head. She was far from okay. But there wasn't a
lot either of us could do about it at the moment.

Hobbled by his ankle restraints, Lucien took short steps
in Kat's direction. But before he could get to her side, Mitch
reappeared. "Stop right there, Boulard."

Lucien froze and glared at Mitch. "Let her go," he demanded.

"I don't think so. You're about to find out what it's like to
lose the one you love. Again." Mitch's eyes turned pure black,
as the black magic that had coated his skin at the defunct
amusement park reappeared.

My vision shifted, and the darkness tainting Lucien's soul intensified. I was working in a constant state of terror now. If we didn't get Lucien out of here soon, he'd be lost. The black heart curse was going to affect the rest of his being. Lucien straightened. If he'd had use of his hands, I was certain Mitch would have been a dead man.

"Do it, Boulard. Cast a spell. Let's see what happens," Mitch taunted.

I could feel Lucien's black magic building. It snaked over my skin, burning with anger and despair. That was when it hit me. Bea had neutralized the coven magic, but the blackness caused by the curse had always been there. If he used magic now, he'd be lost to the other side. He'd be consumed by the darkness. We'd lose him.

"Lucien, no!" I cried. "It's all black magic you're wielding now. Don't let him break you."

My friend turned to me, his pained expression making my heart bang against my breastbone. "What does it matter? If we do nothing, Kat will be lost. I'd rather blow him to smithereens and compromise myself than see her hurt for one more minute."

"She doesn't want this," I pleaded. "If we lose you to this, she'll never forgive herself."

"And if I lose her, I'm lost anyway." The magic kicked up around him, spreading through the room like a storm cloud. He focused on Mitch and started an incantation in Latin. I didn't recognize it, but if it was black magic, I wouldn't.

"That's it," Mitch coaxed. "Take it all in. Show me what you've got."

In my horror, I hadn't noticed Mitch building his own magic. It was subtle, and if I hadn't caught the faint glow around his fingertips, I'd have never known. I didn't know what spell he was building, but he was clearly waiting for Lucien to cast his first. A deflection spell maybe? Whatever it was, it was sure to be too horrible for words. The glee dancing in his eyes told me everything I needed to know.

I took two painful steps and shifted so I was between Lucien and Mitch. "Lucien," I said in my calmest voice possible. "You don't want to do this. Trust me. This is exactly what he wants."

Lucien scowled and glanced away from me, his magic still building.

"Think of all the love you have for Kat," I continued, panting from trying to stay upright.

"Yeah," Mitch added with a sneer. "Think of how much you'll hate me when she's dead. Think of Rissa and how young she was when she died. All because you loved her."

I couldn't stop my own magic from rushing to the surface. And Goddess above, I wanted to unleash it on that asshole. Wanted to call on a portal and send his ass to Hell. Only the veil was closed and my body was too crippled by whatever spell he'd hit me with to do anything.

Was there *any* way to use my magic to counteract it? I was willing to try no matter how excruciating it was, but I had to make sure Lucien didn't turn Vader on me. "Lucien," I said carefully. "He won't get away with this. Do not listen to his bullshit. Listen to me. Your coven leader."

The black magic stopped growing around him. It didn't dissipate, but the cloud turned stagnant. He let out a long, frustrated breath and the magic fled.

I stepped forward and held my hands out to him. He was reaching for me when the house started to rattle around us. I shuffled forward, grasping onto Lucien, and huddled against him. The floors rolled and the lights flickered on, then off, and settled on a dim glow.

"What the hell was that?" I asked no one in particular.

Out of nowhere a loud boom crackled through the house. Lucien and I both ducked and crouched near the floor. When I looked up, three hooded figures hovered over us.

They looked exactly like the one we'd encountered at the amusement park.

Demons! Terror rolled through me. We'd never survive this.

Chapter 21

"You're late." Mitch scowled at the demons.

One of them turned to Mitch, his red eyes glowing. "We don't work for you, witch. We're here for him." The demon pointed at Lucien.

I instinctively shifted so I was blocking Lucien. "You're not taking him."

"Step aside, white witch." The other two demons lowered their hoods. They all had the bright, fiery eyes of a demon, and I was struck by the fact that Chessandra's eyes had looked exactly the same when she'd been talking about Matisse. The difference between angel and demon was very small.

One of them jerked his head toward the back of the house. He took a long sniff and his eyes turned black for a moment. "Angel."

Oh, son of a bitch. He knew Lailah was there. Fear for her exploded through me. If she was captured by the demons, it was only a matter of time before she fell. We were all incapacitated and surrounded by a black magic user and three demons. Plus I still had no idea what had happened to Bea. Life had never looked so grim. My resolve started to fade, and acceptance that I might not be able to pull us out of this set in. I had to try, though. I wouldn't go down without a fight.

"Go," Mitch told the demons. "She is an offering for your assistance in this matter."

A look of deep satisfaction spread over the demon's face, and without a word, he took off in search of the angel.

"No, dammit! What did Lailah ever do to you?" I raged at Mitch.

He shrugged. "Nothing." He moved into the room toward Kat.

Lucien shuffled backward and stood over her protectively. "Stay away from her."

Mitch shook his head the way one would at a petulant child. "I don't want your bitch. I just want you to lay a simple spell on her."

Kat pushed up on her knees and touched Lucien's thigh. "Do what you have to," she said with conviction in her voice. "Even if it means hurting me."

I hurried to her side as fast as I could. Grasping her arm with both of my hands, I said, "No, Kat! We can fight this."

"How?" she demanded. "Neither of you can fight him without dire consequences. He'll use both of you to get what he wants. And in the end you're going to hate yourselves for what you do to me. So don't do anything. Let him hurt me. I'd rather that than let him use you against me." Tears streamed down her face.

Lucien let out an audible groan and fell to his knees. He pulled her to his chest protectively. "Jade, we have to do something."

The pain running between the two of them, combined with the unconditional love, made something inside me snap. I didn't know what it was or where it came from, but my magic shot from the depths of my being like a meteor. Unbearable pain seized my entire body, but instead of collapsing, I rose a foot off the ground, my muscles taut and unyielding. It was as if my magic was keeping me glued together when Mitch's spell was trying to tear me apart.

Power burst within me, traveling the familiar path to my fingertips. The two remaining demons gathered around me, their arms spread wide. Pain pulsed deep in my bones as the magic pressed and pulled at the same time, leaving me tied in knots. The pressure built, and I was certain I was going to snap in two. This was it. I was going to be taken down by a jealous asshole. Not even a demon. No, Mitch's curse was doing this to me and while the war raged, I couldn't even control my magic. It had a will of its own.

"Contain her," Mitch demanded.

But the two demons didn't do anything of the sort. They inched closer, held their hands out, and touched the magic wafting off me. Their faces lit up in sheer ecstasy. And then my body spasmed once more, but not in pain. The spell broke, and all the magic I'd built rushed from me straight into the demons.

They writhed with it, soaked it up, and latched their grubby demon hands on me, determined to steal every last precious drop.

Panic. Sheer terror. Remorse. It all soared through me, overwhelming me, crushing my spirit. But then Kane's image filled my mind. His dark, expressive eyes gazed at me as they had yesterday when we'd lain in bed together, completely full of love. I felt the way his hand pressed to my lower back when we walked together. His soft, demanding lips on mine. I heard his voice whispering our plans for the future, and I saw his profile as I watched him when he wasn't looking.

All that love filled my heart and put me at peace. *No regrets,* I told myself.

"Stop!" Kat yelled, and I watched, completely helpless, as she tried to stagger to her feet.

"Kat, no!" I tried to scream over the roar in my ears. But the house was rumbling again, the walls shaking and the floor rolling. Someone or something was coming.

Lucien, I cried in my head, praying he would hear me. *Use your magic. Do what you have to. Blast a hole in the wall of the house. Just get out. Both of you.*

He turned his head and studied me.

Do it! Save yourselves. More demons are coming.

I swear I saw him give me a tiny nod, and magic built up around us. Black and white, it all mixed together, tainted and ugly. There was nothing pure or good about any of it. All I wanted was for Kat and Lucien to get out. I had no idea where Bea or Lailah were. But I knew the demons were taking everything I had and the three of us didn't have a way to fight them.

The rumble intensified and all of a sudden the door burst open once more, but it wasn't Vaughn. Four men barged in, daggers raised. Light shone from the familiar scrollwork on the handles. Shock and relief flooded me, even as I felt the last of my magic slip away from my control.

Kane. He was here with three other demon hunters.

The hold on me vanished. My body crumpled to the floor. The two demons hissed, and balls of black magic flew at the hunters. One flew straight at Kane. He lifted his dagger, and the magic flowed straight into the scroll symbols on the handle. Another of the hunters aimed his dagger at the demon, and a beam of light seared him in the abdomen. The demon doubled over and then dove to the side and rolled to his feet, coming up fighting.

"Jade?" Kat said, crawling toward me.

I focused on her, too weak to answer. My elation at seeing Kane had fled, and now I was just an empty shell of nothing. No magic. No energy. No strength.

Kat's bound hands landed on my arm. "Take it."

I shifted my gaze from the fantastic magical battle raging around us to meet her eyes.

"Take my energy. You need it," she said.

A lump clogged my throat and tears burned my eyes. I was empty. Had nothing left to give those around me.

"Jade." Kat shook me, panic consuming her. "Do it. Now. Take my energy. We need you."

I shook my head. They didn't need me. I'd failed.

"Look!" She pointed to where Kane and another of the demon hunters were battling one of the demons. The demon was throwing magic, my magic, all over the room. Plaster and brick splintered and cracked. The house was coming down around us and the demons were winning.

Lucien was standing behind us, all that black magic still clinging to him. He was frozen, unable to unleash his only weapon.

"Do it, Jade," Lucien said, his deep green eyes so dark they were almost black. "Take the only gift she has to give."

The love pouring off him, despite the fact that he was so utterly consumed with darkness, touched me deep in my soul. I shifted my gaze to Kat. She tightened her hold on my arm and nodded.

With tears still streaming down my face, I reached for her cooling energy. My own energy was so spent that nothing happened at first. But just as I was about to give up, a trickle of relief flowed into my veins.

"More," Kat said in a tired voice.

Reluctantly, I latched on to the gift she offered and let her energy bring me back from the edge. She clung to my arm, almost willing her strength into me.

"Enough," I forced out and tried unsuccessfully to pulled my arm out of her death grip. I was going to drain her.

She shook her head. "Take it."

"Kat, stop!" I cried, frantic now. She gripped tighter, and her energy flowed freely now. There was nothing I could do to stop it.

She shook her head harder and now tears were streaming down her face.

I snapped my gaze to Lucien. "Get her off me."

"I can't," he said through clenched teeth. "If I touch her, you'll be tainted."

Shit! I jerked, trying to dislodge her grip, and rolled. Her nails dug in, but I brought my knee up and caught her in the hip. She grunted and rolled away. I scrambled to my feet and turned toward Kane.

He was blocking blow after blow from the demon. My magic welled into a pool in my gut. The back spasm was gone, and

I was once again myself. The first thing I did was blast away my restraints, then Kat's and Lucien's. Raising my arms over my head, I tapped into the power pulsing in my chest. It was weaker than it had been, but it was enough.

I focused on the light streaming from the demon, felt it calling to me, and yelled, "Return to me."

The demon froze and then turned in my direction, his body vibrating.

"Return to me!" I yelled again with conviction.

The demon's mouth opened and light shot from him, streaming straight to my fingertips. My familiar magic pooled there. Time seemed to stop as we remained suspended in the moment. My fingers started to burn and the magic burst through, rushing into me, until I thought I would explode with the heady power.

The magic stream suddenly broke and the demon stumbled backward. Kane and one of the hunters charged forward. Two daggers flew, each landing with perfect precision right in the demon's heart. Light swirled around them and fire erupted, instantly incinerating the demon. All that was left was ash.

I spun, frantically searching for the other two demons. "Where are they?"

A loud bang, followed by the sound of flesh pounding on flesh, came from the back of the house.

Kane and the other demon hunter tore down the hall.

I spun back around to Lucien and Kat. She was propped up against the wall, and he was sitting cross-legged in front of her. They were gazing intently at each other but not touching. It damn near broke my heart.

Bea had to restore his magic. How else was he going to combat the blackness eating him from the inside out?

"Are you okay?" I asked Kat.

She gave me a weak nod. "Go, do what you have to."

I sent Lucien a questioning glance. "How about you?"

"I'll live." He closed his eyes, clearly trying to gain control of his emotions. "For now, anyway."

I had to do something. I knew I should wait for Bea, but I couldn't leave him in that state. I gently brushed my fingertips over his shoulder and unleashed a tiny bit of my magic.

His eyes went wide, then he let out a loud cry of agony as he doubled over.

Chapter 22

"Lucien," Kat cried and jerked forward, her hands out.

I jumped in front of her. "No! You can't touch him. Not right now."

"Do something, then." Her face contorted in a mixture of frustration and anger.

I tried to block it out and focus. But I couldn't. My emotional barriers were blown to hell and fear, frustration, and desperation fought for dominance in my heart. I did the only thing I could think of. I filled my mind with all the love and joy I'd experienced over the last few months. Let the memories take over and reveled in them. I had a lot to live for, and so did my friends.

"Lucien," I said quietly but with force.

His head turned to the side as he tried to focus on me. Panting, he clutched at his chest.

"Think about Kat and everyone who's important to you. Let the joy you feel when you're around them push you through this. Find the will to fight for them. You're stronger than you think. Your soul is stronger than ever. Reach deep."

Lucien stilled, but it was clear he was still in a lot of pain.

I turned to Kat. "Keep reminding him of all he has to live for. Make him focus on the good. This is about intentions.

Blackness is no match for pure goodness. Got it?" It wasn't the total truth. Without a spell, the black curse wasn't going to go away. But together they could hold the darkness at bay.

She nodded and started whispering how much she cared for him, what a good man he was, and talked about all the people she knew he'd helped over the years.

His body slowly began to relax and the darkness faded. It wasn't a cure, but it was a start.

By the time I got to the back of the house, the other two demons were gone and Mitch was tearing out the back. He ran full out, leaped, and then climbed the wooden fence. The demon hunters tore after him, but Kane paused and grabbed me around the waist.

He pulled me to him, clutching me tightly. His relief and lingering fear brushed against my psyche. "Thank God you're all right."

I breathed in his familiar musky scent and let the moment sink in. He was here, in my arms, and we both were okay. "You, too," I said with a sob catching in my throat.

He bent his head and brushed his lips over mine. It was gentle, a sweet moment.

When we pulled apart, the cinnamon flecks in his eyes shone back at me. He kissed me once more and then said, "I'll find you tonight. I promise." And without another word, he took off after the other demon hunters.

I watched him disappear over the fence. My heart stuttered in my chest. Kane. My fiancé was a badass demon hunter. And dammit if I hated it yet felt a huge burst of pride at the same time.

I hurried back into the house and followed the sound of Lailah's voice. I found her and Bea sitting in a black-painted room. There was nothing there except a closed chest and manacles screwed to the wall. Bea was holding her head with both hands, and Lailah was crouched next to her, whispering softly. It was a healing chant I'd heard Bea use before.

Even though I was pretty sure we were alone, I sent out my emotional energy just to be sure. My senses touched on

Bea, whose energy was clouded, and I couldn't get a clear read. Concussion most likely. Lailah was angry but also hopeful. Hopeful? About what? That she could help Bea? And then there were Lucien and Kat. They were a mixed bag of complexity that was too much for me to sort through.

There was no one else.

Lailah finished her chant, and a light blue ball of magic manifested in her palm. She brought her hand up to her lips and blew. The spark floated lazily toward Bea and hovered near her mouth. "Swallow it," Lailah said gently.

Bea dropped her hands and shook her head. "You know I can't do that."

"You can and you will," Lailah demanded. "I'm your soul guardian. It's my job to make sure you survive. Now do it."

"Her soul is in danger?" I asked.

Lailah startled and glanced back at me. "Yes. Mitch tried to take it."

I gasped. "How?"

"He hit her with an awful spell." She turned her attention back to Bea, who was staring at the blue orb. "Bea, you have to. Come on. The coven needs you."

"They have Jade." Bea shot me a tired glance.

I didn't have any idea what was going on. Why wouldn't she let Lailah help her? "Bea," I said cautiously. "You can't let Lucien down. Something broke inside him and the black magic is taking over. Without you to restore his magic, he'll be lost to the dark."

After a moment, she opened her mouth and the blue orb zoomed down past her lips, her throat working as if she were swallowing it. She grimaced and slumped back against the wall.

Lailah's eyes rolled into the back of her head and she fell backward.

"Whoa!" I caught her before she hit her head on the fireplace mantel. Her eyes fluttered and she stared up at me weakly. "What just happened?"

Bea sat up, her color rosy pink. Her eyes were bright and she appeared as if nothing had ever happened. "She gave me a piece of herself so I would be strong enough to heal. Unfortunately she's now out of commission for a few days."

"What? There are demons on the loose."

Bea nodded solemnly. "Yes. And that's why we need to get her out of here and somewhere safe."

"Let's go." I propped her up and pulled her arm around my shoulders. Bea did the same on her other side, and together, we carried the limp angel from the house of doom. Kat and Lucien followed us out the front door. Seconds later I was in Bea's car with Lailah while Kat and Lucien followed us.

"To your house," I told Bea. Her place had all kinds of protections and wards. "We need a safe haven."

She nodded. "There's going to be traffic from the parades."

"If it's too bad, together we can cast a spell to clear our way."

Bea cast me a curious glance.

I shrugged. I didn't like using magic to force my will on others. But if there ever was a time for an exception, this was it.

We only needed to cast one spell to get security to let us through a barricade. But it was full dark by the time we stumbled into Bea's small carriage house. After we gently deposited Lailah on the sunflower-print couch, Bea hurried to her kitchen and started a pot of tea. Witch's brew, she called it. To fortify ourselves after the battle.

Kat went to the bathroom for a wet cloth and antibacterial cream. Lucien sat in the chair farthest from us, trying his best to keep his distance.

"Lucien," I said. "Can you do me a favor?"

He lifted his head and nodded. "Anything."

"Call my mom and Gwen and let them know I'm all right. Feel free to fill them in. I'm sure they want to know what's been going on."

"Sure." He stood and grabbed his phone from his back pocket. After a quick glance, he put it on the side table and headed for Bea's landline. "It was dead. Probably zapped in the battle."

"Probably. Bea should have all the numbers in her address book."

"They are," Bea called from the kitchen.

Kat reappeared with the damp towel and a first aid kit. She passed by Lucien and reached out to touch him, but at the last moment, she pulled back. I bit my lip. His cure couldn't come fast enough.

Sitting beside Lailah, Kat handed me the first aid kit. She averted her eyes from my penetrating stare and brushed the hair off Lailah's forehead. With an intensity suited for a brain surgeon, she went to work on mopping the angel's brow.

Over the next few minutes, I applied antibacterial cream to Lailah's wrists, where it appeared she'd been shackled, and then her knees. She'd either fallen or been thrown down. I had, too, but I wasn't wearing a skirt. I doctored my own wrists and then moved on to Kat's, gently swabbing them. She winced but didn't complain. By the time I was done, Lucien was off the phone.

"How'd it go?" I asked.

"About as well as you'd suspect. They want to come over."

"Are they?" Mom was a witch. She would come in handy. Gwen was psychic. And although her visions were always correct, she never shared them. So in this case, she really only was good for moral support.

He shook his head. "They're at the apartment on Bourbon Street. They're never getting out of there."

My eyebrows shot up. "Seriously? I thought they were at Summer House."

"Your mom said something about needing to get the hell away from Hurricane Shelia's saggy boobs."

I couldn't help the burst of laughter that overtook me. At least Kane's mom was having a fun time for Mardi Gras. His dad was probably knee deep in a bottle of whiskey by now. Then I had a vision of Mom and Gwen joining the Bourbon

Street crowd wearing boas and body paint. I shuddered. Yeah, not a good visual.

"Pyper," I said. "I need to call her."

Lucien handed me the phone. She was probably busy at the club, but she'd be worried sick about us. I dialed and waited as the phone rang four, five, six times. Finally on the seventh ring Charlie picked up. "Wicked. This is Charlie and you're missing the party."

I cracked a smile. "It's always a party when you're around."

"Jade? Girl, where the hell are you?"

"At Bea's. Is Pyper around?"

"Yeah, just a sec." There was a rustling noise indicating she might be covering up the receiver. "Jade?"

"Yeah. I'm here."

"Good," Charlie said. "Here she is. Sorry about that. We had a groper."

Ugh. Drunk dudes who thought it was okay to touch anyone they liked because they were in a strip bar.

"Dude. What the hell is going on? I've left you both, like, eight messages," Pyper said by way of greeting.

"Sorry." I grimaced. "It's been a shitty day to say the least. But we're all right." Now, anyway. Sort of. "Kane will call you as soon as he can. I just wanted to check in and let you know we're okay."

There was music in the background, but then I heard a door slam and knew she was in Kane's office. "I talked to Kane briefly after you left the club this morning."

"Oh. Good. I'm glad he got in touch with you." She *was* his best friend.

"No, not good. I'm not happy about this. I can't believe you are." Her tone was more worried than angry.

"No," I agreed. "But there isn't much I can do about it. And he wanted to join the demon hunters. So it is what it is for now."

She snorted. "Right. It is what it is. Fucked up is what it is."

She wasn't wrong. Casting a spell to turn him into an incubus was way over the line. But was it so horrible that he wanted to protect the world from demons?

"Jade?"

"Yeah."

"I'm just worried about both of you."

"I know," I said softly. "That's why I called. I'm at Bea's for now. I'm going to try to get home to Kane's before the night is over. I think Kane is going to meet me there if you need to see him."

She sighed into the phone. "No. It can wait until tomorrow, I guess. I'd just feel better if I could see you both."

"We can come by in the morning. Your apartment. Breakfast?" I could use a little normalcy after all we'd been through today.

"Yes, please. See you early? Eight?"

I had to laugh at her idea of early considering we usually worked the six a.m. shift at the cafe. But I said yes and promised to see her then.

After I hung up, Kat eyed me. "You didn't tell her anything."

"What was I supposed to say? There isn't anything she can do. And she's already worried enough."

Kat rolled her eyes and huffed. "You do that to me all the time. Do you have any idea how irritating it is to care about someone who keeps shit from you?"

I jerked back as if I'd been slapped. "I only do that to protect you."

"Well, stop. It doesn't help. We're in this together. Or haven't you noticed?"

Bea appeared and handed us each a mug of tea. My mentor gave me a look that clearly said she agreed with Kat, but she didn't say anything, and for that I was grateful. I didn't need to be beaten up anymore.

"I hear you," I said to my best friend. "I really do. And you're right. I'll work on it." But I didn't know if I could. Worrying my friends and putting them in danger was more than I could stomach.

Bea smiled at me and patted my arm. "Drink it all down, dear. It will help. We still have work to do tonight." She sat beside Lailah and pressed a mug to her lips. "Drink, now."

Lailah didn't open her eyes. Bea tilted it and when the witch's brew hit Lailah's lips, her eyes fluttered open. She swallowed and sat there looking disoriented for a moment. Blinking, she narrowed her focus to Lucien. Worry shrouded her. "He needs help." She glanced at me and then Bea. "Before the night's out, or we're going to lose him."

Kat gasped and spilled tea down the front of her shirt.

I grabbed her hand. It was what I'd been afraid of. The black magic was going to eat him alive. "We need to find Mitch."

Lucien cleared his throat. "Vaughn will know where he is."

We all turned to stare at him.

Lucien's jaw tightened. "I went to the shop he supposedly works at to see about finding him to help Matisse. But when I got there, the place was deserted. And as I was leaving, he jumped me. Mitch put a bounty on me, and apparently Vaughn Paxton is a bounty hunter."

Kat cleared her throat. "Are you saying the guy who brought you to Mitch's house is Vaughn? The same guy we've been looking for?"

Lucien nodded.

"Mitch fed us the information about Vaughn when you asked him about his brother," I said. "Apparently he decided right then and there he couldn't wait for revenge and must have contacted Vaughn not long after he abducted you. Did you hear him call anyone?"

Kat swallowed. "We stopped at a gas station, but he locked me in the truck. Trust me. I tried everything, even breaking the window." She held up her wrist, showing off a massive bruise. "But it didn't work. He made a phone call, so I guess he called Vaughn then. No one was around, but that's because he spelled the place as soon as we got there. People actually got in their cars and left. It was crazy."

Crazy indeed. That was a lot of magic to dispel. I had no doubt Mitch had made a deal with a demon. He couldn't wield that much magic and not drain himself. I couldn't. Neither could Bea. Not unless he was being fed from somewhere. It explained Lucien's black heart curse as well.

"So? We find Vaughn and we can find Mitch? Is that the plan?" I asked. "But obviously we can't trust Vaughn if he's in Mitch's pocket."

Lucien shook his head. "I don't think they work together. Vaughn didn't seem overly fond of his brother. He was just hired for a job. No questions asked. But I do think he's the place to start." He turned to me. "Unless you think Kane and the demon hunters have a line on him."

"It's hard to say. I can't even contact him. Not unless I go to sleep."

"Don't you know where their headquarters is?" Bea asked.

"Yes. It's not too far from here."

She gave me a gentle smile. "Looks like that's a good place to start."

Chapter 23

Bea and I walked the six blocks to the antebellum home of the demon hunters. Twice I had to stop her from turning around. "It's a confusion spell. Stick with me."

"Goddess above," she said. "That pisses me off."

I chuckled. I wasn't sure I'd ever heard her use that particular phrase.

"It's not funny. Why isn't this happening to you?"

I shrugged. "I don't know. Maybe because Kane brought me here before?"

She huffed and smoothed her salon-dyed auburn hair. "I can't believe they've been in my neighborhood this entire time and I never knew."

"It's a strange world," I said.

She cast me a sidelong glance, and I laughed. This Bea was different. One who wasn't all knowing. It was weird and oddly refreshing.

I clasped her hand as we made our way up the front walk.

"It's frustrating." She waved her hand. "It's like the house is a hologram or something. If you weren't guiding me, I'd for sure think there wasn't anything here."

"It's powerful magic. When I was here last, I felt compelled to turn around, but I could always see the place."

We climbed the steps, and before I could reach for the doorbell, the double door opened. Maximus filled the entry, his large body filling the doorframe.

Bea let out a tiny gasp. "Oh, hello."

He stared at her, his mouth slightly open. Then he closed it as he recovered. "Beatrice. It's been…"

"A long time," she finished.

"Too long." His eyes glowed as he scanned the length of her body, and she blushed.

Oh, holy shit. And gross. The incubus was making eyes at Bea right in front of me, and she was enjoying it. "Okay, that's enough." I stepped between the two of them. "Maximus, we're here on official business."

"Ms. Calhoun," he said, staring over my head at Bea. "What can we do for you? Your fiancé is not here at the moment."

My heart sank. I really wanted to see Kane. "We need to know if your incubi are hunting Mitch, the one who unleashed the demons today."

He tore his gaze from Bea. "The mortal?"

"Yes."

"No. We focus on the demons themselves. Rest assured, the ones you met today will no longer be in existence once the hunters get done with them."

"You just let the offending witches go?" I said indignantly. "Seriously?"

"Jade." Bea put a light hand on my arm.

"It's fine, Beatrice." Maximus stepped back and opened the door wider. "Maybe the two of you should come in for a moment."

I didn't really want to. If Kane wasn't there and they weren't hunting Mitch, I had no use for them, but Bea swept past him, running a hand lightly over his cheek. Lust sparked between them, coating me in an icky film. I wanted to vomit right there on the porch.

"Jade," Bea called. "You're being rude."

I refrained from rolling my eyes. We couldn't have that now, could we? Reluctantly, I followed her into the opulent house.

Maximus led us into his large study and closed the door. "Have a seat. Do you need tea? Water? Anything?"

"No, thank you," I said and sat stiffly on a velvet-covered chair.

Bea sat beside me, her posture refined, and she looked every bit the Southern lady.

Maximus grinned at her. "It's very good to see you."

Her lips turned up into a secret smile. "You, too."

There was silence while they drooled over each other. If I hadn't been so worried about Lucien, I might've thought it was cute.

I cleared my throat. "Um, maybe we should focus? You said you were taking care of the demons, but not the witch. Why?"

He shifted his smoky gaze in my direction. It had zero effect on me, thank the Goddess. "Right. Yes, you see, we are demon hunters. Once we interact with a demon, we're hardwired with an internal tracking. Meaning if one of us battles one, we can all track it. But witches who summon them? No. There's no connection. So we focus on finding the demons. If we find a witch, we'll turn him or her in to the council, but our primary job is to hunt demons, and that's what we do."

"I see," I said. "But isn't that sort of like letting the drug buyers off the hook and going after the drug dealers?"

"It's exactly like that, Ms. Calhoun. There are not that many of us. As you said, we have to focus."

Bea scooted forward. "Can you tell us anything about the witch? Did you know we were being held captive? Or were you already hunting those particular demons?"

He stood abruptly. "You were held captive?"

Bea's eyebrows rose and disappeared under her bangs. "You didn't know?"

"No. I knew about Ms. Calhoun and that's why Mr. Rouquette was sent with a small team. But I didn't know that you were involved." He scowled and rang a bell. One of the demon hunters I'd seen there the day before appeared. "Dawson, what was the intel on today's raid? Is there a report?"

He nodded. "Yes, sir. We interviewed the bounty hunter and the report is being prepared now."

"Good. Make sure I get a copy as soon as it's ready."

"The bounty hunter? You mean Vaughn Paxton?" I asked.

The two demon hunters stared at me for a moment. Maximus cleared his throat. "We do not reveal sources." Then he glared at Dawson. "Be more careful in the future."

Dawson bowed his head. "Yes, sir."

I stood. "He's an incubus. Paxton. I'm already aware. Why doesn't he work with you?"

Maximus gave Bea a look of incredulity as if to say, control your witch. Bea just shrugged.

"Well?" I pressed.

"That is classified information."

"It doesn't appear to be classified anymore," Bea said softly. "I hate to pry into your business, but a few lives are on the line. It would be helpful to know who we can trust."

Maximus's face softened and he bowed his head. "It's not for me to divulge any details of Vaughn's personal decisions, but I think it's safe to say you will not find yourselves in danger around him. If you need him for something, I can call ahead and secure a meeting."

Bea reached out and squeezed his hand. "That would be very much appreciated."

"Consider it done." He gazed at her and longing lit his eyes.

I turned away, feeling like I was spying on a private moment. This guy was Fiona's father. And unless I'd severely misjudged the situation, he was the reason Dayla and Bea were at odds. Matisse had been right. The friction between the New Orleans coven and the Coven Pointe witches was about a man. "Excuse me." I stood. "I need to get some air. Bea, I'll meet you outside."

"I'll be out in a moment, dear."

I shut the door silently behind me and headed for the front porch. I sat on a wooden swing and listened to the shouts of the Mardi Gras parade in the distance. So many people were out celebrating, while Lucien and Matisse suffered. Life was crazy hard for the witches around these parts, though I supposed witches had it hard everywhere else, too. After all, my mother had been kidnapped by a demon when we'd been in Idaho. Power attracted darkness. Wasn't that what Bea had told me once?

When Bea finally emerged from the house, she had a wistful expression on her face. I was dying to ask what was up with Maximus but didn't want to pry. I knew she had been married once and her husband had passed. I was certain whatever had happened with the leader of the demon hunters had been many years ago. On one hand, I was happy she had someone who appeared interested in her. On the other, if we were going to deal with the Coven Pointe witches, this could be a terrible development.

I decided it was best to let it go. "Where to?" I asked.

She held up a piece of paper. "I've got an address. All we need is Kat and Lucien."

"Let's go."

"This is the bike shop," Lucien said.

I checked the address Maximus gave us. "It's the place next door."

"The apartment building?" Kat asked.

"Yes." The four of us—Me, Bea, Kat, and Lucien—piled out of Lucien's Jeep. We'd left Lailah back at Bea's house to recuperate. "The apartment's in the back."

We bypassed the motorcycle shop and slipped through the gate of the apartment building. After climbing three flights of stairs, we stood on his landing. I knocked twice, and Bea rang the doorbell three times. No answer.

I pressed my hand to his door and sent in my emotional energy. Nothing. No one was in there as far as I could tell. "Damn. What did Maximus say? I thought he was setting this up."

"He did." Bea frowned. "I was sitting right there when he called."

"Let's go wait in the car," I said. It didn't make sense to hang out on a crowded stairwell. We all filed back down and were almost out of the courtyard when a shadow caught my eye, and something cool was pressed into my hand. I jerked and thought I saw a tall man with dark hair, but he was gone before I could get a good look at him.

"Whoa." I held my hand up and stared at a white piece of paper. "Did you see that?"

"What?" Bea asked, glancing around. "I didn't see anyone."

"Well, someone was here." I opened the folded piece of paper to find an address written in neat handwriting. "This is across town."

Bea gently took the note from me. "Looks like Vaughn wants to meet somewhere a little more private."

Great. I was all but positive the man I'd seen was Vaughn, and he'd shadow-walked. I tried not to scowl, but time was running out. Lucien was starting to fade. The black magic was creeping over him again. I was terrified if we didn't find an answer for him, we'd lose him. And although Kat couldn't see what I could, it was obvious to me she knew he was in trouble. My zap of white magic earlier hadn't lasted very long.

I drove Lucien's Jeep. Bea sat in the front passenger's seat, and Kat and Lucien occupied the back. I kept glancing in the rearview mirror, terrified Kat was going to hug him or hold his hand, but she seemed to have come to terms with the fact that touching him was out of the question. Instead, they were turned toward each other, talking quietly. I glanced at Bea and whispered, "We're running out of time."

She gave my knee a reassuring pat. "We'll make it."

I wished I could be so sure.

We headed all the way up Canal Street until we were in the Lakeview neighborhood. Most of the houses were new or had been completely redone after Hurricane Katrina, and it had a very suburban feel, unlike most of the rest of the city.

"Take a right," Bea said. A few streets down, we parked in front of a modern-day city farmhouse. The lots on either side were empty. And the house across the street had a construction sign on it.

"Still rebuilding," Kat said to no one in particular.

"Looks like it," I said.

We once again got out of the Jeep and headed to the front door. Only this time when we rang the doorbell, Vaughn answered. His hair was wet as if he'd just gotten out of the shower, and he was wearing only jeans. No shirt, no socks, no shoes, no nothing. And goddamned if he wasn't smokin' hot. I resisted the urge to fan myself. "Mr. Paxton? I believe you were expecting us."

He flashed a sexy-lazy smile. "Ms. Calhoun. It's good to see you well. Our last meeting was an unpleasant piece of business. I'm glad the order was able to get the situation under control."

Lucien scowled. "Under control? You're the one who delivered me there."

His lips formed a thin line. "My apologies to you, Mr. Boulard. I was only doing my job. I can assure you as soon as I assessed the situation, I called in the order." He opened the door wider. "Please, come in where we can talk."

I glanced back at the street. No one seemed to be paying any attention to us. I couldn't help but wonder what this goose chase was all about. "No offense, but you do realize someone could be watching us, right? I mean, anyone staking out your apartment could've just followed us."

He laughed. It was low, sexy, and damned alluring. Jeez. Incubus for sure. Why didn't he work for the order? "They could've, but why would they? As far as they know, you came by my apartment, realized I wasn't home, and left. Besides, there's a spell on the house. Only those invited can see it. We're all safe here. Don't worry about it. Have a seat."

"What about the car?" I asked.

"They can't see that either," Vaughn said, starting to sound impatient.

Okay then. The house was sparsely furnished. A leather couch sat against one wall. Two matching recliners were off to one side, facing a giant wide-screen television. But there was nothing else. Not even a print on the wall. Bea and I sat on the far end of the couch. Lucien and Kat remained standing, obviously still skeptical.

I introduced Kat and Bea and then we got down to business. "I'm here for two reasons. They're both equally important, but one matter is more pressing." I waved to Lucien. "He's been spelled with a black heart curse. One person has already died. And now one of them—" I indicated either Lucien or Kat with a nod to each of them "—is next."

"A black heart curse?" Narrowing his eyes, he studied Lucien. "I see."

"We know who cursed him," I said. "We need the person in order to reverse it."

Vaughn turned to meet my gaze. "And how can I help?"

"It's your brother, Mitch. Can you help us find him?"

Vaughn stood and paced the room. "You're sure it was him?" He didn't seem all that surprised. More like disappointed.

"I'm positive," Lucien said. "We were acquaintances back then. He was there when it happened, and today he admitted it to me."

"Fuck me." Vaughn ran a hand through his lush black hair. "This is going to get messy."

"I suspect it is," I said. "And since the order didn't take him down, I imagine he's on the run or in a safe house until this blows over."

He sat back down. "I can probably lead you to him."

Bea gave him a grim smile of her own. "You're sure about that? You'll be signing your brother's death certificate before long."

Vaughn met her eyes with a cold, hard stare. "Ms. Kelton, I'm a bounty hunter for the Witches' Council. It's my job to take down those who make deals with the devil."

She regarded him a minute and then nodded. "Understood."

Vaughn turned his attention to me. "What's the second piece of business?"

"It's Matisse."

Vaughn's demeanor changed instantly. He sat up straighter, and while he'd been cold and business focused before, now there was something else shining in his eyes. He was good at keeping his emotions masked, but I thought it might be pain.

"She's trapped in a void world, and we need you to help her cross back over." I watched him carefully.

His expression never changed, but emotion certainly rolled behind those intense eyes. "Trapped?"

"Yes, and she'll fade away into nothing if we don't get her out soon."

"And why do you need me?" His tone was unfeeling, but he'd curled his left hand into a fist, and his knuckles were turning white.

"Dayla says you stole something from her. And in order for her to cross, she needs it back."

"What?" Vaughn stood, outraged. "Stole? I took nothing from her."

I gave him a sympathetic smile. "But you did. Do you know what kind of witch she is?"

"Yes."

I leaned in and lowered my voice. "Did you know that after the last time you saw her, she spent a month recuperating?"

It took a moment, but realization dawned in those gorgeous eyes, and he suddenly had a gutted look about him.

Kat gave me a questioning glance, but I wasn't about to answer. It was no one else's business that Matisse had awoken his incubus side.

He looked like he wanted to ask me more questions, but one glance at our audience and he stood again. "I'll do whatever's necessary. Now if you'll excuse me, I need to get dressed." He strode off to the back of the house, calling over his shoulder, "We'll leave in five minutes. Be prepared."

Chapter 24

"How do you want to work this?" Vaughn asked me. We'd parked a few houses down from another place that looked a lot like the house across from the fairgrounds.

I glanced at his muscular arms and the bounty hunter gear in his back seat. "Can you go in and restrain him before the rest of us get inside?"

"Probably."

"Is there a signal?"

"Yeah," he said as he climbed out of the car. "I'll flash the lights on and off. Give me ten minutes. If there's no signal, the plan went to shit and I'd appreciate it if you'd bust in and give me a hand."

Vaughn opened the back door of his SUV, grabbed some zip ties, shoved a stun gun in his pocket, and then jogged down to the dark house.

I waited until he slipped inside to exit his SUV. A moment later I climbed into the back of Lucien's Jeep where my friends were waiting. With any luck, Vaughn would restrain Mitch and we could get this over with as soon as possible.

But as the minutes ticked by, my nerves started to fray. Eight minutes. No lights. Nine minutes. And then when the clock kicked over to ten minutes, Bea opened her door. "We're going in. Kat, it's best if you stay here."

"But—"

"No," Bea said and I was grateful I wasn't the one forcing her to stay behind this time. She was done listening to me. "It's too dangerous."

Kat grimaced, but didn't argue further.

Lucien sent her a grateful smile and then the pair of us followed Bea. But I had to force myself to put one foot in front of the other. It wasn't that I was scared. Not for myself anyway. But while Bea's witch's brew had helped tremendously, I still wasn't one hundred percent, and I had no idea if I could work the spell to reverse the curse. I prayed to the Goddess we didn't totally screw this up.

Taking a deep breath, I grabbed Lucien's hand, more to reassure myself than him. "We're going to get this done."

He nodded, but it was hard to tell if he had any faith left at all.

We didn't bother with a sneak attack. It hadn't worked before. So this time, Bea raised her hands and a sudden blast blew the front door open. The broken door hung at an angle from one hinge. I stood there transfixed, and all I could think about was that it would fall soon.

"Jade. Get it together," Bea demanded. She stepped through the rubble with her magic sparking from her palms. If Mitch came after her, he would likely be flattened in less than three seconds.

My own magic kindled to life with her blast and pulsed through my limbs, ready to be unleashed at the first sign of trouble. But the house was empty. Or it appeared to be. Shit! Had Vaughn played us? Was he working with Mitch?

I turned to get Lucien's take on the situation, but as soon as I did a black blast of fire shot straight at him. I jumped in its path, letting my own magic fly. The two streams collided. Fire consumed my hands, burning so hot, I thought I'd pass out. A scream of absolute terror tore from my throat as the fire started to crawl up my wrists and forearms. I fell to my knees, unable to keep myself upright, and focused on the magic inside me. I could fight this. I had to.

But then a third stream hit the connection. Bea's cooling blue magic joined mine, instantly soothing my burning hands, and slowly, ever so slowly, the fire began to fade. I could barely feel my fingers. Bea's spell had all but numbed them. And thank the Goddess for that, because the blistering was downright awful.

With Bea's strength, we quickly forced the black magic back, and as the connection of the three streams reached Mitch, I took perverse pleasure in watching him writhe in pain. His own spell was going to melt his skin right off.

"Stop!" Lucien cried. "You'll kill him."

At that moment, I hardly cared. The bastard had tried to kill almost all of my friends and burn Lucien alive.

But Bea pulled her magic back, and the shock of it startled me enough I dropped mine, too. But it didn't matter. Mitch was crumpled on the floor in the corner.

Lucien stalked across the room, kicking debris as he went. He kneeled down and touched the witch's neck. "He's still alive. But just barely."

I struggled to get to my feet, unable to use my burned hands. "Where's Vaughn?" I wasn't sure if we were supposed to be afraid *for* him or afraid *of* him. If he was working with Mitch, he could be waiting to ambush us again. Son of a bitch. How could I've trusted him so easily after everything that had happened already? I was only slightly comforted by the fact that Bea had trusted him too.

"Jade, use your magic," Bea said.

"I'm not sure I have anything left."

"Your empath gift, dear. See where Vaughn is."

"Right." As exhausted as I was, I would've thought I'd have no barriers at all. But something was in place, because I was having trouble reading Lucien and Bea. I shook my head and tried again. Then I frowned. "I can't read anyone here." I glanced at Mitch. I'd never been able to read his emotions. And now this very old house appeared to block everything. Was it a spell? Maybe.

Screw it. "Vaughn?" I yelled. "Where in the Sam Hill are you?"

A grunt came from the next room.

I followed, it and when I nudged the door open with my hip, I almost laughed. There was Vaughn, chained to a heavy armoire by his own zip ties. "What happened?"

"The bastard jumped me. Fucking brother. He blames me for what happened earlier today. He's figured out it was me who sent the demon hunters. Did you dust his ass?" he asked, eyeing my hands.

"First of all, he isn't a vampire. And second, no. We need him in order to force Lucien's curse to reverse itself."

Bea came up behind me and spelled Vaughn's zip ties away. He rubbed his wrists. "Thanks for saving my ass."

"One day you'll return the favor," she said. "Now, let's get Lucien's heart taken care of."

We all moved back into the living room.

I turned to Bea. "How is this going to work?"

She pulled a wooden chair over and sat a few feet from Mitch. "Remember the spell we did when you extracted the curse from Kat and forced it back into Lucien?"

Frowning, I nodded.

"That's what we're going to do here. You're going to take it from Lucien and force it back into Mitch."

I opened my mouth but closed it when I realized I had no idea what to say to that. Curing Kat had been hard. Damn hard. But I'd had everyone I loved around me for support. And transferring the entire curse from Lucien to someone else sounded dangerous as hell. But when I thought of Kat and the hope that had been shining in her hazel eyes, I couldn't say no. She'd been my best friend for over twelve years. She'd always been there for me no matter what, and after all this time, she'd finally found someone to love. If I didn't do this, what would happen to him? Or her for that matter?

Saying no wasn't an option. I closed my eyes and wished with all my heart Kane were here. He gave me strength in a way no one else did. Not that he made me more powerful or anything. Not that I knew of, anyway. But his emotional support, the love between us, it always gave me something to hang on to and made me stronger.

I let out a tiny gasp of revelation. That thought had given me an idea. It was no secret Kat was also one of my great stabilizers. If she could do it for me, why not for Lucien?

After fetching Kat from the Jeep, I took a seat on the dirty hardwood floor and motioned for Lucien and Kat to join me.

Kat took a step toward me, but Lucien said, "Wait. Maybe Kat should stay over here. You know, away from the spell, just in case."

I shook my head. "No. She's going to be useful here. Come." My tone was commanding, and all hints of apprehension had left me. I had a plan.

Kat moved first, and Lucien reluctantly followed.

"Lucien, sit next to me." I gestured to my other side, the one Mitch wasn't on. "And Kat, you sit next to Lucien. Then take his hand."

"No," Lucien said. "Not until this spell is gone."

We'd been careful to not let him taint her because she couldn't fight any of the magic off, so he had a point. But if this was going to work, we were going to have to take some risks. "Okay. Yeah. Let's hold off on that for a second. But I still need her. Sit next to him at least."

Kat nodded and sat cross-legged beside Lucien. She'd do whatever I asked. I gave her a grateful smile.

"Jade," Bea asked, her eyes curious, "what are you planning?"

I took a calming breath. This wasn't going to be easy. "I need a way of knowing when Lucien is free from the curse. These types of spells like to linger, right?"

Bea nodded. "Yes."

"Okay, so Kat has the ability to stabilize my energy. She's done it many, many times over the years. And I'm pretty sure due to her relationship with Lucien, she can do it for him. I'm mostly concerned about what pulling the curse from him is going to do to him." And to me, but I didn't say that. I was the powerful white witch, right? "Once I have it all, I want her there to help him stabilize."

"He has been carrying it around with him for a long time. You're probably right." Bea glanced at Kat. "Are you okay with that?"

"Yes," she said without hesitation.

"Kat," Lucien said softly.

But she held up a hand. "I love you. And if there's anything I'm capable of doing, you're going to let me."

The tender look in his eyes as he gazed at her nearly made me break down. I had to glance away. Swallowing the emotion clogging my throat, I said to Bea, "You have to give him his magic back first."

"Of course." She waited until Lucien turned his gaze in her direction and then got to her feet. "Please stand."

When he was toe to toe with her, she grabbed his hands and closed her eyes. "By the power of the New Orleans coven, I hereby restore your magic." Their fingers glowed where they touched, faint at first. Then there was a small, brilliant flash and Lucien's body stiffened. He took a step back and opened his mouth to speak, but before he could get words out, his eyes turned pitch back and the dark magic started to crawl over his skin.

"No!" I cried, certain I was the only one who could see it. Bea and Kat were just standing there studying him. I grabbed his hand and yanked him down. With my other hand, I clutched Mitch's limp one and let my magic build forcefully in my chest. And then I shouted the spell Bea had used not too long ago when we'd rescued Kat. "Goddess of the living, hear my call! We ask for your help, or your mortal son will fall."

Lucien's black magic was crawling over my hands, reversing the numbing effect of Bea's magic. My fingers were on fire again, the blisters screaming in piercing agony. But there was nothing I could do. If I let go, Lucien would be lost for good. And one look at Kat steeled my resolve.

"Reverse the poison that taints his blood. Bring him back to those he loves." The words came out on a choked whisper. The fire consuming my hand was too much to bear. Tears streamed down my face, but I clutched harder, unwilling to let go.

"It's there, Jade," Bea said, cutting through my haze of pain. "The orb you need. Just direct it."

I squinted through my tears and spotted the silver ball of magic I'd conjured. I focused on it and ordered, "Find Lucien's heart."

The orb bounced in front of us and grew brighter as it shot straight to Lucien's chest. He let out a loud gasp, and his body slumped forward. I felt nothing from him.

Panic coiled through my core. Had his heart stopped? *Please Goddess, don't take him. Kat needs him.* I sucked in a ragged breath. What had I just done?

Lucien let out a howl of pain, and it was all I needed to hear. He was alive. Nothing else mattered at that moment. I unleashed my magic, pouring it into Lucien, letting it mix with the black curse. My head spun, and before I could pass out, I used every last bit of strength I had and pulled it back from him.

My veins constricted, instinctively keeping the ugly, tainted magic from entering my system. My stomach rolled. My body shook uncontrollably. Every defense I had was trying to ward off the poison that surely would kill me if I didn't control it.

The agony was such that my thoughts were jumbled. I couldn't think at all. My world was reduced to red-hot, excruciating daggers of pain that ran from my right hand straight through my chest and down my left arm.

The black curse pooled at my left hand's fingertips, pulsating with darkness and evil so strong it threatened to poison me. It wanted to stay with me. Wanted to take up residence in my heart. Promised power beyond any I'd ever known.

"Jade!" I heard the sharp call of Bea's voice but couldn't see her. There was nothing but pain and hellfire. It beckoned me. I was ready to absorb it. Let it overtake me. Submit to the sweet relief of giving up the fight.

Kane's face swam in my mind's eye. He seemed too far away, so far out of reach. I wanted to wrap my arms around him, wanted to touch him one last time. *If you give up the fight, you'll see him soon,* a voice rang in my mind. *Just let go, Jade. Come to me.*

"No. I won't let you go!" Two cooling hands grabbed my shoulders and held on. Cool, clean energy seeped into me, warring with the taint.

My eyes snapped open, and I stared into the fierce eyes of my best friend.

"Do not let it take you. Not now. Not ever." Kat's face was set into a determined expression.

Tears started to fall again, the tracks leaving a tingling sensation over my skin.

"Do you hear me, Jade?"

I nodded.

"Say it. Say you hear me."

"I hear you," I forced out in a barely audible voice.

"Say you'll fight," Kat ordered again.

I nodded again. "I'll fight."

Lucien's hand tightened on my burned one and I nearly passed out with the pain. I groaned and forced myself to keep eye contact with Kat. She was keeping me here.

"Focus now," she said in a soft tone. "Make him take it. Unleash the curse on Mitch. Do it now." Her cool hand shifted and clasped over the one Lucien held. The fire dulled, and soothing relief rushed up my left arm and coiled around my heart.

My head snapped up, and the dam burst. The black magic concentrated at my right hand flooded into Mitch.

His body jerked and convulsed under the invasion. I held tighter, focusing on the clean energy Lucien and Kat were pouring into me until every last drop of pain and agony was gone, forced from my system and into the broken witch who lay unconscious beside me.

I slumped against the wall behind me, barely able to even hold my head up. The room was completely silent. I lifted my head and caught sight of Lucien and Kat sitting next to me, both of them staring straight at me, appearing just as spent as I was. I met Kat's eyes and mouthed, *Thank you.*

Tears filled her eyes as she shook her head, indicating there was nothing to thank her for. Lucien had a tight grip on her hand. His look of gratitude told me everything I needed to know. We'd talk about the specifics later. They'd be fine. We all would.

Then I heard someone clear his throat and Vaughn said, "You better call the Witches' Council."

"Of course," Bea said quietly.

Magic tingled around me in a soft whisper, and a moment later, the air shifted and everything became cooler.

An elderly witch, dressed in a linen suit, appeared from thin air. "What do we have here?" she asked in a surprisingly strong voice.

"A witch consumed with black magic. He's been wreaking havoc for a while now. You'd better take him in," Bea said.

The witch from the council didn't seem interested in talking to anyone but Bea. And that was just fine with me. Someone else could take it from here.

A few moments later, the council witch snapped her fingers, and both she and Mitch disappeared.

I blinked. "Damn. That was easy."

Kat let out a strangled laugh.

I gave her an apologetic smile. "Sorry. I meant the removal of Mitch." I grimaced, catching Vaughn's gaze. "Sorry," I said again. "I know he's your brother."

His eyes darkened. "Stepbrother. And he got what he deserved."

Bea held out her hand, three healing herbs nestled in her palm. "Each of you take one. It'll help."

"Here," Kat said, grabbing them. She handed one to Lucien and held one up to my mouth. "Take it."

I didn't hesitate. There was a time I would have. But not anymore. I swallowed the pill dry and then closed my eyes and waited for its magic.

"Jade?" Bea said.

I opened my eyes. "Hmm?"

"We need to do something about those hands."

I glanced down and gasped as my body started to tremble with delayed shock. "Oh my God." They were bad. Much worse than I thought they'd been. They were lobster red and covered in white blisters.

"We need to get you to my place. I have a poultice that will all but cure that." Bea's expression was confident, and I prayed she was right.

Vaughn walked over to me, his hands stuffed in his pockets.

"Are you available tomorrow? I need to recover before we go after Matisse. If you're still willing, that is," I said.

"Of course," he said, his expression carefully blank as he headed toward the door.

"See you in the morning?"

He nodded and disappeared.

Exhaustion claimed me. My limbs were lead and I wondered what it must be like to be a normal person. I'd never know. But I could dream. Like the mature witch I was, I squeezed my eyes shut and thought of nothing but puppies and chocolate. And maybe Guinness. 'Cause Lord knew if there was anything I needed right then, it was a drink. Or two.

Chapter 25

I must have passed out on the way back to Bea's, because the next thing I remembered was lying in her guest bedroom with Kat beside me. She was gently brushing my hair while whispering something I couldn't quite make out to Lucien.

"Hey," I said in a faint voice. "How long have I been out?"

"Hey, yourself." She smiled down at me. "About an hour or so."

I brought my hand up to brush a lock of hair out of my eyes but paused when I saw all the gauze. My other hand was wrapped, too. I held them up, studying them. My hands and wrists were completely covered. "How bad is it?"

Kat wrinkled her nose. "It *was* bad. Like, really bad. You saw them."

I groaned.

"I said 'was.'" Kat smiled. "Dude, I can't believe how awesome Bea is. She put that poultice on them and the blisters started to go down almost at once. She said they'd be gone in a few hours."

Relief flooded through me. If I never saw a blister again, it would be too soon. Then I shifted to sit upright. The room spun from my sudden movement, and I brought my gauze-wrapped paws up to hold my head in one place.

"What is it, Jade?" Lucien asked.

"Just dizzy. I'll be all right."

Lucien got up from his chair and came around the bed to sit on the opposite side from Kat.

I blinked and wanted to touch his hand but settled for smiling at him. "How are you?"

"Perfect. Exhausted. But perfect."

"And your magic…?" I couldn't bring myself to ask the rest of the question. I wanted to know if he was back to the witch he'd been. If his magic was safe. But I wasn't sure if now was the right time to talk about it.

"My magic is fine. Purer than ever, thanks to you." He touched my arm. "I owe you my life."

I shook my head forcefully and regretted it when my vision blurred. Did I have a concussion? A magical hangover for sure. I steeled myself and met Lucien's eyes. "No. You don't owe me anything but friendship. We're here for each other, always, right?"

"Yes," Kat said softly and smiled at us both.

"Of course, but—"

"No buts," I said, gently. "Seriously, none of us would be here without the others. I've relied on you. You've relied on me. And that's the way we'll continue. We're coven members, but more importantly we're friends, and I know you'd lay down your life for any one of us."

"So would you." His green eyes flashed with emotion.

I blinked back the threat of tears. "Don't do that," I said with a laugh. "I've cried enough for one day."

Lucien leaned in and gave me a light kiss on my cheek. Before he pulled away, he whispered, "I'll take care of her. I promise."

Nodding, I punched him in the leg.

"Ouch. What was that for?"

Wiping away the lone tear with my gauzed hand, I shook my head. "I told you not to make me cry. Now get off the bed. We need to go downstairs. I need something to eat."

They both got up and Kat held out a hand for me.

I brushed her off. "I got this." But when I went to swing my feet out of the bed, my left one got caught in the sheet and my upper half toppled over.

Laughing, Kat caught me. "Yeah, you got this."

I stuck my tongue out at her and grinned as my heart swelled. She shook her head and held her arm out again. This time I braced myself against her and managed to stand without flailing or knocking myself out.

The three of us, battered, bruised, and in need of a week's worth of sleep, walked arm in arm down the hall until we got to the stairs.

"Think you can make it?" Kat teased.

"Better let me go last just in case I topple over. Then I'll have both of you to cushion the fall."

"Forget it," Kat said. "You first."

Kat and I bickered back and forth in jest until Lucien shook his head and swept past both of us. We burst out laughing, and together we followed him.

Bea was at her kitchen table studying one of her spell books. She waved for us to take a seat, while she got up and poured fresh cups of witch's brew.

"Where's Lailah?" I asked. I'd been in the guest room. Unless she was hiding in Bea's room, she wasn't here.

"Jonathon came and picked her up," Bea said.

"Wait, what? Jonathon Goodwin?" I asked, shocked. He was Lailah's ex-mate. They'd had trouble coming to an agreement about the ex part. He wasn't convinced their relationship was over, despite the fact that she was in love with someone else.

"Yep, Goodwin." Bea pulled three mugs out of her cabinet. "He said he had a feeling that she was in danger and came for her."

"Really?" Kat's eyes got wide. "That would suggest that they might be mates after all."

Bea nodded. "It appears so."

Whoa. That was interesting. And disconcerting. Goodwin wasn't my favorite person on the planet. He was an ex-evangelical who'd tried to use me to rile up his congregation and had put me and the rest of the coven in danger. But he was an angel, and it was likely he'd take care of Lailah. So the fact that she was with him wasn't necessarily a bad thing.

Bea placed a mug and a sandwich in front of me, and I smiled up at her. "Thanks. For everything," I told her.

She squeezed my shoulder. "You never have to thank me for anything."

Lucien chuckled. "That's pretty much exactly the same thing she said to me upstairs."

"Yep," Kat said. "I heard it."

"Oh, stop." I rolled my eyes and laughed. "Everyone likes to feel appreciated."

I ate my sandwich in silence as I listened to my friends chatter. Once I was done, I put my hand on Lucien's arm. "Lucien?"

He tore his attention from Kat. "Yeah?"

"Can you take me home?"

I knew Kane was home before I even stepped inside. There weren't any lights on, but I felt his presence deep in my heart. Relief flooded me. He wasn't hidden from me due to his new incubus status. There was nothing I wanted more than to feel his strong arms around me.

Because my hands were still bandaged, Lucien had walked me to the door. He glanced at me. "Do you have a key?"

"Not with me." Everything was still back at the hotel.

He nodded and pressed his hand to the lock. A moment later, he pushed the door open.

"Thanks." I turned and waved at Kat, who was waiting in his Jeep. She smiled and waved back. "Have a good evening," I said to Lucien.

A sheepish grin broke out on his face, and I couldn't help but laugh.

Then I sobered. "No more magic until Bea runs some tests."

"No magic," he agreed. He turned to go, but I placed a hand on him, stopping him, and let my vision shift. The darkness that had clung to him before was completely gone. "What is it, Jade?"

I shook my head and gave him a small smile. "Nothing. Nothing at all. Go. Kat's waiting."

He grinned and strode off, happiness glowing around him like a ray of sunshine. Finally they were getting their happy ending.

"Hey, pretty witch," a welcome voice said from behind me.

I spun, finding Kane wearing only a low-slung pair of jeans, and launched myself into his arms.

"Whoa." He tightened his arms around me and whispered, "What happened?"

I buried my face in his bare shoulder and took a deep, calming breath. "Everything."

"Sounds familiar. Come on. Let's get inside." He pulled me through the door and kicked it closed with one foot.

"Kane?"

"Yeah?"

"What happened to you?" I brushed my lips over an angry laceration on his chest and then pulled back, eyeing his naked torso. There were three more slashes, and he had a bruise on his left cheekbone.

"Demons." He gently pulled me from him and held my arms up, inspecting my bandaged hands. "What happened to you?"

"Black magic witch." I wiggled my paws, pleased when there was no pain. "I think the gauze can come off now."

"Come with me." With one hand on my lower back, he led me to our bedroom.

I sat on the bed and waited while he disappeared into the bathroom. He reemerged with scissors and a damp towel.

"Hands out," he ordered.

I gave him my right hand. "One at a time."

"Right."

I sat there while he took his time cutting the tape and then painstakingly removed the bandage. When he got to the last layer, I squeezed my eyes shut, terrified of what he'd find. If there was even one blister, I was likely to vomit. The cool air caressed my skin, and then after a moment, I felt Kane's lips on my palm. He moved to each finger, tenderly kissing each one.

"How bad is it?" I asked, cracking one eyelid.

"Terrible." His kisses continued, making my entire hand tingle.

The other eye popped open and I peered at my hand. It was red but not beet red. And there wasn't a blister in sight. I let out a sigh of relief and caressed Kane's cheek with my thumb.

He glanced up at me, desire swimming in his eyes. That one look set my body on fire. I wanted him in my arms, needed to be as close to him as possible.

"Kane," I said, my voice husky.

He let out a tiny groan and sat back. "Other hand."

"Huh?"

He gently took my other arm and proceeded to unwrap my other bandage.

"Oh," I breathed. With each new caress of his fingers over my skin, tingles shot like live-wire sparks through my body. The connection was intense and overwhelming, and we had barely even touched each other. It was the incubus thing. It had to be. Every feeling was magnified a thousand times over. And add in the fact that we'd both fought and defeated death, our need for each other was staggering.

Once my second hand was free, Kane pulled me to my feet and clasped both of his hands on the sides of my face and leaned in. Our lips met in a heated frenzy, tongues stroking and warring in desperation and sheer need. Light started to shimmer around us, and I was lost to him. Lost in him.

My fingers curled in his dark hair and I pressed closer, molding myself to him. He tore his lips from mine and ravished my neck, kissing and nipping, until I shivered in pure ecstasy.

"More," I demanded, moving my hands to his shoulders and down his back.

I tilted my head back, giving him more access, and continued my exploration of the muscular planes of his back. My fingers came upon a ragged edge of hot, angry flesh and I froze. "Kane?"

"Hmm?"

"What is this?" I pulled back and ducked under his arm to inspect the gash.

"It's just a scratch."

My breath caught as I suppressed a gasp. The wound started at the bottom of his left shoulder blade and crossed diagonally to his waist. I traced one finger along the edge, and when I got to his spine, he winced. "Like hell it's just a scratch. Have you cleaned these up yet?"

"I showered."

I straightened and put my hands on my hips. "Get the antiseptic."

He gazed down at me, mischief dancing in his eyes. "You're gorgeous when you're being bossy."

I shook my head and strode into the bathroom. When I returned, I pointed to the bed. "Lie down."

He gave me a devilish grin and lay down on his back, but he winced as soon as the angry gash hit the covers.

I sat down next to him and kissed him softly. With my lips still against his, I said, "Stop acting so nonchalant. I know those have to hurt. Let me do something about it."

"This is already helping." He wrapped an arm around me and kissed me again, only slowly and more intensely, the way that was designed to make my body light with fire.

I pulled back and shook my head. "Not until you're fixed up."

"I'm up." He cast his gaze down the length of his body.

"I bet you are." I let my gaze follow his for a moment. My cheeks heated, and he let out a low laugh. Unscrewing the antibacterial cream, I focused on the lacerations and scrapes on his torso. Fear turned my mood sour. "These were all from demons?"

"Yes," he said hesitantly. "But I'm told they'll heal quickly."

I raised one eyebrow. With a little power, I was sure they would. "Is that why you're so eager to get me into bed?"

"What?" he sat up, scowling in pain. "Dammit. No. I want to get you into bed because I want you. I always want you and today was a bitch of a day and the only thing I can think of to make it better is to have you in my arms."

The look of pure indignation, combined with the love pouring off him, made me melt. I wanted the same thing. It was just weird having his new gift influencing my physical reactions. It would take some getting used to. And I was sure it was the same for him. "I know," I relented. "I'm sorry. I want you, too. Now lie back and let me take care of these."

He brushed his lips softly over mine and then settled back against the pillows as I ran gentle fingers over his wounds, mixing a tiny bit of magic into the antiseptic.

"That feels better," he said as I finished doctoring the last one on his chest.

"Good. Now roll over."

His back was a mess of bruises and scrapes. Nothing too serious except the long gash that ran over his spine. I took my time applying the magic-infused cream. He winced and twitched through the entire episode, but by the time I was done, the red had faded to pink and he was breathing easier.

"Okay. You're done," I said.

He rolled back over and managed to not wince this time. "That was incredible. You're handy to have around in situations like this."

I stared at the cinnamon flecks in his dark eyes and felt a surge of love manifest from deep in my heart. "Kane?"

He clasped his hands behind his head. "Yeah, pretty witch?"

"Make love to me now."

Those eyes of his turned molten. "With pleasure. Come here."

I curled up next to him, tracing my fingers over his jaw, down his neck, and back up again.

He kneeled before me and ever so gently peeled my clothes off one piece at a time until I was lying before him naked and wanting.

"Pants," I said, grazing my hand down his abdomen. He shivered under my touch as he discarded his jeans and stood before me in all his naked glory. "You're incredible."

He climbed over my body, marking a path of kisses from my hip to my breast. His lips hovered over my taut nipple as he met my eyes. "So are you, Jade. So fucking incredible." Then his mouth was on me and sensation rippled deep inside, shooting straight to my center. In moments I was writhing beneath him, desperate to feel him inside me.

"Kane," I said on a gasp. "I'm ready."

His hand that had been trailing down my hip froze, and he paused in his exploration of my breast to look up into my eyes. "You're sure?"

"I'm sure." I spread my legs and moved his hand to show him just how ready I was, and when his fingers slid over my slick flesh, I moaned low in the back of my throat.

"So fucking hot," he murmured against my throat. Then he placed his hand back to my hip and pressed his thick length into me. Our eyes locked and we both stilled, taking in the moment. And when Kane started to move, it was slow and perfect as my magic once again spread over both of us, building an intensity that blocked out everything else until all that was left was us, our love, and the magic healing both of our bodies.

Chapter 26

I awoke the next morning in Kane's arms, totally spent but completely satisfied. I smiled and stretched in the pale light of the dawn.

Kane shifted and his eyes fluttered open. "Morning, love."

"Morning," I said sleepily.

He sat up, and the first thing I noticed was all his wounds had healed. I checked my hands. They were still just as red as they had been when Kane had removed my bandages. Well, at least my magic worked for someone.

"You're drained," Kane said, staring down at me.

"Just sleepy."

He shook his head. "No. That's not all." He lowered himself and placed his hand over my heart. "I took too much of your magic last night."

"You needed it more than I did." I'd known exactly how much magic I'd given up the night before. I could have held back, but instinctively I'd understood he needed more to heal his wounds.

Kane shook his head in exasperation. "You can't keep doing that."

"I know. But last night was different. I wanted to. Needed you to be all right after the terrible day I'd had. Can you understand that?"

He stared into my eyes with such intensity, I wondered what exactly he was looking for. But then his gaze moved to my lips and he was kissing me again, lighting the spark with just one brush of his lips. This incubus thing had its perks.

An hour later, we lay side by side, languid and tranquil, and my hands were completely healed.

It was very early in the morning, and Bourbon Street was deserted except for the street cleaners. I peered in the windows of The Grind, spotting Pyper behind the counter. She was by herself, not an employee or customer in sight. As soon as we walked inside, Pyper's head snapped up. Her tired eyes locked on Kane's and she ran into the lobby, throwing her arms around him. "Don't ever do that again."

He let out a low chuckle. "Which part?"

"The part where you turn into a supernatural being and end up spending two days fighting evil. If that weren't bad enough, you didn't even leave me a way to get in touch with you." There were tears in her voice.

Kane ran his hand over her dark hair. "It's okay. I'm fine. Jade's fine. Nothing to worry about now."

I sank into a chair, startled at her reaction. Pyper was my tougher-than-nails, no-nonsense friend. I think I'd only seen her cry twice before, and one of those times was after a spirit had given her a mystical beatdown. I'd known she was worried about Kane, but I hadn't realized she'd been this upset.

She pulled away from him and brushed the back of her hand over her eyes. "You damned well better be." Then she stalked back behind the counter and went to work on a latte and a soy chai.

Kane and I shared a glance, and then both of us slipped behind the counter and helped her get the store ready for what was bound to be one of her busiest days of the year.

At eight sharp, Kane and I stood in front of Wicked, waiting for Vaughn. Lucien had texted him for me the night before with the time and place. Hopefully he hadn't changed his mind. By ten after, I was wearing the bricks down on the sidewalk outside.

"Come on." Kane pulled his key out and unlocked the front door. "It's going to rain. We'll wait inside."

Reluctantly I followed him into the silent club. Charlie wasn't even in yet. Kane flipped the lights on, and from the corner of my eye, I caught movement. I jumped and clutched at Kane's back. "Holy shit. Who's that?"

Vaughn stepped from the darkness and gave me an apologetic smile. "Sorry. When I shadow walked, I miscalculated and ended up inside rather than outside."

"You can just pop in wherever you like?"

"Not everywhere." He strode over to Kane and held his hand out. "Vaughn Paxton. You must be Kane?"

"Kane Rouquette." They shook hands and sized each other up.

"You're new, aren't you?" Vaughn asked him.

"New?" Kane laughed. "I guess that depends on what we're talking about. New to the brotherhood but not so much when dealing with demons and other paranormal shit."

Vaughn nodded. "Yes, by the time any of us make it on their radar, we've usually waged a few battles." Then he turned to me. "What's the plan?"

"No real plan. There's a portal. If what Dayla says is true, as a shadow walker and the descendant of a demon, you shouldn't have any trouble crossing. Ready?"

He nodded. "Always."

"Okay then." I grabbed Kane's hand, and in one blink, the portal appeared just as it had the two days before. "Do you see it?"

"Yeah," Vaughn said, turning to look at me.

So far so good. All of us were in the shadows together. "Kane, are you coming?"

"I'm going to try."

"Good." I glanced at Vaughn again. "Let's jump together." The portal was certainly big enough.

"On three then," he said.

I nodded, and with Kane's hand in mine, I counted. Then I was falling through the whirling haze, and true to form, when we hit solid ground, I landed on my ass. "Son of a... Am I ever going to learn to do that correctly?"

Someone snickered, and I glanced up through the mist to find Kane and Vaughn grinning. Both had landed on their feet. The fog wasn't as thick as it had been before. Something had changed.

"Damn. How did you do that?" I scrambled to my feet, rubbing my ass.

"Skill?" Kane arched an eyebrow.

"Shut up."

He grinned and draped his arm around me. Pulling me close, he pressed his lips to my forehead.

Vaughn was standing a few feet away, his brow wrinkled in confusion. "Where did you say we are?"

"I don't know exactly," I said. "It's a void world in between Hell and our world. Nothing really exists here. And it seems to suck the life from anyone who stays too long."

"And Matisse is here?"

I nodded. "She was yesterday morning. Give me a second." Closing my eyes, I sent my emotional energy out, searching for her. Familiar energy tugged at me. I frowned. It felt like...well, my own. That was odd. I pressed further, and the emotional signature that I thought was mine got stronger, but it was also mixed with someone else's. Matisse's? I couldn't be sure.

Matisse, I called with my mind. *Lead me to you.*

The faint tug pulled me forward. Two steps. Three. Then a dam burst and all I could feel was Matisse's heartbreak. Tears splattered down my face as my heart constricted and cracked. The empty, gutted sensation of being completely left behind touched my soul, and I had to fight from curling into a ball, from screaming with utter disappointment and hopelessness. She'd given up something precious for the man she'd loved. And he'd betrayed her.

An image of a dark-haired man standing with her at the edge of the Mississippi as he told her goodbye flashed in my mind. It was Vaughn. He told her he couldn't be part of her life. That he didn't love her. That he never had. And then he walked away, never once looking back while she stood on the rocks, the cold air chilling her to the bone as her heart hardened right there in her chest.

She'd just been told she wasn't good enough for the man she loved.

My eyes flew open and I glared at Vaughn, my body alive with righteous indignation. *She wasn't good enough for him?*

"Jade?" Kane asked, concern lining his tone. "What's wrong?"

I pointed an angry finger at Vaughn. "He's what's wrong. He used her and then left her."

Vaughn scowled, and his eyes narrowed as he studied me. "I didn't use her."

"That's what she thinks."

Kane placed a steadying hand on my shoulder, and Matisse's emotional energy fled, replaced by Kane's concern.

I shook my head and blinked. "Whoa." I'd never had a vision like that before. Was it a memory? Or some sort of conjured dream state?

"Where is she?" Vaughn asked quietly, his face impassive now.

Frowning, I waged an internal war with myself. Matisse was in enough emotional pain. His presence would only make that worse. But what if he was her only shot to get home? No matter what had or hadn't happened between them, we needed to try. We didn't have any other option.

"This way."

I followed the ever-strengthening trail of Matisse's energy. The mist began to fade as the river and the brick pathway stretched out in front of us. Then I stopped mid-step and gasped.

Matisse was standing on the rocks, her arms stretched out

toward the river and her hair blowing in a nonexistent wind as tears streamed down her cheeks. Gut-wrenching pain was written all over her face. Power sparked around her, a turbulent storm cloud ready to burst. And nestled against her chest was my pendant, calling to me. It *had* kept us connected. Was that why she hadn't faded more in the last twenty-four hours? Perhaps my talisman had kept her safe.

The broken witch, with nothing more than a whisper of power, was gone, replaced by a dangerous powerhouse sex witch. What was driving her power? The talisman? No, that couldn't be strong enough. My gaze landed on Vaughn. His skin was glowing with magic. It was him. The fact that he was near her was giving her the strength to tap her magic.

But she didn't even seem to be aware of us, much less the world around her. If I had to guess, I'd say she was reliving the memory of the day she and Vaughn had broken up, and that was why I'd witnessed it.

"Matisse?" I said quietly, not wanting to startle her.

A bolt of lightning came from the sky and cut through the grayness, striking the water.

Kane tightened his hold around me and pulled me back.

"No," I said. "She needs to come out of this." I touched the magic sparking in my chest and let it pool at my fingertips. I didn't want to spell her, but I would if I needed to protect myself. Or Kane. After the vision, I was leaning toward letting Vaughn fend for himself.

"Matisse," I said forcefully and put a tiny bit of magic behind it.

Her head swiveled and she stared me straight in the eye.

"You're okay." I lowered my arm and walked ever so slowly in her direction. "We've come to take you home."

"I don't have a home," she said, her wide eyes onyx. "He stole it."

"Who? Vaughn?"

She laughed humorlessly. "You could say that."

"Mati," Vaughn said, sex appeal radiating through his deep voice as he moved to her side.

The sex witch stiffened, and her power grew into a force of purple light. She focused on him and her tears vanished. "You're not welcome here." The words were meant to be harsh, but her tone was soft.

Slowly she lowered her arms, but the purple glow only brightened with her turmoil of emotions.

Love, betrayal, and desperation were all mixing together, and she couldn't control it. "Why did you come?" she demanded, angry again.

To his credit he stood his ground. "To restore what I took from you."

His words only added to her agitation. Magic sparked from her fingertips, sending a stream of power to the rocks below her. *Crack!* One large rock split entirely in two. Another shattered.

Vaughn held his hand out to her in a silent offering. His emotions intensified and spilled over as he gazed at her beautiful face. Longing consumed him, along with regret and bitter resentment. For the first time since we'd met, his emotions had come undone, and I had no trouble reading him. "Come back from that place, Mati. Don't let it take you."

Her eyes never left his, and the longer she stared at him, the calmer she became. Her magic continued to come in small bursts, but the uncontrollable whirlwind of power lessened. And when she took a step forward, the sparks disappeared. She seemed almost in a trance, drawn to him in some odd way.

He continued to hold his hand out as she slowly made her way to him. Finally as they came together, Vaughn wrapped his arms around her. They gazed at each other, passion burning between them. Even if I hadn't been an empath, the way they looked at each other, there was no denying the electricity coursing through both of them.

Vaughn's gaze turned tender as he searched her soft features. She stared back, and when her hand came up to rest on his neck, heat sizzled between then, sparking in both of their eyes.

"I didn't know," he said. "I wouldn't have—"

She placed her finger over his lips, silencing him.

He kissed her palm softly then pulled her to him abruptly, wrapping his arms around her protectively.

She pressed her head into his shoulder and held on for all she was worth. The desperate emotional need streaming off both of them almost knocked me to the ground. These two cared very deeply for each other. Whatever had happened between them wasn't permanent. Not if they had the courage to work through it.

"Time to go," I whispered to Kane.

"Huh?" he said, barely able to tear his eyes away from the scene in front of us.

But I didn't answer. I just clutched his arm and imagined us back in the club. The world tilted again, and this time when the spinning stopped, we were in the middle of the empty club and I was cradled in Kane's arms.

I laughed. "Why are you carrying me?"

He smiled down at me. "I didn't want you to bruise your backside again. It's too sexy for that."

"That was thoughtful." I wrapped my arms around his neck and gave him a slow kiss, grateful we were together, grateful the changes in our lives only seemed to bring us closer together. But mostly just grateful we understood each other.

"Hey!" a voice called from behind us.

I smiled against Kane's lips, recognizing Pyper's voice.

"Put her down. What do you think this place is? A brothel?"

"Now there's an idea." Kane lowered me to my feet.

I placed my hand in his and pulled him over to the bar, where we could sit and wait for Matisse and Vaughn.

"Do you think they'll make it back?" Kane asked.

I nodded. "There was so much power bouncing between the two of them, all they need to do is balance it. And now they have that chance."

"Wait, what?" Pyper asked and poured a Diet Coke. She placed it in front of me and then poured one for herself and handed Kane a bottle of water. She knew us well. "Tell me what happened."

I spent the next twenty minutes explaining what I'd seen in my vision and then went into as little detail as possible about the magic exchange between a witch and an incubus.

"So," she said with a sly smile. "Y'all get it on and magic is actually shared between you. Like, when one of you gets off, magic is then exchanged?"

Kane turned a deep shade of red and cleared his throat.

I giggled. "Yeah, something like that."

"And now those two are in some alternate reality getting down and dirty?"

Kane shook his head, but I shrugged and said, "I hope so. It'll probably make it easier for them to get home."

Pyper slammed her hand down on the bar. "Holy shit! Why can't anything like that happen to me? All I get are asshole ghosts following me around. You? You get ghost sex, dreamwalking sex, and now incubus sex. Dude! Life just isn't fair." She shook her head and threw a towel under the counter.

"I could've done without the ghost sex." Kane squeezed my hand.

"But the dream sex was pretty good." I grinned and leaned in, kissing him softly.

"Yeah. Still is," he agreed.

"Oh, God! Stop. I don't need to hear any more. I'm already thinking I might need to slit my wrists." But she laughed and flipped her pink-streaked hair over her shoulder. "Okay. New topic. About this wedding. If you two are done with this mission, what do you think of a Mardi Gras ceremony?"

"You mean today?" I asked, totally surprised.

"Yes."

Kane and I exchanged a glance. Then his lips turned up into a slow smile. "I'm game if you are."

"Of course I am." I glanced at the spot in the club where I knew the portal was hidden. "But what if they don't make it back?"

"You just said you were confident they would," Pyper said. "Right?"

"Sure, but…" Damn, I hoped they did. I turned back to Pyper. "I thought you had a gig body painting tonight."

"I do. But I can spare an hour or two to get you hitched."

I bit my lip. "There won't be any food for the reception."

Kane chuckled. "Are you looking for an excuse to say no?"

"No!" I stood and started to pace. "Just thinking about the logistics. There's the minister, food, getting everyone there, and Pyper has had that party lined up for weeks."

Pyper came around the counter and hopped up on one of the barstools. "After the fiasco the other day, I've been checking into options, and I think I've got everything covered. Ms. Bella has a friend in Cypress Settlement who's registered with the Parish to perform ceremonies. He says for the right price, he can be available pretty much any time we need him."

"For the right price?" Kane asked.

"Hush." She swatted his arm. "You can afford it. And as for the reception, who cares? It's Mardi Gras. Everyone can come to the party I'm working. The man hosting it is a good customer here." She gestured around the club. "He'd have no problem letting the owner, his new wife, and a few friends crash."

Kane tightened his hand around mine. "It isn't exactly what you envisioned. But it would be today."

My heart skipped a beat and butterflies fluttered in my stomach. Yes. I wanted to marry him. My family was still in town, and so was his. That was all that mattered, right? And making sure Matisse and Vaughn made it back from the mist. I knew my answer. I just needed to confirm our mission was complete.

Time seemed to stand still as I burned a hole in the club floor with my stare. I shook my head. "I'd love to. You have no idea how wonderful that sounds, but—"

Light lit the entire club, blinding me momentarily, and was gone just as fast. I blinked and then shot to my feet.

There they were. Matisse and Vaughn. He had his arm around her shoulder and was clutching her to him. Both their faces held looks of wonder, combined with total confusion, as they tried to orient themselves.

"It worked?" Matisse asked him. "We made it back."

"Looks like it." He pulled her into a hug, and the pair held on to each other as if they'd never let go.

My heart did another little flip-flop. It had worked.

She was back safe and sound. Her hand clasped around my pendant as she met my eyes. "This kept me whole while I was down there."

I reached in my back pocket and pulled out the tin. When I opened it, a small ball of magic clung to the stud earring. "Looks like this may have been trying to protect me, too." I held it out to her, but Vaughn took it from my palm. He smoothed her dark hair back and secured it into the top of her ear as if he'd done that a million times before. They seemed so comfortable together it was hard to reconcile the vision I'd had.

"Thank you," Matisse said and reached up to unclasp the necklace.

I held my hand out in a stop motion. "No. You keep it. Please."

She shook her head. "I can't. It's too much."

"No, it isn't," I insisted. "For some reason, it's fortifying your magic right now, and I don't want to mess with that."

She stared at me with uncertain eyes.

"Oh, please. Just keep it," Pyper said lightly. "She has at least a dozen more, I'm sure. You wouldn't believe that bead stash of hers. Beads everywhere. Seriously, if she wants you to have it, you should just take it. Otherwise she'll keep arguing with you about it."

I did my best not to laugh. Pyper wasn't too far off. I did have more, but they weren't infused with magic like that one.

Finally Matisse nodded. "Thank you."

"You're welcome." I glanced at Kane. "I guess the last thing to do is contact Chessandra."

Matisse stepped back and wrapped an arm around Vaughn's waist, her expression hardened with anger. "Well, don't worry.

I'll be in touch." She tilted her head up and looked at Vaughn. "Can you take me home?"

"Of course." With a nod to us, Vaughn took one step and the pair of them disappeared into the shadows.

"So fucking badass," Pyper exclaimed.

I laughed and then turned to Kane. "I'm ready. Let's get married today."

He turned his elated gaze on me and tucked a lock of my hair behind my ear. "You got it, pretty witch."

Chapter 27

Pyper took us to the hotel to grab our stuff and Kane's car. But before we headed back to Cypress Settlement, Kane and I stopped off in Coven Pointe. We'd made a plan to meet Maximus at Dayla's. I'd made a promise to him, and I intended to keep it.

The three of us stood on Dayla's front porch. I turned to Maximus and held out a note card.

"What's this?" he asked.

"You said you wanted to meet with the ex-demon Meri. I called her, and she agreed to speak with you. Just call to set up a time."

"You're a woman of your word, Ms. Calhoun." He nodded to Kane in appreciation.

I rolled my eyes and gestured to the door. "You ready for this?"

He nodded.

"You'd better be," I said, remembering the last time Kane and I had been there. I knocked.

A moment later the door opened, and Matisse stood in the doorway.

"Hello," I said. "I'm so glad to see you made it back here."

"Me too." She smiled. "Thanks to you."

"Thanks to Vaughn," I corrected. All I'd done was convince him to help her.

Her smile faded, and I couldn't help but wonder what had happened once they'd left the club. But it wasn't any of my business. It was obvious they each had intense feelings for the other, but one afternoon couldn't fix whatever had happened between them. "Did you want to come in?" she asked.

I shook my head. "No. Thank you. But we brought someone who really wants to speak with Dayla. Is she here?"

Matisse cut her gaze to Maximus and regarded him with obvious skepticism. "Yes, but I don't know if she wants to talk to you."

"Five minutes," he said.

"I'll ask." She shut the door.

"Do you want us to stay?" Kane asked him.

He smirked. "I hate to say yes, but she's a powerful witch. I'd prefer we had witnesses."

Kane chuckled. I frowned at both of them but said nothing.

The door swung open, and Dayla stood in the doorway, her arms crossed over her chest. Her light hair was piled high on her head, secured with a pentagram hair clip. Interesting. "What the hell are you doing here?" Her gaze bored into Maximus with such intensity I was surprised his head didn't explode on the spot.

Unconsciously, I took a step back.

Maximus cleared his throat. "Dayla, it's lovely to see you again. I just have one question for you."

"What?"

"When exactly were you going to introduce me to my child?" His words were so cold, I actually felt a chill crawl up my arm. His child? Was he talking about Fiona? Had he not known?

Dayla didn't even flinch. "You had no rights to her. You took what you wanted and left. Just like all incubi do."

Whoa. These witches had some serious hate for the demon hunters. I sent Kane a sidelong glance. After a while, would I start to resent him taking my magic for himself? I found it hard to imagine. So far, Kane had been more worried about the magic transfers than I had. As long as he remained considerate, we could work it out.

"I was called to the order, Day. You know that."

"Do not call me Day. You hear me, Maximus? I'm not yours, and you are entirely too familiar."

His nostrils flared in irritation, and I was starting to suspect we should leave quietly. I took another step back, but Kane put his hand on my arm and whispered, "They need to answer a few questions for us first."

"I just want a chance to know my daughter." Maximus pulled out a business card. "She can reach me through that number or the address if she chooses to come by. Make sure she gets it."

"Like hell I will." Dayla went to tear it up, but when she tried to rip the paper she couldn't. She tried again and grunted in frustration. It would've been funny if there hadn't been so much anger flying through the air.

"Only the one it's intended for can alter it. If you throw it out, it will find its way back into your house." He tipped an imaginary hat at her and said, "Good day, milady."

Dayla threw the card, but it floated back into her hand. "Damn you. Why didn't you just give it to her yourself, you fool?"

He glanced back. "Because I wanted it to come from you." He gave her a self-satisfied smile and then disappeared into the shadows.

"That's a neat trick those guys do," I said.

Kane nodded. "Yes it is."

"Can you do that?"

"Yep." He turned to Dayla. "Good morning."

She scowled in irritation. "I am not pleased you brought him here."

Kane shrugged. "I'm not exactly pleased you spelled me without my permission."

She pursed her lips and then forced out, "What can I do for you, Mr. Rouquette?"

"I have a question. It's about this incubus thing. Is it permanent?" Kane asked, surprising me. He'd taken the oath.

"Yes."

"Even though you said you'd lift it once Matisse was found?"

Her eyes narrowed and frustration seeped from her being. Was she frustrated because we were questioning her? We had a right to know. She pushed her bangs to the side and regarded us with fake sympathy. It made me want to unleash a firestorm of magic on her.

She opened her mouth, then closed it. After clearing her throat, she said, "I lied." A second later the door slammed shut.

"I guess that's it then," I said, tucking my arm through Kane's, not at all surprised. Dayla struck me as the type to do whatever she needed to in order to achieve her goal, even if it meant using other people. No wonder she and Bea didn't get along.

"Is it?" Kane asked as we headed back to his car.

"Sure. What can we do about it?"

"I don't know." He pulled the car door open for me and then went around to the driver's side and climbed in. He started the car and let it idle while he collected his thoughts. "But we—well, I—made a life-altering decision without taking any time to consider the ramifications. I wanted to explore our options, if we had any."

"And now we don't," I said, stating the obvious.

"I'm sorry for that." He brought my hand to his lips, kissing my knuckles.

"It's okay. I understand. I really do." I pressed my palm to his cheek. "You're a good man. You were faced with an impossible decision. Either become a hunter or sit back and let other souls be taken. If I were you, I would've made the same choice."

"I know you would've. It's probably part of the reason I couldn't say no." He folded me into his arms, hugging me tight. And when we broke apart, he grinned. "Let's go get hitched."

The sun was low in the sky and streaming in the ceiling-to-floor windows at Summer House when my stepfather Marc and I descended the last steps of the grand staircase. Even though it was last minute, all of our immediate friends had found a way to attend. Kat and Lucien, Lailah and—Lord help me—Jonathon, Pyper and Ian, Charlie and her girlfriend, a handful of the New Orleans Coven witches, my mom, Gwen, and Kane's parents. A few of Kane's friends and his best man were there too. And even Maximus and Bea. It was intimate but perfect.

They all stood as Marc guided me down the aisle, and when I met Mom's tearful eyes, I almost lost it myself. I paused and reached out, squeezing her hand briefly. Last year at this time, there had been no hope of her being at my wedding. Nor my stepdad. My heart swelled, and nothing in this world could've made me happier—except the love shining back at me when Marc handed me off to Kane.

"You're gorgeous," Kane whispered as he leaned in to brush a kiss over my cheek.

"So are you." I scanned his body, taking in his tailored suit that showed off his wide shoulders and slender waist. My body started to tremble with the reality that this was truly happening.

"Relax," Kane said, squeezing my hands. "It's just you and me now."

"For always," I said, getting lost in his gaze.

The minister cleared his throat.

Kane and I turned to face him, and a huge smile broke out on my face. He couldn't have been a day under seventy-five. He wore bright green golf pants paired with a button-down rainbow-striped shirt, argyle socks, and Birkenstocks. He even had a knitted cap to top off the outrageous outfit.

The minister winked at me and then addressed our small crowd. "We are gathered here today to join this witch and this incubus in holy weddedness. Is there anyone here who thinks this sounds like a good idea?"

Everyone laughed.

"Yeah. Me neither. But they look like they like each other, so who are we to judge?"

Kane chuckled, and when he smiled at me, everything else disappeared.

By the time our quirky minister got to the vows, our guests were teary eyed from laughter, and I couldn't think of a better way to celebrate our union.

"Do you, Kane, love this woman?"

"I do," Kane said, humor lighting his eyes.

"Do you promise not to steal all her power?"

"I do."

"And do you promise to feed her cheesecake in bed at least once a week?"

He laughed. "I do."

"Good. And you, Jade, do you love this man?"

"I do," I said through tears of joy.

"Do you promise to give it up when he needs your strength?"

I choked and sputtered on a bubble of laughter. "Yes. I do."

"And do you promise to remember to keep the fridge stocked with beer, especially during football season?"

"Absolutely."

"Good, we have an agreement. The beads please?" He held his hands out, and Shelia ran up to the makeshift altar holding two strands of plastic heart-shaped beads. The minister smirked at us. "It's not a wedding on Mardi Gras without beads."

"You can say that again," I said and nodded in Shelia's direction. She toasted me with a large hurricane glass.

The minister handed each of us a strand of the heart beads and had us repeat after him.

Together we said, "With the beads, we do wed."

"Excellent!" The minister clapped his hands together. "By the great state of Louisiana, I now pronounce you a married witch and incubus." He turned to Kane. "You may now kiss your bride…but don't get too crazy."

Kane swept me into his arms, tilted me backward, and kissed me so thoroughly I forgot where we were…that was, until all the whooping and hollering brought me back to myself. He carefully placed me back on my feet and tucked my arm into his. "That's it, it's official," he said into my ear.

"Yes, it is." I wrapped my hand around his neck and leaned in. "And I wouldn't have changed a thing."

"Yes!" Pyper came bounding up and wrapped one arm around each of us. "Finally! Now let's party! It's Mardi Gras, bitches!"

I laughed. "You heard her. What better way to celebrate a wedding than Mardi Gras?"

We didn't have to say it twice. They all started to file out to their cars. Ever since Pyper had mentioned celebrities and the names Brad and Gerald, they'd all been more than ready to go.

I started to follow, but Kane grabbed my wrist and held me back.

"What is it?" I asked.

He scanned my body, his eyes roaming over my gorgeous, silver-beaded dress. "I just wanted to get one last look at you before we join the masses."

"And something else, perhaps?" I rose on my tiptoes and brushed my lips over his.

He chuckled. "You know me all too well, Mrs. Rouquette."

"Oh, I love the sound of that." I traced my fingers over his jawline.

"So do I, pretty witch." His tone was low and husky. He glanced out the window at our friends climbing into their cars. "Do you mind being a little late to the party?"

The desire humming just beneath the surface of his skin sent a shiver of anticipation down my spine. "No. Not at all."

He pulled me to him, pressing me to the hard length of his body, showing me just how much he wanted me. And as the sound of cars starting and driving off toward the city wafted in through the front door, my husband kissed me again. Then he swept me off my feet and carried me back up the grand staircase.

About the Author

Deanna is a native Californian, transplanted to the slower paced lifestyle of southeastern Louisiana. When she isn't writing, she is often goofing off with her husband in New Orleans, playing with her two shih tzu dogs, making glass beads, or out hocking her wares at various bead shows across the country. Want the next book in the series? Visit www.DeannaChase.com to sign up for the New Releases email list. Look for *Incubus of Bourbon Street coming winter 2014.*